## Anthony Gilbert and The Murder Room

››› This title is part of The Murder Room, our series dedicated to making available out-of-print or hard-to-find titles by classic crime writers.

Crime fiction has always held up a mirror to society. The Victorians were fascinated by sensational murder and the emerging science of detection; now we are obsessed with the forensic detail of violent death. And no other genre has so captivated and enthralled readers.

Vast troves of classic crime writing have for a long time been unavailable to all but the most dedicated frequenters of second-hand bookshops. The advent of digital publishing means that we are now able to bring you the backlists of a huge range of titles by classic and contemporary crime writers, some of which have been out of print for decades.

From the genteel amateur private eyes of the Golden Age and the femmes fatales of pulp fiction, to the morally ambiguous hard-boiled detectives of mid twentieth-century America and their descendants who walk our twenty-first century streets, The Murder Room has it all. ›››

## The Murder Room
**Where Criminal Minds Meet**

**themurderroom.com**

**Anthony Gilbert (1899–1973)**

Anthony Gilbert was the pen name of Lucy Beatrice Malleson. Born in London, she spent all her life there, and her affection for the city is clear from the strong sense of character and place in evidence in her work. She published 69 crime novels, 51 of which featured her best known character, Arthur Crook, a vulgar London lawyer totally (and deliberately) unlike the aristocratic detectives, such as Lord Peter Wimsey, who dominated the mystery field at the time. She also wrote more than 25 radio plays, which were broadcast in Great Britain and overseas. Her thriller *The Woman in Red* (1941) was broadcast in the United States by CBS and made into a film in 1945 under the title *My Name is Julia Ross*. She was an early member of the British Detection Club, which, along with Dorothy L. Sayers, she prevented from disintegrating during World War II. Malleson published her autobiography, *Three-a-Penny,* in 1940, and wrote numerous short stories, which were published in several anthologies and in such periodicals as *Ellery Queen's Mystery Magazine* and *The Saint*. The short story 'You Can't Hang Twice' received a Queens award in 1946. She never married, and evidence of her feminism is elegantly expressed in much of her work.

*By Anthony Gilbert*

**Scott Egerton series**

Tragedy at Freyne (1927)

The Murder of Mrs Davenport (1928)

Death at Four Corners (1929)

The Mystery of the Open Window (1929)

The Night of the Fog (1930)

The Body on the Beam (1932)

The Long Shadow (1932)

The Musical Comedy Crime (1933)

An Old Lady Dies (1934)

The Man Who Was Too Clever (1935)

**Mr Crook Murder Mystery series**

Murder by Experts (1936)

The Man Who Wasn't There (1937)

Murder Has No Tongue (1937)

Treason in My Breast (1938)

The Bell of Death (1939)

Dear Dead Woman (1940) aka *Death Takes a Redhead*

The Vanishing Corpse (1941) aka *She Vanished in the Dawn*

The Woman in Red (1941) aka *The Mystery of the Woman in Red*

Death in the Blackout (1942) aka *The Case of the Tea-Cosy's Aunt*

Something Nasty in the Woodshed (1942) aka *Mystery in the Woodshed*

The Mouse Who Wouldn't Play Ball (1943) aka *30 Days to Live*

He Came by Night (1944) aka *Death at the Door*

The Scarlet Button (1944) aka *Murder Is Cheap*

A Spy for Mr Crook (1944)

The Black Stage (1945) aka *Murder Cheats the Bride*

Don't Open the Door (1945)
aka *Death Lifts the Latch*
Lift Up the Lid (1945)
aka *The Innocent Bottle*
The Spinster's Secret (1946)
aka *By Hook or by Crook*
Death in the Wrong Room (1947)
Die in the Dark (1947)
aka *The Missing Widow*
Death Knocks Three Times (1949)
Murder Comes Home (1950)
A Nice Cup of Tea (1950)
aka *The Wrong Body*
Lady-Killer (1951)
Miss Pinnegar Disappears (1952)
aka *A Case for Mr Crook*
Footsteps Behind Me (1953)
aka *Black Death*
Snake in the Grass (1954)
aka *Death Won't Wait*
Is She Dead Too? (1955)
aka *A Question of Murder*
And Death Came Too (1956)
Riddle of a Lady (1956)
Give Death a Name (1957)
Death Against the Clock (1958)
Death Takes a Wife (1959)
aka *Death Casts a Long Shadow*
Third Crime Lucky (1959)
aka *Prelude to Murder*
Out for the Kill (1960)
She Shall Die (1961)
aka *After the Verdict*
Uncertain Death (1961)
No Dust in the Attic (1962)
Ring for a Noose (1963)
The Fingerprint (1964)
Knock, Knock! Who's There? (1964)
aka *The Voice*
Passenger to Nowhere (1965)
The Looking Glass Murder (1966)
The Visitor (1967)
Night Encounter (1968)
aka *Murder Anonymous*
Missing from Her Home (1969)
Death Wears a Mask (1970)
aka *Mr Crook Lifts the Mask*

# Die in the Dark

Anthony Gilbert

An Orion book



This edition published by
The Orion Publishing Group Ltd
Orion House
5 Upper St Martin's Lane
London WC2H 9EA

An Hachette UK company
A CIP catalogue record for this book is available from the British Library

ISBN 978 1 4719 0992 4



www.orionbooks.co.uk

To Margaret Swayne Edwards
With my love

# PART ONE

## I

THE ADVERTISEMENT appeared in the *Record* on the morning of April 14th and was noted the same day by Mr. Arthur Crook, who tore his way through the paper (said the unromantic Bill Parsons, his indefatigable A.D.C.) like an experienced cook tearing the entrails out of a fowl. It read :

> *Rest and Refreshment.* To a lady seeking the above and able to pay for it, is offered a unique opportunity for complete seclusion in a delightful country house, designed by an artist, situated in the heart of a wood. Two perfectly-furnished rooms, first-class cooking, service, good cellar. Every comfort, perfect quiet. No other guests taken. Write Box O.151. The Record, E.C.4.

" And they fall for it, Bill," marvelled Crook. " They fall for it. And they will till the end of time. And then our hopeful Government thinks it can stamp out private enterprise."

" Murder party ? " suggested Bill, in his laconic way.

" How does it look to you ? " demanded Crook. " Well, do a bit of free translation. Rich dame wanted as sole payin' guest in a house in a lonely wood. No one else allowed over the threshold. Every convenience. I dare say, Bill, but convenient to which party ? Guest or host ? I give you three guesses. All the same "—he tossed the paper aside preparatory to settling down to real work—" some rich fish will bite. That touch about the artist shows the expert. And soon the author of *that* "—he jerked his big aggressive thumb towards the advertisement —" will be singin':

'Now on the Heavenly mountains
Her footsteps pause and stray
Beside celestial waters
She walks in bliss to-day.
And may the devil send us
Another mug this way.' "

He said no more, but Bill knew he had pigeon-holed the matter in his mind. If occasion arose later, meaning if the affair assumed financial proportions of interest to Arthur Crook, Esquire, he could take it out fresh and uncreased. He could forget many things, like the right time for meals or paying his income tax demand or sending his suit to the cleaners, but never important matters like the time " they " opened or advertisements of obvious criminal intent.

## 2

On the same day just such a woman as the advertiser had in mind was preparing to step into the net. Cinema fans would have been disappointed to realise that she was neither young nor beautiful, but from Crook's and the criminal's point of view she fulfilled the one essential condition. She was rich and, at that time, too badly scared by the situation in which she found herself to take any one into her confidence. The second condition was as important as the first.

Mrs. Emily Watson was a widow of fifty-five living in cosy (and quite tasteless) comfort in a house characteristically christened Kozicot in one of London's outer suburbs. Any clever young modern novelist would have known all about her at once by seeing her drawing-room, which was cluttered with easy-chairs, pictures, ornaments, bits of silver, fat cushions with tassels stitched on one corner and pink silk lampshades with silk or bead fringes. Crook would have felt at home there at once, believing that chairs were intended for relaxation and walls for hanging pictures on. Mrs. Watson herself was a short, plump woman with rather too decorative a complexion, heavily-waved hair, a fondness for brooches (of which she had many, all of them valuable—her late husband had seen to that), pendant earrings and if she hadn't bells on her toes she certainly had rings on her fingers. She had as many friends as her position warranted, more acquaintances, really, than she knew what to do with, and one living relative, her nephew, Desmond.

Desmond was the son of her only sister, Marian. When they were girls living in rather impoverished circumstances in West Kensington they had both fallen in love with handsome, charming, selfish Colin Raikes—rake by name and rake by nature someone inevitably said—but Colin had chosen the pretty flighty Marian, a choice that surprised no one, certainly not plump sober Emily. It was towards the end of World War Number One, when people married overnight as it were, when they found time to get married at all, and within the fortnight Colin was back with his unit. Emily worked as a clerk in her father's office and wondered what it must be like to be married to Colin Raikes. Marian speedily told her. For the marriage didn't last. In 1921 Colin, having run through his gratuity and everything he could persuade friends and relatives—Marian's as well as his own—to lend or give him—though, in fact, the one was the same as the other—disappeared overnight, leaving Marian with a son of three. The following year he was killed with a woman companion in a motor accident on the Continent. Emily, meanwhile, had left her father's office and was secretary to Mr. Albert Watson, senior partner of Watson and Ryman, merchants. She earned good money, and still lived at home, so that she was able and indeed eager to help Marian and little Desmond. Marian had, of course, been left practically penniless and she, too, had to set about earning a living. She couldn't, she said faintly, be a clerk or a secretary, but she had certain social gifts, and it was obvious to Emily that she hoped, now she was a widow, to re-marry. She and Colin had been crazy on dancing and her first job was dance partner at a well-known restaurant. But that didn't last long. During her first week a Lancashire lad, having danced twice with her, said with brutal frankness, " Nay, lass, we've had enow of this. Now let's get back and strip." Marian explained indignantly that she wasn't that kind of a girl and, abandoning dancing as a livelihood, found work at a bridge club, where she was extremely successful. After a year or so she was promoted to bridge hostess, a position that entailed considerable outlay on clothes and taxis, but it was evidently a profitable occupation, for she soon branched out into a comfortable service flat and a small car. Later on, when Emily's friends told her frankly that her beloved nephew was no good, a sponger, a scapegrace who only cottoned on to her for what he could get, she would explain everything away by saying that he had never had a settled background. His mother did not re-marry but she had plenty of distractions, and the young Desmond, as he grew older, followed in his parents' footsteps. By the time he was eighteen he knew how to dress, dance, flirt, play bridge and practically any game of chance, and spend money. Making it was a more difficult affair, he explained to his Aunt Emily, whom he always called Penny. As a small boy he had said artlessly on meeting her, " Ont penny," and she, enchanted, had thought he was christening her with a pet name of his own. Even when the truth was explained to her, the name stuck. She was Penny to Desmond to the end of the chapter.

When she was twenty-eight Emily married her employer, as his second wife. She had hesitated when he first proposed, but her mother had said, " Don't be a fool, Emily. When will you get another chance like this, or indeed another chance at all ? You're not Marian, remember," and her father had said, " Good luck, Podge. You know, you'll find it's much more fun sitting at the head of your own table than at the side of your mother's."

So she had married him, and if it hadn't been precisely fun, at least it had spelt comfort and security, and of course it meant she could help Marian more, though she had to do this " on the side." Albert Watson didn't approve of his sister-in-law and pretty soon the two had quarrelled so furiously that Albert wouldn't have her asked to the house, and Marian proclaimed to all and sundry that in any case nothing would have made her come. But the young Desmond had stolen Emily's susceptible heart. Albert was so much engrossed in business that he had very little time for anything else, and Emily made, as they say, a good wife. That is, she was always there when Albert wanted her, occasions which decreased in frequency each year of their marriage. He continued to make more and more money, some of which Emily spent on good frumpish clothes—Albert was a deacon at the chapel and abominated what he called godless fashions—and in collecting a really fine number of brooches, rings and bracelets. For in Albert's simple book of the rules a man's prosperity was judged to a large extent by his wife's appearance as well as by the kind of table he kept and the general appearance—rich, stuffy and comfortable—of his house. So Emily varied his stiff dinner-parties, where she entertained his middle-aged colleagues and their middle-aged wives, where the talk was all of business and servants, with secret delightful excursions to town to meet her attractive nephew. Once she asked Desmond what he meant to do, and he said, " Live, darling," an answer that left her quite unenlightened, though it soon became obvious that living was a very expensive affair. However, having, as she said, neither chick nor child, she was glad enough to help such a charming young man to have a good time. Marian had died of pneumonia shortly before this, and Emily, deceiving her husband deliberately for the first time, said there had been debts, which was quite true, and it wasn't fair to expect Desmond to shoulder them.

" It's even more unjust to expect me to do so," retorted Albert. But, in spite of his displeasure, she managed to finance Desmond under the rose until a piece of carelessness on her part revealed the facts, and Albert promptly had an apoplexy. He was a short man, considerably stouter than his wife, and his sedentary habits and the unnecessary work into which he had plunged for years, weakened his resistance. Twelve months later he also was dead. He had been so busy amassing money that he had never found time to visit his lawyer and change his will, so Emily found herself an extremely rich woman. For a time she was convinced that she was responsible for her husband's death and it took a great deal of tact and special pleading on Desmond's part, as well as reasoned arguments by her friends, to persuade Emily that no man lives for ever, and Albert had been nearly seventy. Desmond, indeed, proved a tower of strength at this time. He had had a number of jobs of recent years, mostly connected with cars; none of them lasted very long or proved very lucrative, but he maintained a high standard of living, dressed, said Emily proudly, like a prince and treated her with a deference and affection to which she had been a stranger all her married life.

"Darling Penny, do shed this guilt complex," he implored her. "Remember that every dog has his day and Uncle Albert wasn't immortal. Now it's your turn. No, don't look so shocked. Do you think I haven't noticed how you gave in to him at every turn for twelve years? Why, you wouldn't even come to a *matinée* unless you were sure he wouldn't come home for tea at five o'clock, when actually he could just as easily have had tea at his office and gone on working there instead of shutting himself up in his study at home."

"He was a good husband to me," said Emily staunchly.

"He didn't go around with chorus girls, I know," Desmond agreed. "But then he found shareholders' accounts more fascinating. It's a mistake to imagine there's only one form of marital infidelity."

She was a little shocked at that, but she had to confess that she didn't really miss Albert much. He had never been there except at his dinner-parties, and she knew now that she had been bored by him for years. It was Desmond who gave up weeks of his time to going through his uncle's papers and giving his aunt advice and offering to come to the lawyer with her—an offer she eagerly accepted, though the lawyer for some reason seemed less pleased to find her bringing an escort when she came to discuss her affairs—and who eventually persuaded her to sell the house.

" There's no sense your hanging on to that mausoleum," he pleaded. " You and Uncle A. always rattled about in it, like a couple of peas, but he regarded it as a business asset, and perhaps it was. Now you understand why I should be no earthly good at business. I should hate the thought of a stately pile hanging round my neck. What you want to do is scrap all your old clothes—once you're out of mourning, I mean, and honestly, Penny, no one mourns for twelve months nowadays—and get the sort of house *you* like and make some friends of your own. You know, you're a young woman still. No one thinks anything of forty these days, and surely it's time you had a bit of fun."

Emily had lived too long in Albert's atmosphere to agree without a struggle, but she did presently, with the lawyer's connivance, get rid of the mausoleum, and buy something smaller and more to her own taste. It was here that Desmond proved invaluable. He persuaded her to buy a little car, which he drove for her and on whose sale, though he didn't mention the fact, he obtained a commission. In it they went round day after day proving that there are three sorts of liars—liars, damned liars and house agents—but eventually she bought Kozicot and furnished it, still with Desmond's assistance, in a manner that made him groan inwardly, but against which he bore up bravely, as indeed he might well do, seeing he persuaded her to get all her stuff through friends of his. When it was all done she asked him about his own plans, and was dismayed to find that he was not only without funds but actually in debt. To Emily as to Albert debts were horrifying.

" My dearest boy, you should have told me. You know I'm only too glad to help."

" Penny, my angel, how could I bother you when you had so much to think of ? I was only too glad to be of service. As a matter of fact, I did pass up something that might have been quite useful a while back, but it would have meant going north immediately and—well, you do need someone to look after you, don't you ? "

" Oh, Desmond, you shouldn't have done that." She was instantly distressed. " You must think of your own prospects. One of these days you'll want to get married, and——"

But he only laughed and put his arm round her, and said, " Not likely. There's going to be a war one of these days, and I don't want my widow to be a charge on the state."

She was dreadfully distressed when he said that. " It creates the wrong atmosphere," she insisted. " If everybody goes about expecting a war we shall get one."

" We shall get one anyway," he told her cynically. " Now, stop worrying about me. I shall get by all right. I always have before. Besides, I dare say it wouldn't have come to much. I don't believe I could stand the dismal north for long."

" Mr. Matthews would have looked after things for me," she insisted.

" And sent you in a whacking great bill. I know these lawyers."

It did cross her mind that Mr. Matthews' bill would be a fleabite compared with the cheque she wrote out and gave to Desmond a few days later, but her native good sense told her she would have had to pay them both in all probability, and it had been delightful having so attractive a young man to dance attendance on her and help her with her choice of furnishings and draperies. Shopmen, she thought naïvely, were much pleasanter if you took a young man with you.

As part return for the generous help afforded during her lifetime Marian had given her sister some bridge lessons and though there had been few opportunities of turning these to good effect while Albert reigned supreme,

Emily now listened to her nephew and took a further course from a girl he recommended very strongly indeed.

" You've got to make some sort of life for yourself," he assured her. " And if you don't learn to play cards you'll find yourself facing a pretty lonely old age."

To everyone's surprise she proved quick and apt at the game, and she soon joined the local bridge club in which she became a permanent star. Indeed, she became something of a bridge fiend and achieved quite a position locally. She gave good parties and was generous with tournament prizes and clever about food—that much at least Albert had taught her.

" If you're going to make a gesture make a generous one," he used to say.

## 3

So, for some years, life went along very pleasantly. She learned not to ask Desmond about his work or his finances, but there were various occasions throughout the year when she could make him presents without appearing too obvious. Of course, some of her bridge friends, who had met him, warned her she was, as Dossie Brett put it, being played for a sucker, but Emily told herself comfortably that poor Dossie was jealous. She was a sharp-faced spinster in the mid-thirties, and her chances in the Matrimonial Stakes, said Mrs. Easingwold, one of Emily's particular bridge four, were pretty low. This Mrs. Easingwold, Dossie Brett, a Mrs. Durrant and Emily, played regularly together every week, and were chosen by the local bridge club to represent them when Southwood played Eltham Way in the annual tournament.

" And even if Dossie's right," Emily told herself, " I've nothing particular to do with my money. It'll all come to Desmond in the end, and if he'd rather have it now, when it's more useful to him, what does it matter ? " (But she did wish dear Desmond would marry and have some dear little children.) Desmond, however, showed no domestic tendencies. He went about a good deal and always looked very handsome and debonair, so she wondered how any girl could resist him. But whenever she spoke of marriage he only said, " The modern woman isn't content to be man's equal, she wants to be his superior. You can't expect a chap to want to marry any one like that."

Then came the war Desmond had always prophesied and he spent several months trying to get accepted for one of the services. Eventually he got into the R.A.F. and wouldn't say a word of what he was doing. Mrs. Easingwold and Mrs. Durrant and Emily all went into the W.V.S., but Dossie Brett became a Civil Servant and dashed all over the country on what she called " hush-hush jobs."

" Though how anything Dossie does can be hush-hush defeats me," said outspoken Mrs. Easingwold. " She's like the crocodile in Peter Pan, you can hear her coming a mile away."

During the war Emily lived in daily terror of an official telegram with the news that Desmond had crashed. She did nothing very important in the W.V.S. and never achieved a photograph in the paper or a meeting with the Queen. Once or twice Desmond turned up on leave, bringing a girl with him, and she privately wondered why he couldn't be attracted by a really nice one, the marrying sort. However, she had to agree that these were no days for marriage, and continued to pray for the end of the war. This came in due course and she attended a Thanksgiving Service; but Dossie Brett said frankly, " Well, I must say I shall miss it. Good old war. Nothing as good as that's going to happen to me again."

Emily thought she was probably right when the country put a Labour Government into power and (said Mrs. Easingwold) sent dear Mr. Churchill into the wilderness, and quiz-masters and cartoonists began to make jokes about longer queues for less food. Then the dreadful thing, the dreadful personal thing, that is, happened to

Mrs. Watson. One day her " daily " came in with the news that a Mr. Abrahams wanted to see her.

" Are you sure he wants me ? " asked Emily. " I don't know a Mr. Abrahams."

" I think he's a friend of Squadron-Leader Raikes," said the girl, who wore slacks and smoked incessantly.

" Oh ? Well, ask him to come in, Doris," said Mrs. Watson, instantly apprehensive. Something, she was convinced, had happened to Desmond. Ever since his demobilisation he had adopted a cynical, not to say bitter attitude that filled her with confusion. She knew, of course, that peace was disappointing, but then she remembered the other war, and knew that Peaces generally are of this kind. Desmond had had a good gratuity but he never seemed to have any money ; partly, she felt, he had got used to letting her help him during the war, when she had, perhaps, been rather reckless, thinking that if she refused him or was niggardly this time, there might never be another opportunity and she would be haunted by the memory of her refusal for the rest of her days. He explained that a fellow wanted a bit of a let up after a war, and added that the Government was making a dead set at chaps like himself—who didn't fancy the Civil Service, but wanted a chance of showing what they could do as individuals.

" They're so infernally illogical," he complained. " They spend years training a fellow to trust his own judgment and then put every conceivable obstacle in his way when he wants to show a little enterprise in civilian life."

Emily agreed that it was very hard, but she couldn't help noticing that other people's sons and nephews were settling down.

" Ah, but they had jobs before the war," Desmond pointed out, and Emily, remembering that he had won a decoration, had not the heart or the courage to point out that Desmond had had plenty of opportunity to get into a pre-war job if only he hadn't found it so difficult to stay in any place for more than a few weeks. Recently he had asked her for a thousand pounds—an advance payment, he'd called it—and she had said that if he would give her some details she would ask Mr. Matthews if it was a good thing, and Desmond had flared up and said he wasn't going to have his future ruined by some old fool who'd sat tight on his backside all through the war, and flung out. Certainly he had come back a day or two later, and they hadn't mentioned the money again, but ever since then she had felt apprehensive.

She stood up to meet Mr. Abrahams, who wasn't in the least what she had anticipated. She had, not unnaturally, supposed that Desmond, faced by her refusal, had gone to the Jews, though Albert had always said they wouldn't lend you anything without security, and quite right too, he had added. Mr. Abrahams was quite a young man, certainly no older than Desmond, and not in the least what she had imagined a moneylender would be like. And it had turned out that he wasn't one. In fact, he seemed as embarrassed as Emily herself. When he had taken the chair she offered him, he said he was very sorry to have to call, but he thought when she heard what he had to say she would be glad he had taken the liberty. She said was it something to do with her nephew and he said Yes, he was afraid it was and, opening his wallet, produced a cheque bearing Desmond's flamboyant signature. This he passed to her. When she looked at it she faltered that there must be some mistake. For the cheque was made out to Mr. Abrahams and was drawn for two thousand pounds.

" I'm afraid there has," her visitor agreed, " though not perhaps quite the sort you have in mind."

" I mean," said poor Emily, contriving in spite of her shortness and plumpness to look dignified, " my nephew cannot have drawn this cheque. He doesn't own so much money."

" That's just the trouble," agreed Mr. Abrahams.

" Then it was quite senseless drawing it," said Emily sharply.

" More than senseless, Mrs. Watson. Criminal."

" Oh no. Not criminal. He—he probably didn't realise it couldn't be met." But even as she said the words she knew they meant nothing.

" I'm afraid we can't believe that. As a matter of fact, he had been warned by his bank that he was overdrawn and that no further cheques would be honoured until he paid in something with which to meet them. As you can see, this one has bounced."

" Bounced ? " She looked at him in perplexity. She had sometimes—not very often but sometimes—heard Albert speak about business. (He had clung to the Victorian view that women knew nothing about money and had seen to it that at least one of them would have no opportunity of learning.) And the word bounced in connection with a cheque had never been so much as mentioned.

Mr. Abrahams explained, and she was more shocked than ever. Shocked and puzzled. Because Desmond couldn't have imagined the bank would honour the cheque, so it was a waste of twopence drawing it in the first place.

" If a man draws a cheque after he's been warned by the bank he becomes liable to criminal action," Mr. Abrahams went on. " The bank may utter a writ against him——"

" Oh no, they mustn't do that." Because even if Desmond had sailed perilously near the wind, and she was uncomfortably certain that Albert would have put it much more strongly and as everybody knew on such a matter Albert was never wrong, still he was a war hero and her only living relative, and if, as of course he must, he married and had children, their father mustn't be an ex-convict. She tried to tell Mr. Abrahams all this in a jumbled fashion, ending up by asking if there was nothing she could do to put matters right, without invoking the police.

" That's really why I came to see you. Mind you, you are under no obligation at all, and it's only fair to warn you that your nephew's reputation in this connection is not very sound. I mean, even if you clear him this time, if you feel disposed to do anything so generous, I'm afraid you can't count on his not—er—trying it on again."

But at that Emily, who was still shocked to the core by what Desmond had done, drew up her five feet one inch and said she was quite convinced that there was a misunderstanding and there had been no intention of deliberate fraud. Mr. Abrahams looked as though he would have agreed with everything Albert had ever said about women and business and let it go at that, only adding that he didn't want to take advantage of a lady's good-nature.

"Good-nature has nothing to do with it," retorted Emily, beginning to feel anger instead of shame. "Naturally if you are owed this amount by a member of my family I should be prepared to discharge the debt."

"I have the papers here," said Mr. Abrahams, and fished some documents out of his pocket. She saw to her horror that he described himself as a turf accountant and realised that this enormous sum was the result of unwise speculation. But, she reminded herself, perfectly honest men speculate. That's how fortunes are made. For Mr. Barton, Emily's father, had been connected with the Stock Exchange and used to tantalise his family by telling them how men rose to affluence overnight by good judgment or good luck.

"And how he can sit there and talk without ever doing anything to make a fortune himself I cannot conceive," Mrs. Barton used to say.

But even Emily had to admit that if you gambled with money you hadn't got which, she understood, was what Desmond had done, you were committing a criminal act, particularly if you drew a cheque that subsequently bounced, to cover your losses.

"If I give you my cheque for a similar amount, and of course there will be no difficulty about *that*, you promise me you will take no action," she observed frostily to Mr. Abrahams.

"If I have my money I've no ground for taking action," said he, simply.

So there and then she sat down and wrote him a cheque and asked for Desmond's in exchange, and when he had gone she burnt the 'stumer' cheque and congratulated herself on having asked for a receipt. Then, courageous and alarmed both together, she sat down and wrote to Desmond asking him to come and see her at once.

He turned up cheerful and debonair, and that was a further shock, but nothing compared with the one that followed. For when Desmond had heard her story he stared at her as if he thought one of them had gone raving mad.

"Penny! Is this a joke? Oh, but it is, of course. You don't really mean you gave that chap two thousand pounds?"

"It was to save you from going to prison," Emily pointed out.

"There was never any question of my going to prison. On my sam, Penny, you ought to have a keeper. Have you never heard of con. men?"

"What are they?" Emily wanted to know.

He told her as tersely as Mr. Abrahams had explained about cheques that bounced.

"This fellow, whom you'd never seen before, marched in and demanded two thousand pounds and showed you a cheque, and you handed over the money without making a single inquiry? Penny, have you gone out of your mind?"

"But—but—he showed me the bill. I've got it here." She took it out of the drawer of her desk and showed it to him.

He pushed it away impatiently. "That doesn't mean a thing. I tell you, you've been absolutely had. I've never heard of this chap, Abrahams, and I've certainly never laid a bet with him. Didn't it even occur to you to get in touch with me before you threw that money down the drain?"

"But he showed me your cheque—the one you signed," protested Emily. She was all at sea now.

" I tell you I never signed any such cheque. I'm not quite crazy. My bank manager wouldn't even need to turn up my account to know it couldn't be met. You've bought it this time all right, Aunt Emily."

He never called her that. She knew he must be furious.

" But—but he was quite certain. And he seemed to know all about you," she urged.

" About me ? He clearly knew all about you. I don't advise you to make a habit of this sort of thing. You'll find yourself not only bankrupt but certified."

She had never seen him in such a state.

" You mean, he invented the whole thing ? "

" I certainly do. Where's the cheque he showed you ? You didn't let him get away with that, too ? "

" Of course not. I insisted on his giving it me there and then."

" Well, where is it ? "

" I—I destroyed it. He advised me to."

Desmond laughed harshly. " I'll say he did. Why, if we had it we might be able to sue him, but as it is you've got no proof that it ever existed."

" There's this receipt. We must see him——"

" I don't suppose he gave you his real name—or his address. I must say I've never heard of him."

It didn't occur to her to ask him how he could be so knowledgeable about turf accountants. She realised it was just the sort of thing he would know all about.

" I shall take it to Mr. Matthews," she said firmly. " He'll advise me what we had better do."

" Oh, he'll advise you to do nothing," Desmond assured her.

" He's got £2,000 out of me on false pretences."

" That's why he'll advise you to do nothing. You see, if it gets about that you gave two thousand pounds to this fellow you say you know nothing about—well, people will think it's a bit queer."

He had to explain that, too, and when she understood him she felt as though the earth were dissolving under her feet.

" You mean, people might think he was blackmailing me ? But why on earth should he ? "

" That's what they'll want to know. They'll say you wouldn't have given it to him without some good reason."

" I thought I had a good reason."

" You mean, you're going to make the world a present of the fact that you thought your nephew was a criminal ? Well, they may believe it, though it won't do either of us much good even if they do."

She realised presently that there was nothing she could do. When they made inquiries they found that no one had ever heard of Mr. Abrahams at this address, and though Mr. Matthews, in whom she ultimately confided, advised her to go to the police, she wouldn't do that. She didn't at that stage suspect the truth, that it was a put-up job between Desmond and his equally unscrupulous friend, but she felt in her bones that she would be doing her nephew a disservice by dragging in the authorities.

" You know, Penny, you really ought to have someone to advise you, to help you keep an eye on things," said Desmond. " No, I don't mean myself—you might think I wasn't disinterested—but someone who could stop you making ducks and drakes of your fortune. Poor old Uncle Albert would turn in his grave if he saw his hard-earned cash being chucked away on rotters like that."

But if the late Mr. Watson had been going to do anything so improbable, he must have been spinning like a teetotum for years, having regard to Emily's transactions with her graceless nephew.

This incident, however, was a milestone in her life. She brooded so much over it, partly because she was ashamed at having believed such a story about Desmond, partly because she did begin to wonder if she was a fit custodian of her cash if she could be so easily defrauded, that her friends began to notice a change in her. She even revoked at the bridge table, which was better proof to them of her mental instability than if she had torn off her clothes and rushed naked round the room.

They talked about it when she wasn't there. Poor old Emily, they said, showing her age. And—Must be a lot older than we thought and Of course now I come to think of it, her husband was about 70. They talked, too, of Desmond, and Dossie Brett, whose pose it was to be very modern—and indeed in that community she was the modern girl *par excellence*—said, " No nephew of mine would be allowed to milk me like that," to which Mrs. Easingwold, who also liked to show her modernity by being daring, made the appropriately coarse retort. As for Emily, she became so obsessed by the affair that she started to mutter to herself when she was out or knitting at home.

" Any one would have been taken in," she declared to an invisible audience. " After all, it was the sort of thing that might happen to any one. If I'd given Desmond the thousand pounds he wouldn't have taken chances."

Then she would remind herself that Desmond hadn't known anything about it, but she had to admit that the pseudo-Mr. Abrahams must have known quite a lot about Desmond. Because—that was the shocking thing—it *might* have been true. There was no chance of getting the money back, because by the time Desmond had answered her summons and explained that all this was nothing to do with him the cheque had been passed. The bank hadn't queried it ; why should they ? Mr. Abrahams might have been a jeweller—she had bursts of extravagance when she bought herself what Desmond called gee-gaws, with a particular stress on diamonds. This was partly because she liked diamonds, and partly because Albert had said to her, " If ever you buy stones don't get pearls or emeralds or any of that lot ; they deteriorate in value according to the fashion of the moment. But diamonds are always money."

Things went on like this for a little while and then her friends began to suggest tactfully that she must be lonely, why didn't she have someone to live with her ?

" I don't want any one." It was Maisie Easingwold who made the suggestion, and Emily simply stared.

" Still, it's a big house just for you."

But Emily countered that by saying she was accustomed to a big house, and Albert would have called Kozicot simply a cottage. Then Providence, in the rather improbable disguise of Dossie Brett, took a hand. It appeared that Dossie's lease had come to an end and the landlord wouldn't renew. Dossie went to the Town Hall about it, but got no satisfaction there. Dossie's house was wanted by its owner, a young service man who had inherited it from his father just after the end of the war, and now he was married and had a baby and nowhere to live. Obviously, if it came to hardship, his need was greater than hers.

Not that Dossie saw it like that. She fumed and raged. All very well to talk about equal citizenship and during the war they were glad enough to back women and their claims, but now the war was over men had preference everywhere, just as they'd done in the bad old Tory days.

" If you were expecting a baby," began Mrs. Easingwold, and Dossie said it was enough to make one. However, there wasn't a thing she could do about it, and she had to start looking about for somewhere else to live. Even the hotels had waiting lists and, as she said, everyone knew that hotel proprietors cheated you right and left and kept putting up prices whenever they felt like it—and Mr. Bevan or whoever was responsible did nothing about them. Then it was that the idea was mooted that she should go, for a time anyway, while she continued to look round, to Emily Watson's. Afterwards no one was quite sure with whom the notion originated. Certainly not with Emily, who was heard to say afterwards, when the arrangement was a *fait accompli* that she'd as soon live with a boa-constrictor and at least Providence had seen to it that boa-constrictors were dumb.

## 4

It was after one of their bridge fours that Dossie, who had been holding forth on her usual topics, unfair discrimination, the lack of interest of Mr. Bevan-or-whoever-it-was and the possibility of finding herself without a roof —literally, my dears, without a roof—that Dossie suddenly turned on poor Emily Watson and said in a joking tone, " How would you like to have me for a blind pig, Emily ? "

Emily genuinely took this for a joke and said something rather smart about not having a sty at her house, and it was a little time before she realised that Dossie was quite in earnest.

" After all, you've bags of room," said Dossie. " And I think rooms get a sort of morbid atmosphere if they're not lived in."

Emily tried frantically to give the impression that she lived in all her rooms in turn, but the others upheld Dossie. After all, they said, she had to go somewhere and for one reason or another, all excellent reasons on the face of them, they couldn't offer her hospitality.

" You'd find me much too stick-in-the-mud for you," protested poor Emily, feeling the fascinated horror of someone who sees a tidal wave travelling straight towards her but can't really believe she's going to be drowned.

But Dossie laughed and said she could be ever such an old-fashioned girl when she liked. Eventually Emily promised to think about it, but on the way back she told herself fiercely that in no circumstances would she have Dossie Brett to live with her. Since Albert's death her sense of liberty had been her mainstay ; she even thought she'd be happier quite poor and free than as rich as a millionaire and have to share a house with Dossie Brett.

The following week the trio, actuated partly by a real feeling that companionship would be good for Emily, and partly by the thought that if Dossie was at Kozicot she couldn't be at Mon Repose or Mi-one, returned to the attack.

" You'd better close with the offer while it's still firm," Dossie warned her. " Mr. Bevan's coming on the war-path any day now, putting in peace-time evacuees, and you'd get a mother and six children in a house your size. Surely, Emily dearest, you'd rather have me than a mother and six children."

Reluctantly Emily admitted that she would. Dossie was such a rattle she was always out and about collecting gossip with all the verve of a city child picking wild flowers. Still, she would be *there*. There was no getting away from that. Finally, she said weakly that perhaps Miss Brett would like to come for a week or two, just till she could find something else to suit her.

" I'm sure you're doing the right thing, Emily," said Mrs. Easingwold and Mrs. Durrant said the same. It had occurred to Emily that Mrs. Durrant might offer Dossie hospitality. Her house was bigger than Kozicot, but Mrs. Durrant said she simply daren't, there was her married daughter to think of.

" I thought she was in Rhodesia," said Emily, whereupon Mrs. Durrant asked her sharply if she'd never heard of people coming back from Rhodesia.

It had been arranged that Dossie should store her furniture—my few sticks, she called them gaily—but when she arrived at Kozicot a van came with her. She was sure dear Emily would understand that she couldn't write except at her own bureau and there was a special chair and a stool and some odds and ends, and she had put in some quite appalling rubbish that she thought Emily would find useful. She kept picking up one thing after another and explaining what each was for, which was just as well, thought Emily grimly, since no one could possibly have guessed.

" She can't have brought all those things just for a week or two," thought poor, distracted Emily, and she was quite right. Emily's friends told her what an admirable arrangement it was and how she'd never feel solitary at night now. So nice to have someone to talk to.

What they should have said was, " To have someone to talk to you," for Dossie was always full of ideas, suggestions, proposals, criticisms. She said she didn't sleep very well and chuckled at herself and said, Uneasy conscience, and Emily could only suppose that when she couldn't sleep she thought up new ways of tormenting her hostess. She was always telling Emily, for instance, that she ought to " get out of herself," she tried to make her follow a time-table, she said blithely no woman need grow old these days, an observation so absurd that Emily couldn't even combat it. It didn't help matters that Desmond didn't like Dossie.

" How's your Charm Girl to-day ? " he would ask, and Emily would find herself floundering in a sea of half-truths about her being really very kind-hearted. . . .

" About as kind-hearted as a black mamba," said Desmond robustly. " She don't like me. That's obvious."

And Dossie would say, " Really, Emily, you make a fool of yourself about that nephew of yours. When's he going to settle down and earn an honest living ? "

Emily was once goaded into retorting, " Earning a living isn't as easy as you seem to think. People like you with independent incomes—— "

To which Dossie replied, inevitably, " You're forgetting I worked all through the war, and though Heaven knows I don't want to blow my own trumpet, I don't think any fighting man earned his pay more hardly than I did."

No one could argue with Dossie when she talked like this, because no one knew what she had done, except that she had been attached to the Home Office and invariably referred to Mr. Morrison by his Christian name.

Emily was afraid that Dossie would drive Desmond away altogether, and for a time it looked as though she might. But one day Dossie said impudently, " I don't think much of the R.A.F. if it can be dispersed by an ex-civil servant, and a female at that," after which she and Desmond seemed to get on a little better. But their manner towards each other was still so off-handed that the truth came to Emily as the cruellest of shocks.

Desmond had been down only a few days before, bringing with him a very delightful man, called Dr. MacKinnon. MacKinnon paid more attention to his hostess than is customary among the young nowadays, when good manners are themselves considered a mannerism, and was so sympathetic that she had the greatest difficulty in not telling him what she really felt about Dossie Brett. Dossie said afterwards, " You seem to have made quite a hit with the doctor. But then doctors have so much experience, haven't they ? " That was the sort of barbed remark she revelled in.

It was about four mornings later that Emily came down earlier than Dossie for once to find a letter from Desmond by her plate. She ripped it open, pleased with him for writing, and began to read. A minute later she was feeling like one of those weeds that wave to and fro in aquaria, only held in place because of the law of gravity (or so Emily supposed it to be) that keeps them fettered to their cranny of rock. The room, in Victorian parlance, went round her. The walls seemed to be actually advancing and she put out her hands to ward them off. This seemed to startle them, for they snapped back into place again. Even so, inanimate matter seemed to have taken life unto itself, for when she blindly put out her hand towards her tea-cup it wasn't there, and she saw it—distinctly saw it—on the other side of her plate. Still, in the face of such a crisis, tea didn't really matter. Desperately her gaze flickered back to the letter she still held in her shaking hand. Perhaps, she thought, this was Providence, who notoriously cares for the weak and the afflicted. Here, before her still besotted vision, was evidence of such a plot as she could never have dreamed. For Desmond Raikes, the unscrupulous, the black-hearted, the morally corrupt young man on whom all her hopes were set, had made that one slip which, say the authorities, all criminals make sooner or later, and, writing both to his aunt and to his friend, MacKinnon, had put the letters into the wrong envelopes.

MacKinnon's name was Percy and Desmond's writing was so execrable that at first she had read the address as Penny.

My Dear Percy (Desmond wrote),

I am not surprised to hear that you agree with me there shouldn't be too much difficulty persuading poor old Penny that she is *non compos mentis* and suggesting that she should enter a hospital as a voluntary patient. For some time now her friends have noticed a great change in her—she is definitely eccentric, as witness her behaviour to that chap, Abrahams—he says she swallowed the yarn, hook, line and sinker and paid up like a bird, which, you will agree, is not the act of a sane person. And Dossie Brett, who, for all she has a face like the back of a taxi-cab, which, poor girl, I suppose she can't help, is a sound ally, could provide any number of instances which would convince a doctor that Penny needs treatment of some kind. I quite see your point about requiring two doctors for a certificate, but if we can make her go in as a voluntary patient we can get over that difficulty. I think if it is put to her strongly enough that refusal on her part now may lead to complete certification later—and if you tell her this she is sure to fall for it as clearly she's fallen for you, another sign of brain softening (nothing personal intended, as you will understand), she will agree. I shall suggest that she gives me a power of attorney while she's under treatment. There may be some difficulty here. She will want to hand over her affairs, lock, stock and barrel, to that ass, Matthews, but I shall remind her that so long as we keep the story in the family there will be no scandal—she can simply tell Matthews she's going away for a time and doesn't want to be bothered with business. In any case, I shall suggest her leaving me an open cheque to meet outstanding liabilities. She won't want to admit to

Matthews that she is unbalanced. You know what lawyers are about wonky old ladies—always an eye on the main chance. And, of course, dear old Doss is in the same boat.

There was some more of it but that was as far as she had got when she realised that a voice was calling her, and she looked round surprised to find the room hadn't changed at all, and that Doris, looking at her in what she could only describe as a very peculiar way, was trying to attract her attention.

" Are you feeling all right, Mrs. Watson ? " she asked in the cheerful democratic manner of her time. " You look very peculiar."

Peculiar, thought poor Emily, desperately. That was the polite word for mad. When old Colonel Houghton got so bad that he had to be shut up, all the neighbours said he had been very peculiar for some time, whereas everyone knew he was as mad as a hatter, but that hadn't seemed very important until he mistook his housekeeper for a pig and tried to cut her throat. Emily pushed her table napkin over the tell-tale letter and said of course she was all right, she had been thinking of something else, and immediately wondered if Doris also was in the plot. If Desmond, if Dossie could be scheming in this heartless manner against her, why should Doris be immune ?

" It's Miss Brett, Mrs. Watson," said the girl. " Not feeling quite up to the mark, she says, and won't be down to breakfast."

" Thank God," thought Emily hysterically. " Thank God, thank God, thank God."

She must have said it aloud, because Doris was smiling broadly and saying in a sympathetic voice, " Talks the hind leg off a goat, doesn't she ? I've often wondered how you put up with it. And she may be not quite herself, as she says, but it hasn't spoilt her appetite. She wants everything the same as usual, and her writing-case and the little wireless and the *Radio Times* and her Boots library book and her cigarettes. You can always tell the ones that have never had to work for themselves. They always give twice as much trouble as any one else."

She marched off, carrying two letters that had come for Dossie, and slammed the door cheerfully behind her. Even after she had gone Emily didn't feel safe.

" I must get away," she kept whispering (but perhaps, she thought, she was saying that aloud, too. Shouting it, perhaps. Perhaps these days she didn't know when she shouted and everybody had noticed it.) The walls seemed full of eyes staring, ears listening. The wind outside the pane was whispering, really whispering, not shouting.

" Mad," it was whispering, " poor Emily Watson. She's mad, quite, quite mad. And she doesn't know, of course. Mad people never do. But she's going away. Going away. Going away." It was like one of those sustained choruses on the B.B.C.

Horrified, she heard her own voice repeat, " Going away " and because at that all the eyes in the wall slanted to stare at her she snatched up the *Record* and held it in front of her face. There was a sort of mist, a mist like madness. She dashed a hand in front of her eyes to clear it away. When it had quite gone she was looking hard at the front page of the paper. And in the very middle of the Personal column she saw the advertisement.

## 5

It seemed to her that it might have been inserted simply for her benefit. So, later, it was to seem to the man who wrote it. Emily read the enchanted phrases over and over again. A lady seeking rest and refreshment—that was certainly herself—seclusion—that was precisely what she wanted. A house in a wood—could anything be more secluded than that ? Wherever Desmond and the false Dossie looked for her, it certainly wouldn't be there. And the final bonne-bouche—no other guests taken. That meant that, even if Those Two did by some miracle of misfortune track her down, they couldn't insinuate their spy into the household. She would, of course, make absolutely certain that there was no chance of this clause being overruled. She would say she had to have complete quiet, and she would offer to pay anything they asked to secure it. Already she was laying her plans. She would take a considerable sum of cash with her ; then she needn't send to her bank for funds. Banks, of course, are supposed to be models of integrity, but Emily was not sure whether, supposing Desmond could persuade Mr. Tennant at the Bank that she was ' peculiar ', he might not reveal her whereabouts. It wasn't Desmond but Dr. MacKinnon who was the real danger, and whatever Desmond discovered he would certainly pass on to his medical friend.

What good fortune, she reflected, that to-day of all days Dossie should be breakfasting in bed. It didn't really mean, as Doris had already pointed out, that she was ill, but of course a late lie-in, as she put it, was a treat to her after years of having to get up and get her own meals. She often told Emily so. Not that Emily minded. She would have liked Dossie to have breakfast in bed every morning, and would have increased Doris' already exorbitant wages, if necessary, if only Dossie had agreed. But when she did once tentatively suggest this, Dossie laughed and patted her hand and said, " I haven't come here to be a burden to you. *Au contraire.*" (Dossie liked to air her French.)

However, this morning she was actually in bed and Emily had time to write an answer to the advertisement before her companion appeared. She told Box O.151 that she was a middle-aged widow who needed complete seclusion for an indefinite period, and thought that his advertisement was precisely what she had been looking for. She said that she was not an invalid, that she was prepared to pay a reasonable sum for privacy, she reminded the advertiser that no other guests were taken, and she asked for a full reply as to situation and conditions. If, she said, the house was adjacent to a railway station or a high road served by ordinary transport, then would he please inform her to this effect, as she wanted real privacy. She added that she needed a rest on account of acute domestic anxieties, and she asked him to treat her letter as confidential. When he replied would he kindly use the stamped addressed envelope she enclosed herewith, as she was anxious to make her plans without being compelled to disclose them.

The envelope referred to was addressed:

Mrs. Albert Watson,
The Country Gentlewoman's Club,
Kimball Street, London, W.1.

and in the corner she printed in capital letters: Not to be Forwarded. It would be simply courting disaster to have a reply sent to Kozicot. Dossie nearly always contrived to come down first, and she never hesitated to paw through the letters and comment frankly on Emily's share.

"You've heard from the fascinating nephew," she would observe. "I couldn't quite make out that hand-writing," indicating some other letter, "but the postmark's Bournemouth. I didn't know you had any friends at Bournemouth."

In the same way, Emily was convinced that when she telephoned from her bedroom Dossie would lift the receiver from the downstairs instrument and listen in, not to the whole conversation, of course, but just long enough to find out the name of her correspondent. More than once she had tried to suggest that she knew Dossie did this, but the whole matter was so sordid that she could never find the right words. Now she knew that in no circumstances would she ever refer to the matter, because Dossie would explain, if explanations really became necessary, that she (Emily) was—well, you know, not quite . . . and one had to keep a check. She could even suggest that it had been Desmond's idea that she should come here.

"I must get away quickly," decided Emily, sealing her envelope, and feeling grateful that there was a post-box just across the road. She snipped the advertisement out of the *Record*, in case, later on, inquiries were made, and Dossie saw the insert and jumped to conclusions. Not probable, of course, but when you were fighting for your existence as an independent person you couldn't afford to take even unlikely risks.

By the same post she wrote to her reliable man of affairs, Mr. Matthews, asking him to send her her will, as she wanted to make some changes, probably add a codicil. She promised she wouldn't keep it long.

Presently Dossie came down, full of breakfast and curiosity, saying as she always did, " Anything amusing in your post ? Mine was . . . " and then long detailed descriptions of her letters which always seemed to come from old school-friends whom Emily had never met, and in whom she could not conceivably be interested. However, Dossie spared her nothing, and when she ran out of breath she nodded meaningly.

" What about yours ? "

" Just bills," said Emily, vaguely.

Dossie looked as though she were going to challenge that, but at that instant the telephone rang. Dossie snatched up the receiver.

" For me," she announced in the sort of voice that requests the other person to go away.

Dossie on the telephone was inclined to be arch, and to roll her eyes and lift her eyebrows, just as though she were talking on television, thought the practical side of Emily. She was sure she didn't want to hear even one side of the conversation, and she went up to her room still thinking of the advertisement. A few minutes later she decided to ring up her hairdresser and lifted the receiver, only to realise that Dossie was still on the line.

" If the Prime Minister ever rations conversation Dossie will die of inanition," she reflected, and was just going to put the receiver back when she heard a familiar voice that wasn't Dossie's speaking from the other end of the line. Her hand stiffened ; then deliberately she put the receiver to her ear.

Desmond's familiar voice said, " For God's sake, Dossie, find out. If she's had that letter we're sunk. She'll disinherit me before to-morrow's sun, and then nobody in London will lend me a bean. I only get by now by quoting her. Old Uncle A. was a pretty grim specimen, but he was as trusted as the Bank of England used to be. What infernal luck that she was down first this morning."

" I'll find out," said Dossie in her odiously confident way. " She's not likely to tell any one, because she'd be afraid they'd agree and in any case I'll get hold of the letter. Then if trouble does blow up we can say she invented it."

Very quietly Emily put the receiver down. This was a complication she had overlooked. Of course, if Desmond thought she had actually read the letter intended for MacKinnon, and it was obvious that by this time he knew of his mistake, he would be desperate. That bit about using her name when he wanted to borrow money was new to her. If it got around that she had cut him out of her will he would not only find his sources of supply dried up, he would probably be stampeded by demands for back payments.

" I wonder if Desmond would really murder me if there were no other way," she found herself thinking. " He wouldn't be able to wait long, because I might be going up to the lawyers this morning. Of course, Dossie will dog me like a shadow if she thinks I know."

Opening her bag, she took out her nephew's letter. She always opened envelopes carefully, and she had not torn this one. If she stuck down the flap with a little fresh gum no one would guess it had been opened. Then she could slip it back into the box opposite, and it would be delivered again to-morrow. She would make a point of not coming down until Dossie had had an opportunity to nose through the post, and by the time she did arrive the letter would simply have vanished.

She heard the little ring that showed that Dossie had hung up, so she got her connection with her hairdresser, always a useful alibi if you wanted to get away for a day, and then went downstairs again. Dossie was hanging about in the hall.

" By the way," she said casually as Emily appeared, " you didn't hear from Desmond this morning, did you ? "

" Why, ought I to have done ? " Emily's face was a mask.

" Only that yesterday when he rang up—you were out and it wasn't anything important—he said he'd be sending you a line, and I thought it might have come to-day."

" Perhaps it will come on the next post," suggested Emily.

She went out of the house, and looking through the french window saw Dossie gabbling away at the telephone again.

" Getting in touch with Desmond, reassuring him," she thought.

When she came back, having reposted the letter, Dossie exclaimed, " Why, there you are. I thought you'd gone out. Desmond rang up."

" For me ? "

" I said I thought you were out, so I said could I take a message. My dear . . . " she began to laugh. " It's just like something on the stage. He did write to you yesterday—I can't think why it hasn't arrived, but I dare say it's something to do with the Government, they seem to upset everything, don't they ? " (Dossie had said this of every Government in turn.) " It seems he's carrying on with a redhead—no, he didn't go into details, didn't think he should confide in an unmarried gel, I dare say, but what do you think ? He wrote to both of you by the same post, and put the letters into the wrong envelopes."

" I wonder what sort of letters Desmond would write to a redhead ? " murmured Emily. " The ones I get are very monotonous, but perhaps he is quite poetical on occasions."

" Now then." Miss Brett was jocose. She even wagged an admonitory finger. " Fair play. You've had your romance, my dear, let the young people have theirs.

I told him, naturally, that when the letter came you'd return it unread."

" I can see you mean me to," said Emily with a sigh. She wondered which of them had thought up the bit about the redhead.

" So that's settled. I do wonder if the fascinating nephew is thinking of settling down at last. He's no chicken, you know."

" He's like the dove that found no repose on earth around," said Emily in one of her rare flashes. " I mean, if he finds it so difficult to support himself, it would be worse with two of them."

" Ah well, you've been lucky," sighed Dossie. " We can't all be rich widows."

Emily said nothing. She was wondering how soon she could hope for an answer to her letter. It seemed to her that every hour was important. Dossie had doubtless been commissioned to act as a spy and she herself must be most careful of everything she did and said. Once she got away from Kozicot to this mysterious house in the woods she would feel safe. From there she would write to her solicitor and add a codicil to her will. She would settle a lump sum on Desmond and tell him that he would not benefit further from her will. He might try and prove she was unbalanced, but by giving him money right away she would weaken his hand. In the meantime, she must preserve good relations with Dossie and somehow contrive to get away before Miss Brett had recognised her intentions. It would be easy to send Doris off for a day; her ex-W.A.A.F. sister was expecting a baby and Doris was always asking for a few hours off to go and see her. As for Dossie, she had bridge appointments and was an inveterate tea-drinker, and also enjoyed meeting friends for elevenses.

" She may be a dragon," reflected Emily indomitably, " but I feel like St. George. I will not allow her to block my way."

# 6

Vyvyan Forrester, the writer of the advertisement, ripped through the replies with a speed and efficiency that Arthur Crook would have admired. There were more letters than you might have expected ; for, contrary to general belief, being rich does not imply being safe. Forrester sorted the replies into three heaps. Those which were hopeless and could immediately go into the fire. Those worthy of a second reading. Those he would certainly answer. When he opened Emily's reply he said confidently to his wife, " Here's our old girl. I'll write to her by return."

" Why does she wish to come here ? " inquired Berta Forrester. She was much younger than her husband, and spoke with a foreign inflection. " What does she tell you ? "

" Wants to get away from her family. It could be blackmail. It could be she's afraid that what she takes for sugar in the bowl is really arsenic. It happens more often than most people guess."

" You'll see her ? "

" I shall ask her to lunch with me at Parkers. That will flatter her, assuming she knows anything about Parkers. Then I can get her to talk about herself and see if she's our money. If she's no good, there are three others worth trying." He read Emily's letter again. " I wonder what she calls reasonable."

His letter reached the Country Gentlewoman's Club on the second post on Thursday. Emily collected it there on Friday. She had some difficulty in escaping from Dossie. She said she was going up to town to meet a fellow member of the Country Gentlewoman's ; they would lunch together and later, perhaps, go to a film.

" Lunch at the Club ? " inquired Dossie, her eyes gleaming.

" No. No, we shall lunch at a restaurant, and I shall be back to dinner."

She wouldn't put it past Dossie to wait in the hall of the Club and if she was told that Mrs. Watson hadn't been in that day except to collect a letter her suspicions would at once be aroused. Even Miss Brett could not think of any good reason for accompanying Emily up to town, so she got her letter without any trouble. She was quite enchanted by the phrasing, the friendliness, the warmth and yet the warning that perhaps the house wasn't quite what she wanted. Since, wrote Dr. Forrester, I have to be in town on business next week, perhaps you would give me the pleasure of lunching with me at Parkers on Tuesday next. Then I can explain the situation to you and you can decide whether it is what you require. I suggest this, rather than your coming down here, as it is a long, slow journey. I will bring some photographs of the house which give a very good idea of its position.

The letter was signed " Vyvyan Forrester " with (Dr.) in brackets and poor Emily was uncertain whether the Christian name was that of a man or a woman. A man, she thought, would have mentioned his wife. But, though she found nothing odd about a man living in a lonely house in a wood, it did seem to her sinister for a woman to live there. Yet how much more reasonable if the writer should be a woman. A lonely woman, lonely like Emily Watson, wanting a friend to share expenses. . . .

" But if it is a woman I shall not go," she told herself, firmly. " It might be Dossie Brett all over again."

Besides, if Desmond did discover her whereabouts and come to call, he would probably enchant " Dr. Forrester." He had a quality of charm allied with complete unscrupulousness, that virtually gave him a full house for every hand dealt. Still, there could be no harm accepting the invitation. Lunch at Parkers would tie her to nothing. If she didn't like the sound of the place or the sex and identity of the advertiser she could simply say, Thank you for a nice lunch, and take the train back to Southwood. From the Club she wrote her acceptance, went conscientiously to a film so that she could answer the tiresome Dossie's questions, and decided that her choice of a picture, which had really been quite fortuitous, was actually providential.

The film was a much-advertised thriller centring round an old lady, rich, of course, as film old ladies have a habit of being, with a much younger companion who was slowly poisoning her. There was, for heroine, a young girl who the vicissitudes of existence had compelled to accept a job as parlourmaid, and when the death was finally accomplished this girl was instantly arrested. Virtue was of course vindicated, and the girl married the private detective who had always believed in her innocence.

Emily was in so suggestible a state that she could convince herself that the companion in question was remarkably like Dossie, both in manner and appearance, and there was even another man who, though noticeably unlike Desmond, seems to complete the pattern. She did not pause to consider that if the film had presented a rich middle-aged woman seeking sanctuary in a lonely house and there being remorselessly done to death she might still have thought it providential. She went back to Kozicot absolutely resolved to go to the house in the wood if the opportunity was offered her.

Getting up to London on Tuesday presented a good many difficulties. So many, in fact, that she almost had a fit of hysterics at the injustice of life that, giving her abundant wealth with one hand, robbed her of liberty with the other. This time Dossie had no engagement to keep her in Southwood, and she said buoyantly, when Emily announced that she had an appointment with her dentist, that she would come up, too.

"Then I shall be sure you don't lose heart at the last minute and go to another film instead of Queen Anne Street," she said in her abominably roguish manner.

Emily felt desperate. Dossie was quite capable of coming to the dentist's with her, and somehow she had to be stopped. There was a period of twenty-four hours when Emily quite genuinely envied the Borgias. Lovely, she thought, to wear a poisoned ring, affectionately clasp Dossie by the hand in saying Good night—though it would, of course, involve some excuse for so formal a gesture—and go happily to bed knowing that by morning no one but an undertaker would be interested in her future —in Dossie's future, of course. But then, if she could achieve *that*, there would be no need to go to the House in the Wood.

In spite of all her efforts, and she very nearly ran a temperature trying to prevent Dossie coming to town without arousing her suspicions, the two ladies travelled up together on Tuesday morning. At Victoria Emily said quickly that she would take a taxi straight to the dentist, and Dossie said at once, " You could give me a lift. I want to go to Debenham and Freebody to look at that dress they were advertising in Sunday's paper."

Emily said innocently, " I thought that was meant for a girl," and Dossie nudged her in the ribs and said, " A woman's as old as she feels. Now you tell the man to go to Queen Anne Street and I'll take the taxi on."

But Emily counteracted that by telling the man to dump Dossie first, and even Dossie could think of nothing to say to that suggestion. As soon as her odious companion had pushed open the swing doors and the taxi had crossed the lights Emily tapped on the window and said she found she was a bit early for her appointment, and would go to her club in Cavendish Street first. She had had the forethought to tell Miss Brett that she was lunching with a friend, and that at least she thought was near enough the truth to get past the Recording Angel, so she wasn't afraid of being tracked to Mr. Masters' surgery.

" I shall go down as soon as they can have me," she decided, " and once I'm there my troubles will be over."

She was never more wrong in her life.

# 7

She had never been to Parkers. Albert Watson thought a woman's place was in the home, and he didn't take his wife to restaurants. He didn't take other men's wives either. He had never been able to understand how men got disgracefully involved with women when there was a whole fascinating world of business to be explored. In business every transaction was just a little different; in his inexperience he thought that all women were exactly alike.

Emily was impressed by Parkers. It was quite small, very quietly decorated, and there was none of that conspicuousness and social brilliance associated with mink coats and fantastic jewellery that made life like something out of Vogue. She herself wore a beaver coat that Albert had bought her as a sort of trade mark, saying that expenditure in this direction was economy really, and you could always get a price for it if you wanted to change over to sables. When she left Southwood she wore quite modest earrings and a simple gold brooch with a pearl heart on it. But in the Club she put on diamond earrings and a very good diamond clip and a bracelet that Albert had given her.

The man she was going to meet recognised the value of all these the instant he set eyes on her, and for once his intention and hers coincided.

As soon as she walked into Parkers her doubts about Dr. Forrester's sex were resolved. This was not the sort of restaurant to which one woman would take another. Dr. Forrester himself was at first sight a disappointment. He looked so very ordinary, a tallish, slightly stooping figure, with a thick, untidy, black moustache and thick but less untidy dark eyebrows. His dark hair was going a little grey and his clothes were quite undistinguished. But she hadn't been talking to him for five minutes before she realised that you can't always judge by appearances, and it spoke volumes for so undistinguished a figure that he should almost at once seem so much at home in this exclusive restaurant. Not that he was known here to the waiters. They didn't greet him as they did several of the clients who obviously made a rule of coming here, but they seemed to sense immediately a man who would expect first-class service, and she was sure that if he came again he would be remembered.

When he had asked her what she would have as an aperitif and had given the order he smiled at her, and said he hoped he hadn't brought her up from Southwood on false pretences.

" I had better warn you at once," said he, " that we live—my wife and I—at the End of Nowhere. In a sense, we're more cut off from the world than if we lived on a desert island, because desert islanders always appear to be discovered sooner or later, whereas, if we were all stricken with typhus and died, it might be weeks before any one discovered us."

He had a charming voice and the friendliest manner conceivable. She found herself thinking he must enjoy considerable professional success, and then the first question popped into her head and before she could stop herself it had popped out of her mouth.

" If you live so far from anywhere, what happens to your practice ? "

" I'm not in practice at the moment. I haven't been in civilian practice since the beginning of the war. I was out in the Middle East for some time, and after they invalided me out I got taken on by a Quaker unit, and went to the Continent, where I worked with the Underground Movement. I was there on D-day.—— "

She interrupted eagerly to say how splendid Mr. Churchill was, and he replied that it was amazing how splendid quite ordinary people were when war brought them up against things. It took a crisis, he said, to show what people were made of. Emily assented with more eagerness than before. There had been a little man, a greengrocer, at Southwood, whom no one thought very much of, his vegetables were never quite fresh, but when war broke out he became a street fire party leader, and when there was a bomb at the end of the road in 1940 he had, unaided, rescued two old people who were pinned down by a piano. Dr. Forrester, disregarding both her lack of logic and also of relevance, said that was just what he meant, and that got them through the soup and on to the next course. She had let him choose a dish for which, he said, Parkers was famous, a dish made with pigeons, and though she disliked the idea of eating pigeons, the restaurant had disguised them so well that she enjoyed every mouthful. During this course he elaborated the situation.

" The house was built, Heaven knows how, by a fellow called Thorold, an artist, who seems to have been as temperamental as artists are commonly painted. What made him choose such a spot I don't know, except that he presumably wanted peace for his work."

" Perhaps he liked the views," suggested foolish Emily, but the doctor said, No, it couldn't be that, because he wasn't a landscape artist at all. He was an impressionist, and some of his work might even startle Picasso. He had left a number of canvases in a big barn adjoining the house.

" As a matter of fact, I met him during the war. He was one of the official war artists, though what made the authorities choose him I can't imagine, except that they seem to enjoy putting chaps on their mettle and making them show how well they can do the sort of job they have never done before. Thorold was very proud of his work, though I don't think he had ever had much recognition. However, he used to say when the war was over he must marry and beget a family to enjoy his posthumous fortune." His face clouded over. " Poor fellow, he never got as far as that. A sniper picked him off before he'd been out six months. When we came back from France, Berta and I, we wanted somewhere to live and accommodation was almost as bad as it had been out there, and I remembered hearing Thorold talk of this odd house of his. So I came down and saw it--I wanted a quiet place myself to get on with a book I was working on, dealing with reactions to fear and Berta wanted to find some place where she could feel safe—the members of the Resistance Movements had forgotten what security was like—and Thorold's relatives, distant admittedly, didn't seem much interested in him and none of them could imagine how any one, bar a lunatic, could want to live in such isolation, so we acquired it pretty easily. That, in a nutshell "—he smiled again—" explains why we are where we are."

" And you like it ? "

Dr. Forrester smiled. " Oh, yes, we like it, but then, we are, perhaps, rather odd people. It certainly wouldn't be everybody's money. No neighbours, no house nearer than a mile, nine miles to the nearest town even when you've reached the main road, and we are nearly two miles from that. Oh, yes "—he laughed at her surprised face—" it's lonely all right. I wouldn't for the world deceive you, and then have you tell me indignantly when you arrived that I hadn't played fair."

" You said modern comforts," hazarded Emily. Outdoor sanitation, no bathroom, and lamps would be going too far.

" We have those. That is, there are two bathrooms, one of which would belong to our guest, and though there's no piped water—in the circumstances you could hardly expect that—we have two excellent wells and in the kind of weather we've been having recently there's no fear of a water shortage. We generate our own electric light and though, for economy's sake, I switch it off between midnight and seven o'clock in the morning—well, there are plenty of candles, though I like to think that the air at The Cottage will persuade you to sleep the clock round. Thorold laid down a very nice little cellar and neither looters nor German parachutists, who are reputed to have come down in large numbers in the woods surrounding the house, ever tapped it, so if you're accustomed, as I can see you are, to good living you need have no fears on that score. Berta is a first-class cook and somehow we seem to do pretty well. Of course, in the country one isn't so restricted to rationed food as people in towns, and there's a farm not far off that supplies all our dairy produce and we can usually look to them for poultry or an occasional duck. I don't think you'd find we should starve you. And, of course," he added, " you could always come into Oxbridge with me when I go in to do the marketing. Or are you bringing your own car ? I ought to warn you—— "

But she didn't let him finish that. She said at once that she had got rid of the car early in the war, after her nephew went into the Air Force and, since she couldn't drive, she found it both cheaper and more convenient to hire a car whenever she wanted it. Though, really, she added, it was amazing how seldom she did want it.

" Then that's settled. By the way, I think you ought to warn your friends that the road to The Cottage is death to springs. Mine have got seasoned to it, but the local hire companies won't send a car up the by-road."

" I shan't be having any friends. As a matter of fact, I don't even intend to leave my address."

" A real rest cure ? " He smiled as the waiter put a ravishing pêche melba in front of them. " I dare say you're wise. After all, your lawyer can manage things for you, can't he ? I dare say you'll let him know on the strict q.t. where you are ? "

No one less astute than Mr. Crook would have guessed from his voice how much hung on that seemingly casual question.

" No," said Emily firmly. " I shan't even tell him."

She thought the doctor was looking at her in rather an odd way, and this impression was confirmed when he said in a very gentle and sympathetic voice, " Mrs. Watson, I don't wish to appear intrusive, but I am a doctor and you are, I think, contemplating coming to my house. Have you perhaps a particular reason for wishing to go into seclusion just now ? "

He was so kind, so helpful, that she took a lightning decision. She had to share this burden with someone, and there literally wasn't a soul in her own circle to whom she could speak.

"I had better put my cards on the table," she acknowledged. "I dare say it isn't really such an unusual situation as I imagine. I am a very rich woman and I have a nephew who—well, I suppose to him it seems unfair that I should have so much money without having to work for it, though, actually, I did have to be Albert's wife for many years and perhaps that constitutes some sort of claim—in any case, Desmond is fonder of my money than of hard work. And you'll understand, after all the dangers he underwent in the Air Force, I find it difficult to keep refusing. And yet every time I weaken it makes it worse for him in a way."

"I think I understand," agreed Forrester. "You think, if you disappear for a short time, he will have to stand on his own feet?"

"It's worse than that," admitted Emily. "I really don't think he would stop at anything to get this money if I don't give it to him whenever he asks. It's really for my own safety that I'm leaving home."

"You really believe your nephew has criminal intentions against you?"

"It's not that he dislikes me particularly," amplified Emily Watson. "But he must have money, and if one of us has to be—to be shut up, he'd sooner it was me. I really am in more danger than I can make you understand," she continued in a rush, though, had she been able to realise it, she was in worse danger now than she had ever been.

"I quite see you feel worried and anxious to get away, and I think it's a very good plan. Your nephew certainly won't find you at Swinnerton and even if he did—well, if you wanted any help I should be glad to give it. Still, I dare say you'll find that once you are out of the way and can't be tapped, so to speak, he'll begin to understand he must stand on his own feet."

"The trouble is," she whispered, "I'm afraid he—he—the fact is, he doesn't seem to have quite the same standards as most people. I know, of course, the war did make a good deal of difference ; as he says himself, you can't train people for violence and a complete disregard of other people's property, including life, and expect them to come back and settle down perfectly normally."

" Can't you ? " said the doctor dryly. " It's what most of us have to do, all the same. Still, I agree there may be a transition period. You know, from what you tell me—and you must remember that I speak from a wealth of experience—I think, perhaps, you're worrying yourself unnecessarily. Naturally, I don't know your nephew and you do, but I have met a great many young fellows who have been through the same sort of thing, and again and again they seem obsessed with the idea that life owes them something, and they want to collect it. I believe myself that idea is responsible for a great deal of the lawlessness everyone deplores. If you're not there he will have to try and collect from someone else. But most people are fairly well armoured. If you will allow me to say so on such short acquaintance "—and here he gave her his most charming smile—" I think you are probably too sensitive. I mean you are too ready to take everything he says at its face value. Young men have a way of talking very wildly, but a great deal of it, consciously or otherwise, is merely for effect. No, I'm much more concerned for you than I am for him, and I can't help feeling that in your circumstances you could hardly find a better place than The Cottage. I forgot to mention, by the way, that we are on the telephone, so you won't feel cut off from life. If you suddenly want to contact your lawyer or your banker or any of your friends you've only to put a call through. I always think the knowledge that you can walk back as easily as you walked in is very reassuring."

" You have made me feel better already," Emily acknowledged. " But, really, I have talked a great deal about myself. Do tell me about your wife. She doesn't mind the loneliness ? "

" I don't think she would call it lonely. After all, she

has me and it's not often we're separated even for a night. And after those appalling years in occupied France, particularly after she joined the Resistance Movement, she finds trees—the house is surrounded by them, as I think I told you—quite comforting. You see, until now, she has never felt safe. You can sympathise with her there to some extent. It wasn't the Germans who alarmed her; they were the known enemy. It was the familiar friend who might, after all, prove a traitor who kept their nerves at full stretch. Or the girl who brought the milk and made some casual comment on the way the war was going—you could never be absolutely certain she wasn't in German pay, wasn't trying to trip you up, to learn something that might cost you your life. It was never possible to relax. The very people in the same house might betray you. I can see from your expression that you do understand."

"Yes," she said softly. "I understand."

She thought of Dossie Brett, living in her house, Desmond coming in with his charming inconsequent air and delightful ways, the friendly MacKinnon—oh, yes, she understood.

"All she has to fear now," continued Forrester—she thought it an endearing trait, the way he talked about his wife—"are ghosts, and those don't bother her. By the way, how do you feel about them?"

"I'm like your wife. If ghosts are the only enemies I have I shall be safe enough."

"The neighbourhood is popularly supposed to be haunted. I dare say you've heard that certain localities are supposed to be chosen by ghosts. I know of two or three in England, not particular houses, but whole neighbourhoods. It would surprise you to know how superstitious contemporary country folk can be. One hears of native tribes subscribing to this belief or that, and one says, Oh, well, they're natives, but you can find the counterpart of that in our own country at the present time. There's no one in the village who would come near The Cottage after dark. Even tramps keep away. You or I might hear an owl hooting—we have a good many owls—but the villagers know it's the ghost of some girl who died in the woods and whose spirit is imprisoned in a tree—that sort of thing." He went on talking with so much spirit and such obvious knowledge of and absorption in his subject that she forgot they had met less than an hour ago. When it was her turn to speak she said, " There are only two things to be settled now. Terms—and when I can come."

" I warned you the terms are high, at least I hoped the advertisement gave that impression. Berta and I talked things over and at first we thought of advertising two vacancies. There would be certain advantages, from the point of view of the guests, I mean. They would be company for one another and that might be a good thing. But then, it occurred to us that the kind of guest we were angling for would prefer privacy and more space. You see, if we had two we could only offer a bed-sitting-room to each of them, and then they would share the bathroom, and—I don't know why it is, but more bad feeling seems engendered by bathrooms than by wills, and no one can put it more strongly than that. And then, they mightn't get on together, one might be cantankerous, and it's not like running a hotel where people can leave next day if they don't like their conditions, or at all events, go out to the cinema and the shops. At The Cottage there is nothing—I can't stress that too strongly—but the house itself and the woods. There are superb views, wonderful air, and, as I say, there's a weekly excursion into Oxbridge, but to any one who has lived a full, busy life it may sound bleak. We are asking fifteen guineas a week to cover everything, including wine."

Emily Watson was a very rich woman, and the circumstances of her life were such that she never spent anything like her income in the course of a year. Mr. Matthews invested it as wisely as possible to obtain the best results, though you needed to be a wizard, he told her, to be able to foresee what the Government had up its sleeve. Still, fifteen guineas a week for a limited period didn't seem to her an outrageous sum in return for what she would get. So she smiled and said, " If I had a nervous breakdown and went into a nursing home, as I probably shall if I stay in Southwood, I'm sure it would cost me more than that, and everything would be extra."

" I can see you're a philosopher," he said. " Well, then, about references, if you've really made up your mind—— "

She looked at him in dismay. " Is that really necessary ? You see, if you're going to ask for references it is going to ruin my plan. I know it would only be Mr. Matthews and the bank, but—you don't know Desmond. He would pretend I had lost my memory or something if I didn't turn up at the end of a fortnight or so and he might bully Mr. Matthews into giving away my address, and though I don't say he would go down to The Cottage he would certainly write, and all the good of my rest would be undone."

" It's usual," murmured Dr. Forrester.

" But only to make sure that—that you will get your account settled," said Emily eagerly. " If I give you, say, a fortnight in advance—or a month if you'd rather—wouldn't that dispose of the question of references ? "

It was the Abrahams affair all over again. It never went through her mind that in such an arrangement both sides should provide a reference.

" It would certainly simplify matters," Forrester agreed. " And, of course, if you make all your transactions in cash even the bank won't have to be admitted into your secret."

" Then that's settled." She looked immensely relieved. " Now when could I come ? The sooner the better. In fact, to-morrow—— "

He laughed. " Oh, I'm afraid that's rushing things a little too much. And I'm sure you won't be able to shut up your house at such short notice."

" I still haven't made you understand," said Emily painfully. " Every additional day is dangerous to me. You've no idea how curious they are. Even my letters are examined. That's why I asked you to write to my

Club. And if you should need to write again, though I don't see why, please send it to the Country Gentlewoman's."

" I see your point, but all the same I'm afraid to-morrow would be too soon for Berta."

" Is someone with you now, then ? "

" Oh, no. You'll be our first guest, and I hope the experiment will prove satisfactory to us both. But I don't go back to Swinnerton till to-morrow night, and Berta will want a couple of days just to make everything shipshape. We haven't been using these rooms, you see ; they've been shut up ever since we moved in, and the house had been empty for so long before then it'll take two days to have them the way we'd like you to see them. How about next Monday ? "

" I couldn't wait till after the week-end. Surely they would be ready by Saturday ? And even if they aren't quite in order I'd still sooner come down then."

" Very well. Saturday, then. There are only two trains to Oxbridge, where I'll meet you in the car. The morning train leaves King's Cross at 10.28 and arrives at 2.13, and the afternoon train leaves at 1.59 and is a little slower. It arrives at 5.16. If you drop me a card to tell me which train you'll be taking—— "

" I shall come in the morning," said Emily decisively. Dossie always went out first thing on Saturdays with two shopping bags and by the time she got back Emily would have gone.

" If anything happens to make you change your mind send me a telegram," said Forrester, ordering a liqueur with the coffee. " By the way, if you're thinking of doing any shopping in Oxbridge might I suggest pound notes ? We're a very backward community and fivers probably wouldn't be accepted as legal tender."

" I think we've settled everything," she told him a quarter of an hour later as he saw her into a taxi.

He smiled and watched her drive off. " Yes," he murmured under his breath. " Yes, my dear Mrs. Watson, I think we have."

# 8

When Emily returned to Southwood she found Dossie in a state of considerable excitement about some amateur theatricals in which she was to take part. She said, " You know I always wanted to go on the stage, but my family were difficult. They said it was a hard life, but what they really meant was that a daughter at home has her uses. As for hard, nothing could be harder than nursing my mother." She looked grim. Emily was shaking with apprehension because she was afraid that Dossie would suspect something. As a rule, she asked innumerable questions when Emily had had a day in town, but to-night she was so much interested in this new development that she seemed to forget everything else. Emily asked cordially what part she was going to play and discussed the possibility of getting just the right clothes. She said she thought she might have something put away upstairs, and offered to look through some of the trunks. Albert had always said, " Keep what you've got unless you're offered a good price for it ; you never know when it may come in useful." It was only when Dossie casually murmured that Desmond was going to help with the stage management that her fears raised their heads higher than ever.

" Desmond ? " she repeated. " What on earth does he know about acting ? "

" Why, Emily, he's absolutely cut out for it. I tell him he ought to go on the stage—suit him much better than regular work—but he says you have to start young, and, as I'm always reminding you, he's no chicken. Oh, no, Desmond's future is obvious."

" What does that mean ? " asked Emily sharply.

" He'll marry some well-to-do widow and live on her very comfortably, and she'll be so pleased to have a handsome husband a good deal younger than herself, she'll think she's made a good bargain."

"In that case," said Emily, concealing her rage, "they will both be satisfied."

"By the way," Dossie added carelessly, "that letter of his did arrive, and I sent it back to him. I knew that's what you'd wish me to do."

"You might have left it to me to return it," was Emily's dry rejoinder. But she didn't pursue the subject. The last thing she wanted to do was to arouse Dossie's enmity. So later in the evening, when Dossie began to exhibit her normal signs of curiosity she said casually she'd been to Parkers, and explained that Parkers wasn't a hat-shop as Dossie seemed to think, but a restaurant. When Dossie said enthusiastically that they must go there together one day she changed the subject and hoped Dossie wouldn't notice, but really—Dossie and Parkers simply were unthinkable.

For the next two days she made her secret plans. She resolved to take no one into her confidence until she was safely out of the house. She would leave a letter for Dossie saying that, on medical advice, she was going away for a short time and she wanted no letters forwarded. She would write the same to Mr. Matthews. There would be no need to write to Maisie or Mrs. Durrant, because Dossie would tell them all she knew and probably quite a lot she didn't. She would take a considerable sum of money with her and also her diamonds. The obvious thing, of course, would be to lodge them at the bank, but if she did that there was the chance of questions being asked. Besides, thieves don't visit places like The Cottage. They're too remote. Thieves like places where the getaway is easy, and, in any case, no one would expect to find about twenty thousand pounds worth of diamonds in a solitary house in a wood. On Wednesday and Thursday she began to sort her clothes. This she would take, that could stay in her wardrobe. Her obviously town clothes would be out of place at Swinnerton. All she would need there would be a woollen frock, two suits, a short coat—the brown suede would be best—sensible shoes, perhaps one evening frock, though when she would wear that she couldn't imagine. Still, once she was gone, she knew Dossie would rampage through her wardrobe, and if she saw an evening gown was missing would assume that Emily had gone to some hydro—Torquay, say, or Bournemouth. She would tell Doris she could have Saturday morning off—she didn't come on Sundays, of course—and while Dossie was out she would make her own getaway. Instead of buying her ticket at the local Cook's Agency she would go to London on Friday and get it at Harrods or some big place where she wouldn't be identified. Then she would get a taxi—or no, taxis on Saturdays were always difficult, she remembered, she would hire a car. But eventually she decided in favour of a taxi, because the car would be traced, and the driver might remember the address on the labels.

"Criminals must be exceptionally clever people," thought Emily, exhausted by so much planning, "they always have to be one jump ahead of the police. It's not surprising some of them get caught, it's much more amazing that any of them get away."

And then, when she thought she had prepared for every contingency all her careful planning came to nothing, for on Friday morning Desmond telephoned in his usual light-hearted way to say he wanted to come down and see her that afternoon, and he would be bringing MacKinnon with him.

"He hasn't forgotten you," he said teasingly. "You made a tremendous hit. You know, Penny, you'll be giving me a step-uncle yet."

Emily, taken unawares, said she would be delighted to see him about four o'clock. She didn't dare invent an appointment in case Dossie took her to task about it, and her suspicions were aroused. In any case, it didn't matter because by four o'clock she would be in the train en route for Swinnerton. Luckily, Dossie was going to be out most of the day, and Doris always went out between lunch and tea. She said it was usual if you stayed to cook the dinner. It had often been very inconvenient, but to-day it suited

Emily perfectly. When she had hung up the receiver, Emily began to make her plans. She had intended to go to London to-day and buy the ticket, but now she must start in good time and get the ticket at the station. She picked up the telephone to send a telegram to Forrester warning him of her arrival, but put it back, remembering that such telegrams can be traced. She could put through a trunk call from the central Post Office where nobody would notice her, particularly on a Friday when it was always full of people drawing Old Age Pensions or taking money out of the Post Office in order to have a good week-end. When Dossie came into the room she told her that Desmond had rung up, and while she spoke she watched her face to see if the news came as a surprise. But Dossie only said, " That's a bit of luck. I was going to ask him for some advice about the play, but if he's going to be here he can tell me then."

" He's bringing Dr. MacKinnon with him," Emily continued.

But either Dossie really hadn't known or else she was a better actress than Emily had realised, for she only put on one of her arch looks, and said " Dossie's a good girl. Dossie doesn't poach," and then, before Emily could suggest it, she added, " By the way, Doris has had a letter from her mother. She's had a fall and wants the girl over for the week-end. I said I'd ask you if she could get off midday."

" She might have asked me herself," returned Emily dryly. " She's not usually so backward."

" Still, you'll let her go, I suppose," Dossie urged.

" She'd go in any case," was Emily's retort. She thought Dossie looked relieved. She began to gabble something about all the jobs she had to get done before lunch, and she wondered aloud if she hadn't better warn Maisie Easingwold that she wouldn't be able to keep to their usual bridge schedule now she was going to be so busy with the theatricals. Emily sat like a statue, feeling as though her purpose must be obvious to any one. Go, go, her mind was screaming, but just before she reached the pitch of saying something Dossie must remember later, Miss Brett collected her large efficient-looking bag and marched out. Emily watched her from the window to make sure she didn't come back within a minute as she sometimes did, saying she'd forgotten her cheque-book or her umbrella or something, adding, " One of these days I shall forget my head," but when Dossie was really out of sight she set about making her own preparations. She must go to the bank, draw a really considerable sum of money, she must contrive to pack without Doris realising what she was doing, she must telephone and make quite sure that someone would meet her at Oxbridge. Even if the doctor couldn't come himself he could surely arrange for a car from a local garage. True, he had said the garages wouldn't send their cars to The Cottage, but Albert had taught his Emily that there's practically nothing people won't do if you offer them enough money. And she had reached the stage where money seemed very unimportant indeed.

She packed everything neatly and quickly in two suitcases, which she locked and pushed under the bed. She drew a cheque for two hundred pounds, wrote her notes for Dossie and Desmond—both D's she thought vaguely as she addressed the envelopes—and drew another smaller cheque to cover household expenses during her absence. Since Dossie was supposed to be paying her own way she really was only responsible for Doris's wages, but she added something for emergencies, and put that into Dossie's envelope. She would leave the letters on the hall table when she left the house. Then she wrote a guarded letter to Mr. Matthews, simply saying that she was going into the country for a short time and asking him to look after matters for her. There was no one else, she decided. It seemed queer to think you could step out of your niche so easily.

At the bank she manœuvred to get a newly-returned clerk who didn't try to engage her in conversation as Mr. Webb or Mr. Jenkins would have done, and though he seemed surprised when she asked for the amount in pound notes, he only said, "I'm afraid it will be rather a cumbersome packet."

She said, "I don't care for five-pound notes," and took the money. It wouldn't be possible to conceal the size of the cheque if questions were subsequently asked, but at least single pounds couldn't be traced, and she had the feeling that she was going away for a very long time. That, too, might have been prophetic if she had stopped to examine it. At the Post Office she had to wait a little time, burning with impatience, while the girl obtained her connection, and when at last she put the receiver to her ear it was a woman's voice who answered her. It was curiously flat, a guarded voice, she thought, as though the speaker might at any moment clap the receiver back.

"It must be the wife," she decided. "Of course, she's so used to treachery she must feel apprehensive every time the bell rings."

"Is that Mrs. Forrester ?" she inquired. "My name is Watson. I had arranged to come down to-morrow, as your husband will have told you, but I've had to change my plans suddenly."

The voice sharpened. "You are not coming ?"

"Oh, yes. But I'm coming this afternoon instead. Will you tell your husband, so that he can make arrangements for someone to meet me ?"

"This afternoon ?" repeated the voice. "There is some mistake. Mrs. Watson is not expected until to-morrow."

"I've just explained about that. It's imperative that I should come this afternoon. Is Dr. Forrester out ?"

"Yes, he is out. Please do not come to-day."

Emily gasped. "But your husband assured me you had no one in the rooms I am to occupy. It can't be inconvenient—that is, if it is I am very sorry, but I simply must come down to-day."

A voice from the exchange said, "Thr-r-ree minutes," and Emily cried quickly, "Don't cut me off, please. It's urgent. Mrs. Forrester, will you please tell your husband——"

"It is no use. He cannot meet you this afternoon."

"Then I'll get a car at Oxbridge. There must be a garage there."

"That will be impossible. My husband should have warned you. The Oxbridge Garage will not send cars so far."

Emily knew a sense of absolute defeat. She could not remain where she was; it would be better to go to Oxbridge and chance being met. If there was no sign of the doctor she would try and get a car, offering any price, and if it did prove impossible she would put up there for the night. She had looked up Oxbridge on the map and saw it was a market town of some size, which must boast two or three respectable hotels. She tried to explain all this to the woman at the other end of the line. Mrs. Forrester did not argue any more. She simply said, "I will tell my husband, but I do not know what time he will be back. It would be better to stand by the first arrangement."

Emily felt she would scream but the next moment this difficult and unpleasant woman had slammed down her instrument. Emily was so much perturbed that she almost forgot to pay for the telephone call, but her resolution to leave Kozicot that afternoon was stronger than ever. There was no time to be lost. She hurried back to the house and found Doris preparing to get off.

"I've put your lunch on the table, Mrs. Watson," said that independent girl. "My word, are you sure you're feeling all right? You look ever so queer. I should have a nice lay down this afternoon, if I were you."

Emily said she had hurried back and she thought there was thunder in the air, it always gave her a headache. Doris agreed cordially that her Mum was just the same, and added that the dinner was all ready and was in the frig. Doris talked a basic English that involved using as many abbreviations as possible. She said it saved time.

"Miss Brett said she wouldn't be in to lunch," Doris continued. "But you see, she'll be in to tea all right."

Emily controlled herself while Doris, still talking, pulled

on her high boots, tied on a fantastic fur-bordered hood, offered a few remarks about Mum, giggled and said wouldn't it be a lark if she was to find herself an auntie by the time she got back, and at last took herself off. Emily found herself unable to touch food. A sort of panic invaded her. Suppose she couldn't get a taxi? Suppose it wouldn't take her as far as King's Cross? Suppose they got held up in a traffic jam and missed the train? Suppose no one did meet her at Oxbridge? She compelled herself to answer her own questions. If she didn't get a taxi she would have to get a car. If she got a taxi and it wouldn't take her to King's Cross, then she must take it as far as she could and get a second one later on. If she started in good time she wouldn't miss the train. If no one met her at Oxbridge she would find somewhere to sleep. . . . She put the last remaining toilet articles into her case, warmed up some coffee and drank it hurriedly, put her letters on the hall table and went down to the end of the road, feeling that Dossie and Desmond and possibly Dr. MacKinnon too, were hidden somewhere close at hand. But luck was with her. A taxi came almost at once, the driver made no difficulty about taking her into London on the understanding that she made it worth his while, and she reached the station with nearly half an hour to spare. The train was in, however, and she secured a first-class carriage to herself. Not until the train drew out of the station did she dare relax. Even then the thought flashed through her mind that Dossie was somewhere on it, but she dismissed that. If Dossie had really been following her she would have stopped her getting on to the train.

"Now, at last I am safe," Emily whispered to herself. She had never made a greater mistake.

She had to change at Great Cottleston and, as might be expected in the second year of the peace, there were no porters, and she had to manage her two suitcases, her umbrella, her rug, her jewel-box and her bag without assistance, but the connection was in no hurry and she was comfortably settled long before the last stage of her journey began.

When the train stopped at Oxbridge the first person she saw on the platform was the doctor himself. She drew a deep breath of relief as he came towards her.

" So you were able to meet me after all. I am so glad. Your wife seemed to think——"

" Fortunately, I telephoned after your call came through and she told me what had happened. I was able to postpone an engagement and meet you here. I really couldn't bear the thought of you sitting up all night in the waiting-room, always supposing they would allow you to stay there."

" I was going to a hotel," said Emily.

He shook his head. " You wouldn't have got in. There's an Agricultural Show on, and every place is packed. I believe you can't even hire a bed under a shop counter."

" I'm sorry if I've inconvenienced your wife," said Emily; " but the fact is, I simply couldn't be at Southwood this afternoon. My nephew telephoned that he was coming down with a friend and—well, it was quite impossible for me to meet them."

They had passed through the barrier by now and Emily saw a Rolls-Royce standing by the kerb. Admittedly it was not of recent vintage, but it bore its years sturdily.

" I did tell your wife I would get a car," continued Emily, but he smiled for the first time and said, " When you see the road leading to the house you'll understand why Bertha was so sceptical. Cars from Oxbridge simply don't come to The Cottage."

" Because they think it's haunted ? "

" It could be that, though I don't believe it is. No one, you know, is afraid of ghosts in daylight."

He packed her luggage into the car and opened the door next to the driver's seat.

" You'll have to get in this side if you don't mind. The other door is locked. It's not very safe, and I don't want to lose part of my luggage on the way. When I next go into Oxbridge to shop I'll leave the car at the garage there and get them to put it right."

Emily opened her bag to take out a handkerchief, and uttered a small exclamation of annoyance.

"Oh, dear, how stupid! I meant to post this letter from town. It's just to let my lawyer know I'm going away for a rest."

"You can post it from here. It'll only be delayed by a day. The postman comes about eight o'clock and collects our letters in exchange for whatever he may bring. Of course, if he hasn't got anything he doesn't come, and then we have to walk down to the high road and post our letters there."

"That won't trouble me in the ordinary way," Emily assured him. Now that the journey was over and she was actually in the car en route for The Cottage she was weak with relief. By now Dossie and Desmond would have read her letters. She wondered if they would try and trace her, but she had few fears on this score. She had covered her tracks too well. Her only mistake had been this letter to Mr. Matthews. If it were posted from Swinnerton it would bear an unmistakable post-mark.

"I think," she said, "I won't post it just yet. My nephew is sure to try and find out from Mr. Matthews where I am, and there can't be anything so important during the next few weeks that I should have to go back to London. No, I won't run any risks." And deliberately she tore the letter into fragments and scattered them out of the window. She had no notion then of the appalling significance of her action.

# 9

They did not talk very much. The drive seemed to Emily very long, but then the road twisted so much it was impossible to get up much speed. Also the weather, that had been fine and clear in Southwood, was foggy here, though Forrester assured her that by the time they reached The Cottage they would be above the fog.

" We're very low down here, and we get the mists from the River Bent. But we shall leave all that behind once we start climbing."

After that he fell silent again and they went on cautiously through the murk. It came over Emily suddenly that she was going to a mysterious house to stay with strangers, that no one knew where she was, that she dared not return to her own house, and that she had no safe refuge anywhere in the world. Albert used to say that money could buy anything, but she knew he was wrong. It hadn't been able to buy him an extra year of life, and it couldn't buy her security now. For, of course, she couldn't stay at The Cottage for ever.

She needn't have bothered. Forrester never intended that she should.

The road, so far as one could see it, stretched as far as the sky. It was a considerable time since they had passed any houses, and the land, Emily noticed, seemed poor and untended. The scenery also was becoming wilder. Where one hill sloped up to the skyline there was nothing to be seen but coarse grass and stunted trees, bent like old witches by the powerful winds that must come sweeping across the countryside. The evening light fell suddenly, covering everything in a dim blue dusk. Now she was aware of the quality of the silence, not rarefied or pensive, but sombre and brooding. It wasn't surprising that the locals believed in ghosts. Even a townswoman, stranded in such a landscape, might hear anonymous voices, see what were only trees by day assume new shapes, the trunks groaning and stirring, the black branches becoming ensnaring arms, the twigs clutching fingers. She shivered, and Forrester said at once, " Cold ? It's not very much farther. And Berta will have a blazing fire for you and some hot tea."

She forced a smile. " That will be very welcome." It was absurd to feel apprehensive. There was always a solemnity, a sense of things moving to their close, at such an hour in the country. In towns, of course, it was different. Lights came out, traffic roared, you could hear the neighbours' wireless sets all down the street. Just as she was wondering if this road would ever end the doctor turned the car into an opening so narrow it had been invisible in the dark. A minute later she began to realise why no garage would send a car to The Cottage. The path climbed steeply, and was little wider than a cattle track ; and, thought Emily, about as rough. Even with Forrester's excellent and practised driving she was almost bounced out of her seat.

" Hang on to that strap," he advised her. " I had it put there for that purpose."

" Do you live at the end of the lane ? " asked Emily, wondering how much longer this nightmare drive would take.

" Not so far as that. The end is a sort of No Man's Land of desolation. Even the resolute Ministry of Agriculture couldn't do much with it. It needs draining, and I doubt if it could be done satisfactorily. Even if it could the cost wouldn't repay you. In bad weather the fields at the top of the wood are a morass, and though I've never ventured so far myself there are local stories of people being bogged there. When they hear the wind they'll tell you it's the cries of those who were lost among the trees and never got out. Still, you won't need to wander far into the woods. Thorold laid out quite a charming garden and Berta and I have got it back into order. In good weather it's very pleasant to sit there." Then he laughed. " I believe you are agreeing with the villagers that the place is haunted. Ah, but you're not seeing it at its best. Wait till we get a brilliant day, as we so often do even in the heart of winter, birds singing, air like champagne. I don't believe you'll ever want to go back."

At last the car slowed down and Forrester began to turn it carefully. It was a difficult piece of work with a car so large and a road so narrow, but he accomplished it skilfully enough, and then got down to unlock a great iron gate that was hung in the hedge.

" How on earth did any one bring that up here ? " she exclaimed, and Forrester said, " That's often puzzled me, too. But that's the sort of chap Thorold was. He wanted a gate here, so a gate there must be." He had taken a large key out of his pocket and was turning the massive lock.

" Do you always keep it fastened ? " said Emily, feeling a fresh pang of foreboding.

" Only when I'm away. Berta prefers it because it means no one can get in. I admit the possibility of tramps is remote, but it does exist, and she's quite alone here."

Emily looked startled. Somehow the tone of the advertisement had suggested some form of domestic service. She said as much. Her companion shook his head.

" You wouldn't get a local woman inside the gates. I often wonder what Thorold's reputation really was. No one here talks of him and apparently he was very seldom seen. It was odd, you know, a man as rich as that, for he'd need a considerable fortune to build the house in a place where the price of every service would be at a premium, thanks to its distance from even comparative civilisation, coming to such a spot. And this gate, so far as I can make out, was always kept locked. I asked if he had people to stay but no one seemed to know, or if they did no one would talk about him. He didn't give much away, either—a queer chap in every way."

He had unlocked the gate while he was talking and had driven the car into the drive. The garage was quite close to the gate and, he assured her, almost half a mile from the house. She shivered, not altogether because it was cold. It seemed to her, too, not merely odd but menacing to think of a human creature, not apparently hopelessly disfigured, deliberately choosing to isolate himself here. After a minute or two, however, the house burst into sight, blazing with lights, the front door ajar, and Mrs. Forrester waiting for them on the doorstep. The contrast was so great that her heart gave a great thump of relief. Glancing at her watch, she saw that it was only six o'clock. In town it would still be light, though here the immensity of the woods seemed to cloud the entire landscape, forming a barrier between earth and sky, and casting a dark shadow of their own.

The car stopped and he jumped down and opened the car for her to get out.

"Berta," he called, "I've brought Mrs. Watson. I believe she thought I was driving her over the edge of the world. I'm sure," he added in friendly tones, turning towards Emily, "you're longing for tea. I could do with a cup myself, and I think it might be a good idea to put something stronger into it. And now, come and get warm. One thing, living in the middle of a wood, we're never short of fires, no matter how many fuel crises sweep the country."

While he was talking Emily was accustoming her eyes to the sudden contrast of electricity and firelight with the darkness from which they had just emerged. In the majestic hall a fire burned with a welcoming glow; the fine staircase led to a square landing whose windows gave a view that, in daylight, must be magnificent, over the woods; everywhere was warmth, cheerfulness, a sense as though life here moved eagerly. Forrester was taking down her baggage, dumping it inside the door, saying that he would bring it up in a minute. Meanwhile, she must get warm, and then Berta would show her her quarters.

And now for the first time Emily turned to face the woman who would be her hostess and the sole companion of her own sex she expected to see for weeks. And she received a tremendous shock. From the voice on the telephone, from Forrester's own appearance, and from the general circumstances, she had expected a middle-aged housekeeper, but the girl who came forward to greet her could hardly have been more than twenty-five, and if she wasn't precisely beautiful she had distinction, which was better than beauty because it was more enduring. She was not very tall, but slender and elegant in her plain black frock with no ornaments anywhere. She had black eyes under a high white forehead, black hair drawn back from an oval face to reveal small, shapely ears, high cheek-bones, fine hands with long, strong fingers. When she spoke it was almost impossible to realise that hers had been the flat dogmatic tones heard earlier over the telephone that day. Yet, even at the time of their first meeting Emily was struck by something out of key as it were; it took her some time to realise what it was, for she was not accustomed to such considerations. But presently she discovered the clue. Berta Forrester was young, attractive, fascinating in a way that young women seldom were in these days when their chief aim seemed to be to assert their equality with their brothers; yet she was utterly devoid of the spirit of youth. Emily Watson was old enough to be her mother, a married woman of some experience, a householder, even a personage in her own small world, yet she had the feeling at that very first encounter as though she were talking to someone who had progressed far beyond her both in experience and in knowledge. It was the war, of course, what she had been through, what she had seen, that had killed some spring of vitality. For all her distinction, the soft tones of her voice, the promise of that lovely mouth, those purely-sculptured brows, she was empty of joy.

"And what," thought Emily, vaguely appalled, "made her marry this man who is old enough to be her father, not even a particularly attractive man, though presumably he has money? I can't believe she is in love with him. I suppose he brought her safely out of occupied France and she married him out of gratitude."

Seen against the background of dark wood and golden light she was like an Old Master, giving an impression of strength far beyond her years. Oh, there was mystery here all right, the house, the setting and above all, the young mistress of this spacious solitude.

Berta Forrester gravely held out her hand. " I am glad Vyvyan was able to meet you," she said. " Now you know where we live you will understand why I said no garage would send a car here. Oh, we have tried, when we first came here and petrol was short, but nothing, no money that we could offer, could help us."

Forrester sent his wife a quick glance. " Everything is ready, Berta ? " he asked, and her eyes came obediently back to his.

" Everything is ready," she agreed, and Emily thought, " Why, I was wrong. She does love him. She's infatuated with him, this rather plain, quite unromantic looking man. I believe he is a hero to her." And she realised how little she knew about either of them, how little, for that matter, she knew about life. Her own experience had been a series of persistent shocks during the past few weeks—Desmond's callousness, Dossie's duplicity, and now the relations between these two apparently utterly dissimilar people.

" Tea, Berta," her husband reminded her, and the girl said, " I think, after that long journey, Mrs. Watson would prefer tea quietly in her room. I have lighted fires, everything is warm. You see "—she turned with a faint smile to the visitor—" no one has lived in your part of the house for so long. My husband and I only use two or three rooms. The last owner perhaps entertained a great deal." Her lovely mouth twisted. " But you are our first visitor. I hope if there is anything I have forgotten you will tell me. We wish you to be comfortable here."

" I am sure I shall be," said Emily in a warm voice. " But—do you actually look after everything yourself ? It must be a great deal of work."

" No." Her voice was uninterested again now. " Just the two of us. The rooms we do not use remain shut up. Indeed, I shall be glad to have a little more to do."

She had taken up the lighter of Emily's suitcases and

was leading the way upstairs. Her husband followed with the heavier luggage. Emily herself carried her bag, umbrella and jewel-case. As she mounted she realised that the doctor had been right when he spoke of Thorold as a wealthy man. Everything about the house spoke of taste and the ability to satisfy it. Heavy brocade curtains hung at the windows, the furniture was all period, carpets were fitted from wall to wall, there were fine pictures, beautiful china—it was all as unlike one's conception of a furnished lodging as could be imagined. For some reason this made her uncomfortable.

"Did Mr. Thorold have no relations?" she asked suddenly.

The doctor from behind answered her question. "Only some rather distant cousins with whom he hadn't been on terms for a considerable time. Apparently they put the property, lock, stock and barrel into the hands of an agent. But even with accommodation so hard to come by practically no one nibbled until we came along."

"I should have expected them to put the furniture and china up to auction," murmured Emily. "It would have fetched a huge price."

"I don't think they ever came to look at it. And then the difficulty of getting it to some accessible place would be so great—no, I fancy they were thankful to get what they could for the place as it stands. Thorold was an odd fish," he added, as Berta opened the door of a room on the first floor, "he had his own codes, moral and social, which didn't make him precisely *persona grata* with his kith and kin."

The room into which Berta Forrester had led her seemed to Emily the acme of luxury. It was a sitting-room with a table laid for tea and drawn up to a blazing fire. Through a partially-opened door she saw the bedroom where also a fire was burning. Emily moved across to the grate and held out her hands to the flames. As she stooped above them she saw that someone had been burning papers here; a fragment floated on to the hearth, only partly burned, and she bent and picked it up.

It was a woman's writing and the words that were still decipherable read: *any affection for me* . . . and underneath . . . *for the sake of old times.* . . . The writer was clearly in an emotional state for the writing was very unsteady and sprawled over the page.

Berta Forrester looked over her shoulder. "Why, that is one of them," she said. "Just think, Vyvyan, when I was clearing out that cupboard in the corner I found a bundle of papers I had not noticed, thrown right at the back. They were letters, quite old letters, years old, that had been written to Mr. Thorold—at least, I suppose it was Mr. Thorold since no one else has ever lived here. They were all from women." Again her mouth twisted, more from scorn than from disgust.

"Did you read them?" Forrester sounded genuinely curious.

"I glanced at one or two—they might have been important. But they were all alike. Women's letters always are." Suddenly she struck her hands together. "They are such fools, they know nothing. Do they think you can keep a man by begging him for love, as if it were a kind of charity? Oh, it is clear what kind of a man this Thorold was."

Emily shivered and Forrester said at once, "You are cold? Berta will bring your tea——"

"There is no hurry," she told them hastily. "It's just—I feel sorry for those women, so many of them, and I suppose all deceived." Albert had never deceived her, but Desmond had, and Desmond's form of deception was harder to bear than Albert's infidelity would have been.

"To be unhappy in love—that is a little thing. There is so much else." That was Berta again and Emily thought, "She knows too much, much too much." And again she speculated on the bond between this oddly-assorted pair.

Forrester left her after another minute saying she must be sure to ask for anything she wanted, to which she replied quickly that she would be very comfortable here. But after he had gone she knew that wasn't true. This was not a comfortable house for all its luxury. The human element was too disturbing. But she was interested—keenly so. Later on perhaps Mrs. Forrester would begin to trust her, even confide in her. One of Emily's motives in marrying Albert was the hope of a family, but this had never materialised. She didn't think Albert minded much; he was almost too busy to notice if the nursery was occupied or no. If I had had a daughter, reflected sentimental Emily, she would have been about this girl's age.

She had to admit, however, when Berta returned with an excellent tea beautifully set out, that no daughter of hers would have been like this study in black and white, like an Old Master, who stood beside the table asking gently if anything had been forgotten. Still, she felt her pulses quicken. She had been a little afraid she might be bored in the country, but the human problems with which she already found herself surrounded had taken her mind off her own troubles. After tea she began to unpack. The wind was rising and came battering at the windows now concealed by long velvet draperies. In the wood the trees sighed and creaked. She had the sense of being shut away from all normal life. Yet the comforting feeling of being under a roof, with doors shut and curtains drawn, while the storm broods outside, drove away her doubts.

When Forrester came up before dinner to ask her what she would like to drink she remembered that she had not yet paid her first week's instalment for board and lodging. When she raised the matter he smiled and said there was no hurry, "Not," he added, "now that we have you on the premises." Seeing the startled look on her face he hastened to explain, "The only idea of asking for something in advance is to make sure that you aren't misled by one of these changeable women who decide at the eleventh hour they'd rather go to Worthing or the Lakes, and leave you flat, with all the other applications rejected."

She said, more to make conversation than because she was really interested, "Did you get many replies?"

And he told her, "An amazing number. I always am surprised at the quantity of people who are apparently anxious to get away from the familiar. Sometimes the reason is obvious, but in the other cases I think it's largely a matter of overrunning your engine and realising you must rest if you're not going to break. I saw so many good fellows break for no other reason during the war," he added.

"I suppose so. Did you meet your wife in France? She is so striking——"

He said gravely, "She was one of those cases, though in such circumstances it wasn't at all surprising. But she's young and she's brave. Everything will come right for her. I hate," he added abruptly, "to see beauty spoiled and I promised myself that, where failure had to be faced so often, in this one case at all events I would succeed. And I shall, I have no doubt of that. If she had been going to break it would have been before this. I am particularly glad for her sake that you answered my advertisement. It will be so good for her to have a friend, someone she can trust."

Emily, opening her wallet and peeling off the requisite number of notes, murmured, "You're not afraid it may be too lonely." And he told her, "She won't be lonely now. But an absolute break with the past was essential. I tell you this, Mrs. Watson, because I can see you are a person who can be trusted. She must put everything that belongs to that time behind her, begin a new life. It's one of those cases where the past and the present can't be joined. There is so much she needs to forget, so much she has lost that she can never recover. I know you won't hint to her that I have said this to you. I don't think she will tell you herself. She is very reserved and her experience has taught her how dangerous speech may be."

## 10

During the days that followed Emily, with a wisdom that gave the lie to Desmond's contention that she was out of her mind, made no attempt to force Berta Forrester's confidence. When they met, as for instance when the girl brought in her meals or came to take them away, they exchanged a few words, but they did not touch on the personal until one evening when Emily had been at The Cottage for a week. On her first evening she had feared she might find time drag. She had brought a number of books and magazines with her, and she had supposed that when she had read all these she could obtain others at Oxbridge. She went to Turners Library and Turners always claimed that their main advantage was that even in quite small towns they either had a branch or had made arrangements with the local bookseller to convenience their clients. But to her surprise the time passed more swiftly than she had ever known before. Indeed, for the first time in her life she felt herself free of the tyranny of the clock. She had no engagements to divide up her day and, therefore, she lost that sense of urgency that dogs people who live by routine. She was like someone who has always lived on a limited income and had to think twice before expending a shilling; now she was a millionaire. All time belonged to her, and she very soon began to luxuriate in the leisure and tranquillity that were now her portion. Forrester had spoken no more than the truth when he said that the situation of the house was unique and the views magnificent. The garden, though small, was charmingly set out, and in fine weather she took her book or her knitting there, intending to read so much, get to such and such a stage of her work, and always before she had reached her objective it was lunch-time or tea-time. No one came to the house; Berta always seemed busy, but there was no sense of fluster or bustle.

She did far more than Doris or any of the girls who "obliged" householders at Southwood would contemplate, but she remained the cool, mysterious figure of the first evening. Forrester did not again touch on the subject of his wife, and Berta might have had no history for all she spoke of it. At first it seemed strange not to be writing letters and to wonder whether the postman had brought anything on the morning delivery, but within two or three days she accepted her solitude, even revelled in it. She no longer thought, How long shall I stay? How long will they be prepared to keep me? She took each day as it came. She was so convinced that Desmond could not track her down that she didn't even wonder how he was managing without her, or what plots he and Dossie hatched in the little house that she had liked so much but that, in comparison with The Cottage, seemed fussy and pretentious.

At the end of the first week she paid Forrester for the second time and then went into her bedroom to prepare for dinner. She had always changed her dress when she was Albert's wife, and although the war, with its accompanying air raids, had made so much formality absurd, she still made some alteration in her appearance. To-night she put on a dark-red, velvet dress she seldom wore at home, having a secret feeling that the neighbours thought it too young for a woman of her years and build. It was delightful to feel she was in a *milieu* where she was, at all events, free from that kind of criticism. When she had fastened the belt she remembered a pair of diamond earrings Albert had given her when he secured the Tracey contract, which were among the most handsome of all his offerings. She opened her jewel-case and, not seeing them precisely where she expected to find them, she impatiently shook the whole collection on to the rose-coloured quilt. Although she was not one of those women who make a fetish of jewels she had to admit that, seen against that vivid background, themselves taking the light from the pedestal lamp beside the bed, they had a dazzling beauty. It had been Albert's practice to celebrate every success by some piece of jewellery, quite regardless of its use. Brooches, a pendant, three bracelets, ear-rings, clips, they lay tumbled before her. The fancy took her to try on various ornaments she had not worn for years.

"Like a pearlie at an East End show," she told herself, fixing the earrings into place, pinning a diamond fall at her waist, clasping bracelets three deep on her plump wrist, putting brooches wherever she could find place for them. The effect was startling, all those brilliant stones winking in the light, the ear-drops dangling, the bracelets clinking softly.

She was looking at her reflection in the long mirror, more fascinated than admiring, when a low gasp startled her. Looking up, repressing an exclamation of alarm, she saw the girl, Berta Forrester, standing in the doorway, staring at her in amazement and, she thought, an ungovernable longing. Emily felt remarkably foolish.

"I was tidying my jewel-case," she said, "and remembering how long it is since I wore many of these pieces."

She began to unpin the brooches as she spoke, and to draw the rings from her fingers.

"I came to see if you were ready for dinner," explained Berta. "I did knock, but you did not hear me." She came closer, then said simply, "How beautiful they are. I never thought I should like jewels again."

"But why not ?" asked Emily in amazement.

The girl shrugged. "In the war I have seen stones, yes, as lovely as some of those, bartered for a place in a jolting wagon, a corner in a barn, a bag of food, a pair of shoes. And I thought how little they were worth in fact. I despised them."

"I understand that," agreed Emily. "I have felt the same myself."

The girl looked at her with a new alertness. "You, madame ?"

"Yes. Over here, during the raids, when any moment might have been one's last and all the money in the world couldn't buy safety, I used to think how valueless personal possessions were. They couldn't protect you against bombs or buy you any of the intangible things by which we live."

"And yet," said Berta, coming still closer, as though fascinated against her will, "the war is over and the stones remain, while of the people who owned them there is nothing left. Sometimes I think it is possessions and not the possessors who have eternal life."

"You shouldn't be thinking things like that at your age," exclaimed Emily. "You are so young, most of your life is still before you."

"A new life—perhaps. But the old one—Vyvyan tells me I should forget. It is finished, done with. He tried to explain. He took up a knife and cut a slice of bread from the loaf on the table. That slice is the past, he told me. It no longer belongs to the whole loaf. That is how it is with me. My first husband—oh, yes, I was married very young to a man who died in the war as a prisoner—my father who also died doing forced labour in Germany—they said it was pneumonia—my two sisters—all of them belong to the past. But once"—and here life suddenly seemed re-born in those dark eyes, that severely-controlled mouth—"I also had beautiful things. Gustave was so kind. It was only when we became the slaves of the conqueror that I saw how little they were worth, and I said, I will never desire jewellery again. It is nothing—nothing. . . ." In the passion of her feeling she opened and closed her thin, strong hands as if to emphasise their emptiness. "I thought at least I was strong there. And yet—to see them again. It is like seeing life come back to a dead world."

She heard her husband calling and turned at once. "I must go. You will forgive me, Mrs. Watson. I was taken by surprise."

The incident made Emily feel uncomfortable. She was one of those women who would have been just as happy with imitation jewellery, but she had sensed in the girl's impassioned tones a depth of feeling she herself could not understand.

"I wish I could give her something, a little brooch,

say," she thought to herself, "but it would be too difficult."
However, opportunity might offer itself later. For the moment it seemed as though the girl had forgotten the incident. When they met again she was perfectly calm and impersonal. Yet, lying awake that night, Emily thought, "I have established contact at last. Presently she may confide more in me."

She had discovered, in this strange house set in a wood, seemingly a million miles removed from civilisation and the usual trivial pursuits of men and women, what she had wanted for years—an absorbing interest. And whereas, on her arrival, the very thought of Desmond or Dossie could throw her into a transport of apprehension, now she could spend a whole day without remembering their existence. It was as Berta had said—they belonged to the past, these two to the present, and she refused to contemplate a future in which inevitably they must reappear.

Towards the end of the second week she thought she would go into Oxbridge with the doctor, get her hair shampooed, change her library books, see if she could pick up any of those women's magazines that were produced precisely for people like herself, and do a little general shopping. She suggested to the doctor that she should accompany him the following day, which was Friday.

"I know that is your market day," she added.

"Why, Mrs. Watson, why didn't you mention it this morning?" exclaimed Forrester. "I had to change my plans this week. I needed to see a dentist and I went in this morning. I've made another engagement in the opposite direction for to-morrow. Was it something very urgent? If so, we could telephone."

"You can't get my hair shampooed by telephone," said Emily, half-laughing, half-annoyed at this postponement of her excursion. "But perhaps to-morrow. . . ."

"Saturday?" He looked doubtful. "You'd never get an appointment with the hairdresser for Saturday at such short notice. And the library and Sewell, the bookshop, close at one. How about Monday? Everything will be open then, and I have a perfectly clear day and could put the car at your disposal for as long as you want it."

Since none of her errands was urgent Emily agreed, and the doctor added, " It looks to me as though it's blowing up for rain in any case. Not a good day to visit the hairdresser."

He was quite right ; it rained hard in the afternoon and she was glad of the sitting-room fire and the comfortable tea-tray that Berta brought up at the usual time. When she took it away again there was a slight exchange of remarks in the passage outside that Emily could not avoid overhearing. As Berta emerged she was apparently met by her husband who said, " Did you ask her, Berta ? " and the girl said hurriedly, " No. I thought perhaps she would think it strange. It is no matter. . . ." Then the voices died away as Forrester went downstairs with his wife. She wondered what they were discussing. He must certainly mean herself. And what was it they had intended to ask her ?

Forrester satisfied her curiosity when he brought up her drink as usual.

" Mrs. Watson, to-morrow is my wife's birthday and I want to celebrate her first birthday in her own home since the outbreak of war. Naturally we can do very little in the way of festivities, but we should be so glad if you would join us for dinner that night."

Mrs. Watson accepted at once, but " Oh dear," she said. " What a pity you couldn't run me into Oxbridge yesterday. It would have been such a pleasure to find some little thing . . ." And she spoke with absolute sincerity. She really loved pottering round the shops and picking up odd things, a pudding-cloth, an ironing-board cover, a coloured string bag, an art silk table-runner.

" Oh no. I do beg you—if you would simply bring yourself. . . ." It was strange how attractive even a plain man can be when he smiles, Emily reflected. Even Albert —but Albert had never smiled, only grinned ferociously when he defeated an adversary, so it was impossible to say if he could ever have looked attractive.

Presently it seemed to her that here was the opportunity for which she had been wishing a week ago. Now, without fear of giving offence, she could pass on to Berta some little trinket—not the diamond fall, of course, or the ear-rings—there was a little diamond brooch that she never wore now, but one she had liked very much at the time. It had been given her, not by Albert, but by her long dead-and-gone Aunt Fanny, and was shaped like a bird, with ruby eyes. Yes, Berta should have that. Her heart glowed with pleasure as she embedded it in cotton-wool and put it in a tiny blue Chinese box secured by a minute sliver of ivory.

She took it with her when she went into the long drawing-room with its beautiful hangings and cabinet of old Chelsea, the following evening. A great fire burned in the hearth, a tray of cocktails stood beside it. Berta was still in black but to-night she wore a plain gold chain given her, she said, by her husband. Emily pushed the little box into her hand.

" For me ? " Berta opened it eagerly. " Vyvyan, see what Mrs. Watson has given me. Diamonds and rubies. Oh, it is charming. How can I thank you ? See how pretty it is." She put the brooch on and showed it to her husband.

" I told Mrs. Watson we didn't ask her for the hope of getting something for ourselves," was Forrester's comment. " Yes, it is quite charming. Victorian, I think ? " He looked at Emily, who began to tell them the trinket's story.

" I hope it carries no tale of ill-luck," said Forrester pleasantly.

For a minute Emily thought he disapproved of her bringing a present, but presently a less agreeable thought struck her. She wondered if Forrester had deliberately invited her in the hope that she would give Berta something out of her jewel-box, and was disappointed that it was nothing handsomer. However, as the evening progressed, she put that idea out of her mind. There seemed no doubt about Berta's pleasure. Several times Emily caught her looking affectionately at the gift. At her husband's request, warmly backed by Emily, Berta sang after dinner, and then they gathered round the fire and talked, while Forrester repeatedly filled their glasses.

"I shan't be fit to go into Oxbridge to-morrow," Emily warned him. But he laughed and said people didn't get intoxicated on good liquor. He talked of the future, less his own than that of the medical profession, for, he assured his audience, he intended presently to return to practice, when his book was finished. Berta seemed to throw off her pre-occupation and began to speak of her pre-war existence with such warmth and clarity that Emily could conjure up a picture of the family, father, mother, three daughters in their secure French home.

"Rozanne always said she would go into a convent," Berta told them. "Felice wished to marry and have nine children. I wanted to go on the stage. In those days we were all sure we should get our wish. It is a good thing no one can read the future."

Forrester put out his hand and covered hers, and because she feared a momentary break in Berta's control Emily broke into a quick account of her own earlier days. They responded eagerly, plying her with questions, asking about Marian and Desmond, seeming absorbed in what was after all a not very exceptional record. When they broke up shortly before midnight she couldn't quite remember how much she had told them, but she had a feeling that she'd let her tongue run away with her. Still, she reflected vaguely, it didn't matter. They were outside her normal purview. It didn't seem important what you said to strangers, because after a bit you went away from them, and forgot as completely as you were forgotten. It was when you were dealing with neighbours or relatives you had to watch your step.

She tripped over the rug in her bedroom and said aloud very solemnly, "Watch your step," and Forrester's voice from the corridor asked, "You are all right, Mrs. Watson?"

" No thanks to you if I'm not," she called back, thinking she sounded saucy. " All those cocktails."

She was suddenly so tired she could hardly crawl into bed, but when she did sleep she had a sort of nightmare in which the handle of her door turned and turned and she lay watching it by candlelight. But when at last the door began to open the light went out, and she screamed. She must have screamed in her sleep and waked the others, because she was aware of Berta, wearing a dark dressing-gown, coming over to her bed.

" You are ill, Mrs. Watson ? A temperature ? The 'flu perhaps."

She struggled for self-possession. " It was absurd of me. I had a nightmare." She laughed weakly. " I warned your husband he was making me drink too many cocktails. . . ."

But after Berta had gone all desire to laugh left her. She felt too ill to care about anything but her own misery.

" How can people get regularly drunk if this is how they feel the next day ? " she thought. She took a large dose of aspirin and lay down again and what with exhaustion and the drug she presently drifted into sleep. When she awoke the day was bright about her. Her watch said eight-thirty, and she jumped out of bed, remembering that this was the day she was to go to Oxbridge. But long before she had finished dressing she knew she wouldn't go. She was so dizzy she could scarcely get across the room ; her head ached and the very notion of letting a hairdresser touch it made her feel faint. When Berta brought in her breakfast she exclaimed in amazement at her appearance.

" But, Mrs. Watson, you are ill. You look feverish. I will call my husband."

In spite of Emily's protests she called the doctor, and he came in looking troubled.

" What's this, Mrs. Watson ? A temperature ? And you feel faint ? "

He seemed quite a different person this morning, not the entertaining host, but the doctor, kind but sensible.

He wouldn't let her say her condition was the result of too much drink the night before.

" Why, you had no more than Berta and less than I. You're not going to ask me to believe that two or three mild drinks are going to have this effect."

" When you're not used to them," protested Emily, " and they were very strong."

At home, of course, the ladies gave small cocktail parties mostly to members of their own sex, though sometimes a husband was pressed into service, but the proportion of spirits to orange juice or lime or whatever was available for purposes of dilution was very small indeed. Some of the hostesses, explaining gaily that they couldn't get a thing from their wine merchants and didn't know how to get into the Black Market, bought ready-made cocktails in expensive bottles, and a few patronised the newly-opened wine and spirit stores that sprang up like mushrooms in the year following the war, and in many cases offered their patrons practically teetotal refreshments.

" I'm afraid it's a bit of a chill. You'd better take things easy for a day or two and Berta will give you a light diet," said Forrester at length. " Now, Mrs. Watson, there's nothing to be anxious about. You'll be as right as a trivet in a couple of days. Just lie quiet and keep out of draughts."

That advice was easy enough to follow, and Berta took a good deal of trouble concocting appetising dishes. Emily had to admit that she wouldn't have been nearly so well looked after in a nursing home, where she would have paid as much as she was paying here, with innumerable extras. She felt considerably better by Friday, but agreed that it would be wiser not to attempt the journey to Oxbridge. In any case, Forrester said, he would be making a special trip the following Wednesday and she could have the whole day to wander and explore.

This was such good sense that Emily could only agree, inwardly wondering whether anything would happen to prevent this excursion also. However—three times lucky as Maisie Easingwold was perpetually saying, and she drank her cup of hot Ovaltine on the Tuesday night full of quite irrational pleasure at the thought of the morrow.

" I must be losing my sense of proportion," she told herself as she switched off the light. " Fancy thinking an outing to a little country town an adventure. It will be interesting to see what Oxbridge really is like."

But that, in fact, she was never to know.

## II

Next morning everything seemed to favour her plans. The sky was a brilliant blue, the wind kind, the birds sang riotously, leaves fluttered against the window-pane, the bathwater (as always) was deliciously hot, breakfast her favourite bacon and tomatoes. At ten o'clock she was waiting in the hall, wearing in honour of the occasion her newest hat, a fantastically high-crowned affair with veiling down the back, and white gloves.

Forrester came from his part of the house, carrying an assortment of bags and baskets for the shopping. When he saw her he stopped and laughed.

" Mrs. Watson, you're not putting one over on me, I hope ? You look as though you were planning an elopement."

Emily laughed, too. She had a pretty laugh, youthful and sweet. He thought that she must have been attractive before she let herself go, but such thoughts didn't occupy much of his attention and he forgot it again a moment later. When he opened the door and they came into the drive, for she was going to walk down to the garage with him, the sweetness of the air, the scent of living things, the brilliance of the day, was like a welcome.

" In weather like this," she said impulsively, " I'm always so grateful I wasn't a stillborn child."

He laughed outright.

They walked down to the garage chatting easily. She waited while Forrester drove out the car and opened the door for her. It was ridiculous, she told herself, to be so happy at the prospect of what Dossie would call a piffling little outing. But all the same she was. She felt that Desmond and Dossie and all they represented were a million miles away, or rather that she was behind a barricade where they couldn't touch her. Sooner or later, she supposed, she would have to emerge, but even her few days here had given her a sense of security, a new courage. Now she was ashamed to think how easily she had let herself be stampeded. At the gate, Forrester got out again to unfasten the lock, and before he rejoined her he opened the blue home-made letter-box nailed outside. The postman put any letters that might arrive for the house in this box and collected any that had been put there for that purpose.

" Knowing I was going to Oxbridge to-day I didn't come down earlier," he explained to Emily. He took out a single envelope and stood looking at it.

" Nothing for me ? " said Emily foolishly.

He turned at once. " I thought you said you hadn't given your address to any one."

" I haven't. I don't know why I said that. I suppose really there's no reason why I shouldn't write to Desmond now. It's not likely he will care where I am, unless he wants help, but perhaps it looks a little strange my disappearing into the blue without a word. It almost lends colour to his ridiculous suggestion that I was on the verge of a nervous breakdown."

" I'm not sure you weren't when you arrived," said Forrester, putting the letter in his pocket. " It's not surprising seeing the circumstances of our lives at the present time. This," he slapped his pocket lightly, " is from another lady who wants what she calls a safe retreat."

Instantly Emily took alarm. " You are not thinking of having someone else at The Cottage ? "

But if she didn't realise how much safer she would be with what Dossie liked to call a stable-companion, Forrester did.

" I told you Berta and I agreed to have only one guest at a time. All the same, you will give us due notice when you think of returning to your own house ? My wife tells me that it's much simpler if our visitors follow one another with a few days between them than a few weeks. I don't pretend to follow her logic, but since the main burden, if you won't misunderstand me, falls on her I feel I must meet her as much as I can."

" Yes, I know what she means," said Emily quickly. " You get into a routine. And if you let too much time elapse between one guest and the next you—you spoil the rhythm. But I wasn't thinking of going back just yet. I feel so much better since I came here. . . ."

" If I may say so, you look much better, too. If I were a millionaire I'd organise a chain of houses where people bothered by domestic stress could recuperate. The trouble is that, like all good things, rest and refreshment are expensive, and one wants to be sure that the refugees, so to speak, have enough space not to get under one another's feet."

" I'm not sure that's really a very good idea," said Emily surprisingly. " This sort of rest is ideal, because you're away from all the people who know your particular circumstances. If you had a number of housewives under the same roof they'd spend their time discussing their individual problems, and they'd become quite jealous if someone else seemed to have had a worse time than themselves."

" I see you understand your sex, Mrs. Watson," was Forrester's retort, but he made it in so absent a tone that she turned to look at him. He wasn't looking at her, he was staring at the car that seemed, now she came to notice it, to be behaving rather oddly, stopping and starting again, and then havering. Wishing to seem sympathetic, Emily inquired, " Is something wrong ? " but there was no apprehension in her voice. Cars, she knew, were unpredictable monsters, but men like Forrester and Fletcher, who had been Albert's chauffeur, knew how to deal with them. She sat back placidly, watching the doctor open the bonnet of the car.

"Do you know anything about cars?" her companion asked in tones muffled by his attitude over the car's internal organs.

Emily had to confess that she did not. Fletcher, she explained, had always looked after the car. She had once suggested learning to drive but Albert thought better not. Forrester lifted his head and reeled off a list of technicalities that might have been Bantu for all they conveyed to her. Woman-like she translated freely.

"You mean you can't make her go?" Even then she didn't quite believe it.

"It seems like a hoodoo. Every time you try and get into Oxbridge something happens to prevent you." But he smiled as he spoke, as if to show he didn't really believe in superstition.

Disappointment woke sharply in her. "You mean, you can't mend it? Oh, but surely if you tinker with it a bit you can put it right."

"I wish it were as simple as that. People imagine that when you buy one of these extravagant cars, that's the end of your liability. They're wrong. That's where the liability starts."

She looked round her. The world looked so right, so new, as if it had been enamelled overnight. She couldn't really accept that for the third time her excursion must be postponed.

"There's only one thing to be done," the doctor continued. "I'm a fairly good mechanic. I needed to be out in France where one often had to depend on one's own efforts. It's all a matter of getting the particular spare part. Darling may have it. I shall have to jump a lorry into Oxbridge. For some reason there are always lorries going that way. The difficulty is to get one coming back. It's an extraordinary thing," he continued contemplatively, "that they all seem to go to Oxbridge never to return. What happens, I wonder, to cars—and people—who go but never come back?"

He saw Emily's surprised eyes fixed on his face and apologised, both for his inattention and for the car's failure.

" You'll think Providence has some particular reason for not wishing you to see Oxbridge," he said, " and perhaps it has, though I can't conceive what it is. Mrs. Watson, I can't tell you how sorry I am, and, believe me, I do intend to get you into Oxbridge yet. But not, I fear, to-day."

There was nothing for it but to climb out of the car with as good a grace as she could muster, and say it was disappointing but, after all, only a pleasure deferred.

" What will you do with the car ? " she inquired.

" Leave her here, of course, till my return. There's no choice."

" Suppose some other vehicle wants to pass her ? "

" It won't. Nothing else ever braves the lane. Why, where would they be going ? "

" They might be coming to see you," she rejoined lamely.

" Oh, I don't think they'd be doing that," said Forrester in confident tones. " We have no local friends who would be likely to look us up without warning."

She heard herself say, " No friends are better than false friends," and he turned in some surprise and exclaimed, " Why, that is what Berta says. But it's a wrong attitude towards life—warped, unnatural. People in that condition are like invalids—you must treat them gently but never yield too much to them, only enough to cure them."

It was a long time since he had spoken of his wife and she found herself wondering what it must be like to be married to a doctor. Surely one could never feel towards him as one would towards an ordinary man. Here she realised that Forrester was waiting for her to go before he set out on his journey, so, accepting a message to Berta, she turned reluctantly away. It was particularly unfortunate that this accident should have taken place on such a fine day; she felt she could not return to the house, nor did the thought of the garden satisfy her.

" I might explore the woods a little," she thought. " I know they are supposed to be dangerous, but if I keep the doctor's advice in mind never to lose sight of the house, nothing can happen to me."

With this thought she went back to the house as fast as her black patent leather shoes would carry her. She would change into a more comfortable pair, tie a scarf over her head, put away her gloves and bag, and make the best of what promised to be an unusually beautiful day. She told Berta what had occurred and Berta said sympathetically, " That is tiresome for you. I tell Vyvyan a car is more trouble than it is worth, but he says we could not live here without one. But he would do better to have something smaller and of more recent vintage."

" It's not very easy to get cars," suggested Emily sensibly. " Have you had this one long ? "

" It was Mr. Thorold's. It was in the garage when we bought the house. He must have been a rich man to have such a large car, but Vyvyan says it was our good fortune. But we should be better off with a little modern one."

" Do you never go into Oxbridge ? " asked Emily, politely.

" No, no. No, that would never do. You see, I have had enough of crowds. Now I like peace. But one day perhaps we shall return to Paris. When things are better. I shall like that."

" I believe he keeps her here against her will," reflected Mrs. Watson compassionately. She went up to her room to make the necessary changes in her attire, and found to her annoyance that she had dropped a glove on the way from the car. Despite the doctor's assurance that no one ever came that way, which meant that a dropped glove would be as safe after lunch as it was now, it did not occur to her to postpone going to look for it. The weather might change—you could no more depend on the weather than on the Government's latest move, she considered—and the glove might be soaked ; or, she thought hazily, there were magpies, predatory birds, who might think a good skin glove the very thing to line a nest. She put on the comfortable shoes, the shabby gloves, the hearty homespun scarf over her grey hair which looked wilder than it did at home, though that wasn't her fault.

"I'm sure I've done my best to get you waved," she told her reflection in the glass.

She didn't find the glove by the time she had reached the garage, and she thought that probably she had dropped it in the car. She pushed open the gate, took a few steps to the left—and stopped dead. Stopped and stared and began to whisper to herself. Then she took a few more steps—and a few more—but it was no use. She had known that at once. She stood perfectly still, considering, doing a sort of mental arithmetic in her head. And while she waited there horror crept out and touched her on the arm. Already she knew she had turned a corner and she could not go back.

For there was no sign of the car anywhere. It had absolutely disappeared.

She did not immediately appreciate the situation. She looked all round her, at the hedge spilling over with cow parsley and the ditch thick with weeds, even up into the trees as though the great cumbersome thing could have taken wings, like a car in a film, and flown into the branches. In her present state she would hardly have been surprised to see it couched there, peering down at her like an enormous grey bird. But, of course, it wasn't there. There was only an ordinary black crow, looking down at her with what she thought was derisive amiability. And even he appeared to find her disappointing, for after a moment he spread his wings and flew away.

"But it was there," Emily told herself stupidly. "It was there not ten minutes ago. And he said there was something wrong, it would not work."

Stooping down, she saw that there was an even track of car tyres in the muddy surface of the road, going steadily towards the high road, and she began to follow them for no special purpose, except, she supposed, to see exactly where they led. They led where any sensible man —Arthur Crook, for instance—would have anticipated— as far as the main road. So Forrester had been lying when he said there was something wrong.

" And there is something wrong," she told herself in hushed tones. " Something I don't understand."

Forrester's voice came back to her memory. " You'll think Providence doesn't mean you to go to Oxbridge." Substitute the doctor for Providence and—was that the answer? This, as he had reminded her was the third time she had been prevented. The first time he had made what seemed a quite reasonable excuse, but now she remembered that Thursday was early closing day. Was it likely, particularly if he had to see the dentist, that Forrester would have chosen that particular day, when the town after one o'clock was dead? She hadn't thought of that before. Then on the second occasion—surely a doctor should have been too wise to give her so much to drink without realising the effect it might have. But now she was beginning to wonder if the cocktails were responsible. There was her nightly hot drink prepared by Berta—what if he had slipped something into that to make sure that she couldn't make the journey next day? But why? That was the point. Why? She stood at the end of the lane watching the infrequent traffic. She had a vague idea of hailing a passing car and asking to be taken into Oxbridge, where she could get a train for London. Janes, said Arthur Crook, never have the sense to cut their losses. She reminded herself that she was wearing old clothes, that she had only a little silver in the pocket of her coat, shabby gloves, no luggage. Why, I wouldn't have enough to buy the ticket, she reflected. Again the question as to motive rose to trouble her.

For by this time she was convinced that Forrester intended to prevent her going to Oxbridge. Even a woman as foolish as Emily Watson could realise that. And as she stood there, thinking, it came to her for the first time how unwise she had been, how completely she had put herself into the hands of these two strangers, of whom she knew absolutely nothing but what they chose to tell her. She didn't know even that Forrester had worked in France during the war or that Berta had taken part in the Resistance Movement. She knew nothing at all —except that the doctor had been startled when she spoke of the possibility of receiving a letter, that he had jumped at her suggestion of bringing cash to The Cottage and paying him in single notes each week.

" He means to keep me here till my money's exhausted. But even that isn't a good enough explanation. He could get someone else." And then the horror that had stolen out from nowhere as she stood by the gate of The Cottage gripped her fiercely. For the first time she saw the peril in which she stood. For supposing she should disappear, what proof was there that she had ever been here at all? She had taken the most elaborate precautions against discovery, had refused to leave her address even with Mr. Matthews or her bank manager, had written no letters and, logically, had received none, had spoken to no one on the telephone, had not set eyes on one of the locals, not even the postman. She thought she knew now why Forrester had been so anxious that she should not attempt to hire a car locally on her arrival. That would have advertised her existence in the neighbourhood. Pitiless memory conjured up another vision—Berta standing motionless, her eyes wide, her body tense, at the entrance to her (Emily's) bedroom, with the diamonds scattered helter-skelter on the quilt. She had not attempted to conceal the size of her roll of notes; Forrester must realise she had brought a considerable amount of money with her. She had obtained emergency cards before leaving Southwood, so even her ration book could not be checked.

" All the same," she told herself restlessly, " I don't really believe it. There's some other explanation. That kind of thing doesn't happen."

Crook could have told her it's happening all the time, that having money doesn't make you safe. The only safe thing is to be poor and obscure, and if you can contrive to be plain as well—and it's surprising how many people do—so much the better. To be rich, middle-aged, to have quarrelled or at all events have cut yourself off from your only living relative, is to hand your fortune to the first scoundrel you meet, with parsley round the dish. She remembered, too, the doctor's story, recounted in his mild unemphatic voice one evening when he brought her her cocktail, of parachutists of all nations who were reputed to have come down in the woods and whose bodies had never been found. If one extra body should presently lie out there, the body of a foolish middle-aged woman, who would know? Besides, there were ponds in the woods. . . . She found she was shivering violently. This was odd, because she wasn't in the least cold. In fact, now she thought about it, there was something menacing about the brilliance of the weather. Everything was glossy with heat, even the dust on the road was turned to gold. Perhaps, though, that was what was wrong with it. English weather is like that. Unlike the English character, it knows nothing of compromise. Either it is bitterly cold with a driving wind, or it rains fiercely or the whole countryside is obliterated by fog. Or else you get this irrational heat. No two days are alike. You can't plan. And now with the heat came a great stillness. At the moment no traffic was passing, and Emily realised that in all her visible and audible world there was no sound of any sort. The very birds were silent, the leaves hung from their boughs as though they were painted on the air. And she remembered what the village said about the woods, how the trees sometimes took human semblance, twigs becoming fingers, roots being painfully pulled up from the earth, the whole wood slowly beginning to move with crouching steps to surround her, to crush her, so that even if any one did come looking for her she'd be unrecognisable.

She had the sense to know that in a moment hysteria would supervene, and no one in as tight a spot as hers could afford such a risk.

" There are two things I could do," she told herself firmly, putting her square chin in the air. " Either I can go back and try and ring up a garage and offer them anything to come and take me away this afternoon or I can at least somehow get in touch with someone else in this part of the world. If the Forresters know I've spoken to people, told them my name, some of my history, then they wouldn't dare—wouldn't dare . . ." Well, jeered Common Sense, wouldn't dare what ? What is it you're afraid of ?

" Wouldn't dare try and get rid of me," she whispered.

There was, of course, the third alternative. She might refuse ever to re-enter The Cottage, but to arrive at Oxbridge in her present dishevelled state, penniless, minus her baggage and (most important of all) her diamonds, was unthinkable. For she couldn't prove in a court of law that she had ever brought the diamonds down to Swinnerton. There was, of course, the little brooch she had given to Berta, but she could easily conceal that. In short, to arrive thus would be to support Desmond's and Dossie's contention that she was utterly unbalanced. Therefore, her best course was surely to lift the receiver the instant she got back and get in touch with—whom ? With Desmond ? Or Dossie ? Impossible. Both were too treacherous. Either would be capable of writing immediately to Forrester, explaining that she wasn't quite to be trusted and if her suspicions were correct that would be playing straight into his hands. Her lawyer then, prim and purposeful Mr. Matthews. She tried to phrase the conversation in her mind. These things weren't as easy as they sounded.

" Oh, Mr. Matthews, this is Mrs. Watson of Kozicot, Southwood. At the moment I'm staying at a place called The Cottage, Swinnerton, with a Dr. Forrester. I want you to make a special note of the address. (Why ?) Because I think I'm in danger. (Again why ?) Because three times I've been prevented from taking a motor drive."

Oh, it was useless. To begin with, he would want to

know why she came here in the first place, why she came so furtively, how it was she took her diamonds with her. It wasn't possible to say that she had been afraid the Desmond-Dossie combination would steal them in her absence, because the obvious thing in any case would be to leave them at the Bank. Then, too, there was always something ominous about staying at a doctor's house in a remote part of the country. If you were young, people suspected scandal; when you were older they said there was probably some mental deterioration. Why, she, the least malicious of women, had said it herself when Helen Fortescue suddenly disappeared, and though certainly it had been true in her case, just the same thing would have been said if it hadn't. She might write, of course, but if Forrester didn't intend any one to know she was staying there he would see to it that the letter didn't go. The safest thing would be to try and get in touch with the Oxbridge Garage—Darling, Forrester had said—and try to persuade him to send up a car. Even if he refused she would make a point of mentioning her name and her home town, and then if sooner or later, as must inevitably happen, inquiries as to her whereabouts were set on foot, he might remember. But it was a slender hope. It would be far better if she could meet someone face to face, someone who would realise at once that she was perfectly capable of looking after her own affairs.

Fired with resolution she began the homeward journey. For the greater part of the distance the road went uphill, so it was no use pretending you were a racehorse and making too hot a pace. During the last minutes, life, that had seemed static, seemed to start again. The trees stirred a little, a bird (a wild duck ? she didn't know) went winging through the skies that showed an alabaster finish. And in this new, more sanguine mood she began to notice her surroundings. So it was that when she had gone a short distance she noticed a gap in the hedge that she had overlooked in her hurried walk down to the road. Once, she supposed, a gate had hung there. It was there no longer, clearly had not been for some time, but there were traces of a path leading into the wood and on the reasonable assumption that this path led to a dwelling she plunged in. The little path twisted and turned, but she argued that if she refused to be beguiled off it she could not lose her way and pressed obstinately on. Her efforts were rewarded when, at the next twist, she saw a house—the merest cottage really—a few yards away. It was standing in a rather desolate bit of land that someone had rather half-heartedly tried to rescue from the surrounding woods, but nothing flourished there now but some huge cabbages run to seed and some straggling runner beans which came up apparently to defy the world, since they were clearly uneatable. She hurried forward. It would be easy to find an excuse for disturbing the occupants. She would begin by saying that she was staying at The Cottage, that her name was Mrs. Emily Watson and that she had lost her way. After that it would be simple; she might even learn something about the mysterious Forresters. Then, as soon as she got back, she would tell Berta of the encounter, and that surely should prove her safeguard. She had got it all worked out so well that it came as a blinding disappointment to discover that the cottage was empty, and not merely empty, but uninhabited. More, it had been uninhabited for some time. The windows were broken, the roof badly damaged, the whole place was tumbledown almost beyond repair. Sick with disappointment she walked round the crumbling walls, and was surprised to find a spade leaning against the rotten back door. A spade, she thought, argues someone nearby, at all events a spade that has clearly been used not long ago. For though the earth on it was caked it was not covered with spiders' webs or mould; someone had used it in the course of the past week or two. From this she argued that the owner must be working in the neighbourhood and even if he wasn't visible at the moment—having his elevenses or something, she supposed, though where he could have elevenses in the heart of a wood she couldn't guess—he would probably be back quite soon. A phrase she had heard in an American film came into her mind. Stick around. That was what she would do. After a minute or two it occurred to her that he might be inside the cottage. There was no trouble about opening the front door. Even if someone had wanted to lock it he couldn't have done so, because the lock was rusty and broken. Inside everything was intensely primitive. There was a low-ceilinged room with ivy growing on one of the walls, and an ancient rusty range in one corner. A staircase rose from the back to the second storey and there was a cupboard under the stairs. A big rusty hook was fixed in the centre of the ceiling, and by this time she would hardly have been surprised to find a body hanging from it. She advanced to the foot of the stairs and called softly, but without result. The stairs themselves looked dangerous, but she mounted cautiously and looked into the two minute rooms on the upper floor. There was no furniture in either and the floorboards were unsafe. Baffled she came down again. Her resolution to be seen by someone was so strong that she was prepared, if necessary, to wait here all day. Back in the little kitchen-living-room her glance fell on the cupboard, and though she didn't anticipate any assistance in that direction she obeyed a woman's natural impulse and crossing the uneven stone floor she pulled the door open.

## 12

She would have said she was prepared for anything. But she was staggered and completely flummoxed by what she saw. Someone had screwed three hooks into the back of the cupboard and from one of these hung a hat. A woman's hat, majestic, dignified, a great black velvet pancake mounted on a brim like a full moon, the whole decorated with a band of broad black petersham ribbon and a steel buckle. In its dowdy assurance, if you could employ such an expression about a hat, it was more impressive than if it had been one of these pieces of modern nonsense that draw all eyes. Emily, who was by no means a fool in all ways, registered several incontrovertible facts about it on sight. It was, clearly, an elderly woman's hat. It was expensive, it was well-made, it was at least five years old, since such ribbon hadn't been procurable for a very long time, and it had not been in its present position very long. The cottage was so damp that ivy could grow on the inside wall; the cupboard, presumably intended for coal, was so damp that if you put your hand on the wall it would come away clammy; yet there was no tarnish on the buckle. Nor was the velvet mildewed. She stood staring at it, wondering how such a hat could be in such a place. She thought of all the possible solutions—for instance, the owner might be picnicking in the woods and think she would leave her hat where it would be safe. But even Emily couldn't buy that one. Then perhaps a younger member of the party had hidden Gran's hat just for a joke. But she couldn't buy that one either. Because there simply wasn't a picnic party. In this quietude you would hear even gentle voices, and the picnickers couldn't have flown here, and if they had come in a car where was it, and anyway who was likely to choose this remote spot for picnicking? No, there was some other explanation, though what it was she couldn't imagine. Stepping nervously inside the cupboard, with a dread of hearing the door suddenly click to behind her, she lifted the hat from the hook. It bore the name of a well-known provincial milliner. Partington, Bath. Emily had stayed at Bath and actually been inside Partington. That seemed to create a link with the owner. All the same, only quite an ancient party would dare put this erection on her head, and what in the name of Heaven was an ancient party doing in a tumbledown cottage in a remote wood at the other end of Nowhere?

The obvious answer did not, at that time, occur to her.

As she replaced the hat she tripped on a bit of slate someone had left on the floor, and her purse fell out of her pocket and distributed its contents all over the place.

She groped for them, shillings and sixpences, a little powder compact, a very pale-red lipstick, the latch-key of Kozicot. As she straightened herself she got the idea that the hat had moved round on its hook. She was sure that she had hung it buckle uppermost, but now the buckle faced the floor. Suddenly terrified she stepped out of the cupboard, slammed the door and fled back into the hot sunlight. It was absurd, of course, she knew that. Hats are inanimate, they don't have personality, they can't twitch themselves round on their hook or hop down and get behind the impertinent tourist, slam the door shut and then go back and watch you suffocate.

" Desmond's right," she whispered in horrified tones, " I am going mad. It's just the thought of what could happen." To die in the dark. To die—like the proverbial rat—in the cold cloistered dark.

She flung a wild look round her. The spade was where she had originally found it. Whoever had been using it wasn't there any longer. Whoever had worn the hat wasn't there either, but for the moment she didn't connect the two.

When she came out into the lane once more Fate gave her one last chance. If she didn't take it she was lost. She had thrown away the first one when she decided not to go along the road and try and hitch-hike her way to Oxbridge. Then, security had been no more than at arm's length ; but she walked away from it, deliberately Now she had another opportunity. There was still time to reconsider that ill-advised decision. Forrester—one enemy—was at Oxbridge. His wife was up at The Cottage. Poor doomed Emily Watson stood hesitating between the two. There ought to be some indication in the atmosphere when a life and death decision has to be made, a hush or a clamour—anything out of the ordinary. But Nature takes no notice. All Emily thought was that it was a little cooler. It did pass through her mind that it might be best to go back and look for a telephone box, but common sense assured her that you only found these comforting red boxes in civilised places like Southwood.

No one would dream of erecting one on a lonely road linking Oxbridge with the next town. If there was a box it would be an A.A. one and so of no use to her. So, her decision made, she turned her face towards The Cottage.

" All this yap about female intuition," said Crook, with a fine show of indignation, after Dossie Brett had dragged him into the case. " Where does it get you, Bill ? Down among the dead men, that's where."

Long before she reached her ill-starred destination Emily was echoing the poet, Christina Rossetti, " Does the road wind uphill all the way ? " and getting the same response. She wasn't young and she wasn't slender and, taking one thing with another, she had had a nerve-racking day. The refreshing air which had sprung up while she stood in the lane, looking first in one direction and then in the other, had been as deceptive as Forrester's surface charm. Soon she ceased to be aware of anything but the broiling sun, the menacing woods, her swelling feet in their brown leather brogues. When at length she panted through the gates of The Cottage she looked what Doris would have called a sight, her hair straggling over her neck, her face dripping with perspiration, her heart leaping like a hooked fish. She had one particular thought in her mind. Before Berta intercepted her, before the doctor returned, she would telephone the garage and make her own position abundantly clear. She even gleaned a faint sense of pleasure at the thought of arriving unexpectedly at Kozicot and perhaps catching Desmond and Dossie engrossed in some new plot for her ruin.

Her plan went wrong from the start. For one thing, Berta was on the step waiting for her, and as soon as the pitiful dishevelled figure came within shouting distance she began to come towards her, exclaiming, " Mrs. Watson ! I have been so troubled. I thought you had gone into the woods and were lost. My husband warned you that no one, not even he, can find his way among the trees. Where have you been ? What has happened ? "

Emily leaned against the newel-post in the hall and said with as much dignity as she could muster, " I told you—

I went to look for my glove. At least, if I didn't tell you, I meant to. I thought I must have dropped it in the car."

" And did you find it ? "

She suppressed an hysterical laugh. " I couldn't even find the car." Berta said nothing ; she was watching her steadily. " Did you hear what I said ? " repeated Emily. " I couldn't even find the car. Doesn't that seem to you queer ? A big thing like a car just vanished like—like that." She extended her hand, palm upwards and blew into it, as though dispersing a handful of dust.

" It is quite simple," Berta assured her. " No doubt Vyvyan found that he could make her run, after all. He is a very good mechanic."

" In that case," demanded Emily reasonably, " why didn't he let me know ? It was particularly arranged that I should go to Oxbridge to-day."

" Perhaps he looked for you and you were not there."

" I was up at the house. He couldn't have looked very hard."

" Then no doubt he had some reason. No, Mrs. Watson, do not ask any more questions. I have always found that when something inexplicable happens it is best to say nothing."

Emily looked as though she could scarcely believe her ears.

" Nothing ? But—oh, of course I was mad." Mad to come, she meant, to a lonely house in response to an advertisement, to waive the question of references, to conceal her whereabouts from everyone.

Berta, however, was answering her seriously, gently. " Oh, no, you must not say such a thing, Mrs. Watson. You must not allow yourself to think it. You are not mad, you have just had very severe nervous strain, naturally you require a rest. You should trust my husband, he has seen so many cases like yours. Absolute rest is essential. It is only for a little while. Then you will be as well as ever you were."

Emily felt terror clutch her round the heart. " What are you saying to me ? Oh, I should have known. Would normal people want to live in the middle of a wood, cut off from civilisation ? "

" 'Would normal people wish to come to visit in a house in a wood, cut from civilisation ? ' That is what I asked my husband when he spoke of his plan. 'But no one will come to such a place,' I said. 'Only crazy people and we do not want them.' But he answered, 'Do you not think, Berta, that someone must care even for the crazy ones ? Often they are the most helpless, because they have so few friends.' You see, Mrs. Watson, fear is a wild animal and during these last years he has been unleashed and has roamed through the world, biting and infecting. And those wounds must be healed. Every letter we received, and you would be surprised how many there were, said the same as yours, that the writer wished to escape, not perhaps from life itself, but from the framework of her personal life. When he saw those Vyvyan said, 'Here is something we can do. They are like people who are being crushed by the crowd, crushed by anxiety, trouble, oh, by many things. Here they can escape.' That is why you came, Mrs. Watson, isn't it ? To escape. And you have been here for two weeks of perfect calm. You are better. Isn't that so ? You are less afraid of the world you have left than when you arrived ? "

Emily listened, hypnotised. Because, running through this farrango of nonsense, was a golden thread of fact. She was better, or had been until to-day. Why, only this morning, preparing for the excursion, she had thought that, peaceful though it was here, safe (as she supposed), yet she would wish to put a period to her stay. She had seen herself laughing in Desmond's face, telling Dossie she could pack her things and go, confessing that she knew all about the plot. So brave she'd felt—only a few hours ago. Now she realised the trap in which she was caught.

" You mean—your husband intends to keep me a prisoner here ? " It was what she had thought earlier on. Oh, she'd been mad all right, ever to come back here. Mad, indeed, ever to come. And if Berta didn't agree with her, Arthur Crook certainly would have done. But then, to him, women were always one remove from common sense. " The fact is," he used to say, " there ain't enough brains to go round, so the Almighty had to stuff up the gaps in women's heads with cotton-wool, and most of the time it don't make any difference."

" Prisoner is an ugly word," said Berta gently. " Whatever he does, Mrs. Watson, it is for the best."

" Ah ! " cried Emily, with an ugly laugh that startled her more than her companion, " but whose best ? However, it won't be quite so easy as he imagines. I intend to go this afternoon. I shall get a car."

She moved towards the telephone. Berta made no attempt to stop her. " I intend to ring up the garage for a car," she announced. " Your husband told me its name."

" It will be no good," Berta assured her gently. " They will not come."

" People will do most things for money," retorted Emily grimly.

But Berta only repeated, " Ask them, of course, offer them any bribe you please. But they will not come to this house."

" You mean—— ? "

" I mean only what I have said, Mrs. Watson. That the garage will send no car here."

Suddenly she understood. Forrester had foreseen this contingency and guarded himself against it. Neither Darling nor any other garage would take any notice of calls from The Cottage, because they had been warned. . . . Warned of what ? That there was an unbalanced woman in the doctor's care, someone not responsible for her actions ? She saw part of the hideous picture, but not yet did the whole horror burst upon her.

" Then I shall walk down to the high road and telephone from there," she announced as quietly as she could. " The luggage can be sent for later. My diamonds I will take with me. I shall go at once."

" And when you reach Oxbridge, Mrs. Watson, what will you do then ? There is an Agricultural Week on there.

You would never get a room. And there is no train to London to-night. Besides, if you wish to go there is no need to be melodramatic. This is not a prison, whatever you may think. When my husband comes back, if you explain to him what you wish to do, you will find he will not try to prevent you." She spoke very calmly, almost with sympathy, yet behind the quiet words was an implacable purpose. Emily Watson knew that the younger woman had cleverly contrived to put her in the wrong, and she knew, too, that she would have to fight if she was not to be defeated. She struggled for composure.

" Your husband will hardly have thought of preventing my getting in touch with my lawyer," she suggested, and in spite of herself her voice sounded shrill, and the words tumbled over one another. " I shall put through a trunk call. You can, of course, charge it on my bill."

Berta made no attempt to stop her. But neither did she go away. " Have you thought what you are going to tell your lawyer, Mrs. Watson ? "

" Of course. I shall give him my address and say that I wish to see him in the course of the next two days, that I am coming to London to-morrow. . . ." As she heard herself say these words she suddenly felt safe. She took down the receiver and asked for Trunks.

" There's no need to do that," said a voice at the other end. " We can put you through right away. What's your number ? "

She gave it and added Mr. Matthews' number. " It's urgent," she added. It seemed an eternity before the voice said, " Number unobtainable."

" It can't be," she almost screamed. " It's a lawyer's office. I must get in touch with him. It—it's a matter of life and death. Please change the line."

But though the operator was very obliging the reply was the same. Number unobtainable. Mortified, utterly downcast, Emily replaced the receiver. She had no vision of Forrester standing where she stood now, and saying, " I think I should warn you that I have an afflicted lady under my care, who may try to get connections to London or other large towns to people with whom she is not acquainted. I should take it as a favour if you could assure her that the numbers she gives are unobtainable." He couldn't have got away with that in a large town, but in Oxbridge, since there was no Swinnerton exchange, your neighbour's concern is your own. It was commonly supposed that the lady in question was Mrs. Forrester, and the villagers had all manner of conjectures about her, from the old man who thought she was a vampire to the old woman who swore she was a witch.

Emily, meanwhile, felt suddenly quite frantic. She knew the despair of a man isolated on a rock, watching the rising tide and knowing that before long it will cover his refuge and sweep him away without trace. She thought wildly of making a dash for it, but it wouldn't be any good. She was sure now that she never went anywhere unwatched, and she saw herself stealing hurriedly down the lane, being followed by a ruthless Dr. Forrester in a great grey car. The lane was so narrow there was hardly room for a pedestrian and a car of that size, and she could in imagination feel the wheels catching up with her, hear her own shrill scream as they rolled her over. . . . Even in the ditch she wouldn't be safe. Desperately she laid hold of herself; a nervous collapse now was precisely what Forrester hoped for. He could then either dispose of her, and how convenient the wood would be, or get her certified. In the latter instance he could call in Desmond to bear him testimony, assuming he could find out Desmond's address, and she reflected with dismay that she had just made Berta a present of Mr. Matthews' name and telephone number. Summoning every iota of self-control, she moved away down the hall.

" I don't understand what you have in mind," she said in shaking tones and quite inaccurately ; " but, naturally, if I wish to leave this house I am a perfectly free agent."

" Naturally," agreed Berta. " If you will wait till my husband returns I am sure he will be ready to fall in with any arrangements you have in mind, though I know he feels that a little more rest will set you up completely.

It's perfectly natural that the war should affect the nerves of all of us. But it would create a very odd impression if you were to try to escape, as though there was some reason why you should not behave like a normal person."

To Emily, however, it now seemed clear that unless she could contrive her getaway before the doctor's return she might only achieve it in a coffin or a strait-waistcoat. A coroner, she thought, would believe Forrester's evidence, if he said she had thrown herself under the car. Any coroner, she supposed, would believe a woman was unbalanced who crept away furtively with all her jewels and a large sum of money in bank notes, without even leaving her address with her lawyer. Now she thought with longing of that letter to Mr. Matthews that she had so light-heartedly destroyed on the afternoon of her arrival. And if Forrester offered details of peculiar behaviour while under his roof, Berta would unhesitatingly confirm them, and there would be no one to oppose him. Besides, both Desmond and Dossie would confirm her mental instability, with MacKinnon in support. Emily felt like the author of the Psalms complaining that he was hedged in on every side. She thought of trying to send a telegram, but by this time she was convinced it would be a waste of time. No, any action she took must be taken from outside the house. After what had happened she supposed she would never find the gates unlocked. Forrester would be far too wary to give her an opportunity of getting out and telling her story. If she wrote a letter and left it to be posted she would be in no better case. She would have no proof that it would ever be given to the postman, and she would, in fact, be playing into the enemy's hands, since she would be providing him with an address to which, if he chose, he could write. No, her one hope was to write and personally hand the letter to the man when he came to The Cottage. She knew he arrived between seven-thirty and eight o'clock, when there was any post to be delivered. She must, then, take her letter down to the gate and hand it to him in person. In that way she would prove the fact of her existence to a third person. She would say, " I am Mrs. Watson and I am staying with Dr. and Mrs. Forrester. This is a letter to my lawyer in London. . . ." But even so the doctor might explain that she was mentally deranged. . . . Still, it would show that she was actually on the premises. At this stage she found herself wondering if she really was out of her mind. Because things like this, she believed, don't happen. Crook could have told her they're happening all the time, and if they didn't people like himself would be queueing up for the dole. But she had never heard of Arthur Crook, and wouldn't at that stage have trusted him an inch if she had met him. Her notion of lawyers was a race of men like Mr. Matthews, suave, dignified people speaking in Public School accents. A man accustomed to strut about in ready-mades of bright-brown material and to sport vulgar, brown bowlers would have suggested a tout or someone in league with Desmond and Dossie.

Looking up, she saw that Berta was still watching her. Again she had the impulse for flight, now, instantly, while the gate was still unlocked and Forrester out of the way. But as she moved Berta said unemotionally, " No, Mrs. Watson, that is no good. I can see what you have in mind, but it is too late. Listen ! "

Emily cocked her head but heard nothing. " You are wrong," she said excitedly. " I am going and I am going at once. If there is no train to London to-night, then I'll go to a hotel at Oxbridge ; if there's no room at the hotel I'll sleep at the station. If they close the station after dark, then I'll go to the police. You can't stop me."

But Berta, still unmoving, repeated her former warning. " No, Mrs. Watson, you cannot do that. As I told you, it is already too late.'

Emily, engrossed in her fight for liberty, had heard nothing, but now, to her horror, she saw the door begin to open. Then Forrester came in.

" I'm afraid I haven't such good news for you as I had hoped," he said, smiling to his visitor. " About the car, I mean."

" I didn't expect you to have any good news," retorted Emily, white to the lips.

He looked surprised. " I thought you said you didn't know anything about cars, Mrs. Watson."

" Enough to know that this one will never be able to take me into Oxbridge."

He looked more astonished than ever. " Oh, it's not so bad as that. I hope to get her back to-morrow night, in which case we could have our excursion on Friday. If not——"

" Why do you trouble to lie to me ? " demanded Emily, now almost beyond the borders of common sense. "Even if you did get the car back to-morrow, and for all I know it's in the garage now, something would happen between now and Friday to prevent my going out in it. But it doesn't really matter as I shan't be here on Friday. I—I have to get back to town unexpectedly."

" I wonder how you heard that," said Forrester in his pleasant voice. " I thought you said you hadn't given the address or the telephone number to any one." (Was it imagination or did he shoot a wary glance at his wife ?)

She thought in desperation, " He must know I've had no letters. I couldn't get them without their passing through his hands first. And they know there has been no telephone call, because Berta is never out of the house."

Before she could speak the doctor continued, " I do hope this absurd affair of the car has nothing to do with your lightning decision. It was only this morning you spoke of staying on for a while."

" Yes," said Emily, rushing headlong on to the spear, " it is what you call the absurd affair of the car. You see, I happen to know there was nothing wrong with it. It was just an excuse, and your wife has explained to me that you never intended to take me to Oxbridge. Now, whatever your reasons, I'm not interested (though that, of course, wasn't true either), but it was a trick, and I won't stay anywhere where such tricks are played on me."

Forrester did not look one whit discomposed. " I'm sorry you should jump to such an unfounded conclusion.

As a matter of fact, after you had gone back to the house, it occurred to me that the car was very near the head of the slope, and if only I could push her the intervening few yards she might run down to the high road of her own volition. Once there, I could probably persuade a lorry driver, for a consideration, to give her a tow into Oxbridge. And that is precisely what happened. I could hardly suggest taking a passenger in a towed car . . . and I think," he added more coldly, " you must have misunderstood my wife if you think I was deliberately bamboozling you."

" I said that if you could not take Mrs. Watson in to Oxbridge it was for a good reason," returned Berta quietly. " You have now told us what the reason is. But Mrs. Watson is determined to leave us at once."

" That strikes me as rather unreasonable," objected Forrester.

Now that he was in command of the scene Emily had to admit that he reduced the whole melodramatic situation she had created to an incident that might take place anywhere, but her previous conviction was so strong that no amount of reasonable argument could now have shifted her.

" It is a very plausible story," she agreed ; " but all the same, I intend to return to Southwood and nothing you say will prevent me. I propose to go to-morrow."

" Without the car ? "

" I shall telephone this garage——"

" I warned you before, that is a waste of time. Not Darling or any garage in Oxbridge will send a car out to The Cottage. No, Mrs. Watson, I beseech you to be reasonable. If you insist on carrying out this sudden change of plan, then I will accompany you to London on Friday, if possible——"

" You will accompany me ? There is no need for that."

" I think so. I don't consider you are in a fit state to travel alone."

All her fears came crowding back upon her. " But that is absurd. I came alone."

" Would your relatives—your nephew—have permitted it if you hadn't slipped away when the coast was clear ? And—isn't that really why you came as and when you did ? If you'd confided in them would you have been allowed to come at all ? Believe me, Mrs. Watson, I speak as a doctor and I tell you that the first time I met you I realised you were suffering from severe mental strain. I hoped that a reasonable period of rest under ideal conditions would set you right, and I must admit that I have seen a considerable improvement since you came here. But I still shouldn't feel I had discharged my duty to you if I let you go off unaccompanied, particularly in your present rather excitable frame of mind."

" What are you suggesting ? " asked Emily in a frightened voice.

" Nothing in the least alarming. If you will give me the name of your doctor or some responsible person, a relation for choice, I will accompany you to London, to-morrow if you wish, and deliver you into safe hands. Or if you like to give me the name of some friend or relative who would accept the responsibility, I will write to him or her and get him to come down to Oxbridge. I haven't the smallest wish to keep you here an hour against your will, but I shouldn't be doing my duty as I see it if I let you go off really for a whim, for I have proof that twenty-four hours ago you had no thought of leaving this house, without assuring myself that you had a destination and every chance of reaching it."

" Perhaps," said Emily, throwing up her head, " you would like to send for the police."

" The police ? " Now he looked really puzzled.

" Then we could go thoroughly into the matter. You would soon find that you can't keep people against their will."

" When the police or any one in authority had heard what I had to say, they would agree that my view is an eminently reasonable one."

" And what have you to say ? "

He returned gently, " Must you make such heavy

weather of this, Mrs. Watson? Believe me, I've only your interests at heart. And I'm prepared to accept your word for it that you don't know how serious your condition is."

"Considering you've never examined me as a doctor..." Emily began indignantly.

"I wasn't speaking of physical condition, but nervous. For instance, do you realise that you walk in your sleep?"

She blinked at him, like someone struck suddenly between the eyes.

"That's nonsense. I never have."

"They always say that, and generally they're quite sincere, the sleep-walkers, I mean. They don't know. The usual thing is for a person who is sleep-walking to return to his or her bed whenever they have done whatever it is their sub-conscious roused them to do. In your case——"

"Yes," she said breathlessly. "In my case? What are you going to suggest is the reason for sleep-walking? Though, mind you, I don't for an instant admit it."

"Two or three times my wife and I have found you in the hall by the front door," he told her. "You're always feeling over the surface, trying to get out. You don't know the various locks and bolts we employ, and since in sleep-walking you act on instinct not intelligence you have never got farther than the door. But it's perfectly obvious to a medical man that you are trying to escape from something—or someone. That bears out my first impression, when you admitted to me that you wanted to get away leaving no trace, because of some vague threat against your security or possibly your life. I don't quite know. It's an impulse of fear, you see. Fear is pressing on the mind as some growth might press on a vital part of the body. You see what I mean? You have to remove the physical growth by operation if health is to be restored, and where the obstacle is mental, then its cause must be removed. I haven't asked you for your confidence, and I do not ask you for it now, but you have some fear in your mind that is beginning to dominate you. If you are not careful it will dominate you entirely. I speak only for your own good. As you know, fear is my particular province——"

"Yes," cried Emily fiercely. "Oh, what a fool I've been. Why didn't I see that before? That advertisement of yours was simply to lure people down here and terrify them out of their wits so as to give you data for your wretched book. But you needn't think you've succeeded with me. The danger in which I stand isn't imaginary. . . ." But at the expression that crossed his face as she spoke these words, her spirit wilted as suddenly as a flower attacked by flame. That's what they all say, his expression said. Now her danger was greater than it had ever been; Forrester had scored his first important victory, for in that instant there was sown in her mind the seed of self-mistrust. She might say scornfully, This is all a plot, all lies, but the tiny doubt nagged like a worm in the bud. Suppose it is true? Suppose I do walk in my sleep? Suppose that's why Dossie has been privy to this plot? Perhaps other people at Southwood know, and that's why they were so insistent that I should have someone to live with me. Suppose . . . If . . . They hadn't changed their manner towards her, because you don't stop knowing as rich a woman as Albert Watson's widow simply because she becomes a little odd. But—hadn't she noticed something, something indefinable, during these past weeks? At the time one didn't think—but now, looking back . . . Here she glanced up to find Forrester watching her intently. Fearful of self-betrayal—for it was true that nowadays she sometimes spoke her thoughts aloud without realising what she did—she murmured something incoherent and went to her own room.

# 13

And now she was waging a desperate fight against the hysteria that is the onset of madness. Like someone trapped in a shivering sand she fought her way back to firm ground. Once she lost her footing, then all was lost. Once she allowed Forrester to persuade her that she was, in fact, mentally unstable, reason would slip like that poor lost one floundering on the sinking sands. I must keep cool. I'm imagining. This is 1947 when such things don't happen. Why, it's sheer Victorian melodrama. But here she made the discovery all women in danger are bound to make some time or another, that melodrama isn't peculiar to the Victorian era. It belongs to no time and affects no one class of the community. This isn't Chicago, you remarked to your neighbours when one of the Sunday papers featured some particularly horrible atrocity—just as though.Chicago were like hell, a state belonging to some other phase of living, not a place you could visit in the same way as you visited London or York. People don't do these things in a civilised age, you told yourself and your friends, and then you opened your paper and read of some frightful tale of ill-treatment of a child or some woman tortured in marriage. And perhaps one day people would be talking just that way because of some body that had been found—or some woman wrongfully imprisoned in an asylum—and this time they wouldn't be able to say, This sort of thing doesn't happen in one's own circle, because the woman would be Emily Watson of Southwood, owner of a nice modern villa called Kozicot, and what happened to Emily Watson of Southwood might happen to Mrs. Smith of Kozicot, Epsom, or Brighton or Eastbourne. A phrase she had sometimes heard in church floated through her mind . . . no respecter of persons. She clenched her fists and beat them softly against her half-maddened brain.

"There must be something, something I've forgotten. If I could get in touch with the villagers . . . don't they gossip about this household when they're alone? Of course they do. How does the doctor explain things to the garage and the telephone operator? Don't send a car. Don't take any calls." That was enough to make any village gossip. Ah, but that was where Berta came in. Forrester would have allowed it to be known that he had married a heroine of the Resistance Movement. It would be enough for this country community that the girl was a foreigner, almost as alien to them as a blackamoor. They called the inhabitants of the next county foreigners; they'd be ready to believe the most fantastic stories about a Frenchwoman. Tradesmen didn't call, Forrester did all the shopping. Very likely no one had ever seen Mrs. Forrester. The telephone never rang, visitors never came. . . . And then, with a fresh shock, she remembered the hat in the derelict cottage. She hadn't taxed the doctor with that. If she had, what would he say? Another fragment of a diseased imagination, perhaps. Still, the hat was there. Ah, but perhaps by to-morrow it wouldn't be. If she told any one about it, if she ever got away and established contact with the rest of the world, perhaps it would have gone by the time investigations were set on foot. And in that case who would believe her? Expensive frumpy hats don't blossom by nature on the walls of coal cellars. But if no one saw it but me—no one but me. . . . It must have been about then that she took her second step into the dark. Sitting shivering on the window-seat she began to whisper, "Suppose I'm wrong? Suppose it was an hallucination? Suppose there was never a hat there, really, at all? Why, perhaps I dreamed the whole thing, perhaps even the cottage was part of my dream."

The human mind is astonishingly adaptable. In spite of the shock of the morning, the quickening of her rather sluggish intelligence into a realisation of actual and deadly peril, Emily found herself within a few hours behaving in a carefully normal manner, so that no one who wasn't in the secret would have guessed that her life had, as it were, turned turtle since morning. When Berta brought up her lunch, for amazingly the whole affair had only occupied a couple of hours, she found (and she did wonder where the car really was, if Forrester had really driven it into Oxbridge and left it there or if it was hidden in some much nearer place) both women were elaborately normal in their manner. Emily observed that it seemed to be clouding over and she thought she'd sit quietly by the fire with a book, and Berta said her husband thought the storm that was clearly on the way would hold off till the next morning. They exchanged a few more phrases and then Berta went back to her own quarters and Emily forced herself to eat her lunch just as if this were an ordinary day and her mind were not riven with fear. All the time she was making plans. It seemed improbable that she could get away unobserved and she was sensible enough to realise that if she did such precipitate action would lend colour to Forrester's assertions of her mental instability. No, the obvious thing was to contrive to get in touch with Mr. Matthews, at the same time behaving in a perfectly normal manner so as to allay suspicion here. Matthews might think her story a bit queer, but she remembered how Albert used to say that no lawyer worth his salt took sides against a rich client. All that afternoon she sat by the fire planning what to say. She resolved to omit all mention of the hat she had found ; it might prove to have no more to do with the case than the traditional flowers that bloom in the spring, and in any event, other people's affairs were best left alone. That was another of the sagacious Albert's dicta. She further resolved not to set pen to paper in the house itself. She could not protect herself against sudden interruption by one or other of the Forresters, and if it were known that she was writing letters they would watch her movements like a pair of lynxes. No, to-day she would plan exactly what to say and to-morrow, after breakfast, she would casually announce her intention of going a little way into the woods. She would wear her oldest clothes, her low-heeled shoes, leave hat and gloves and even her bag in her room. Then they would know she wasn't trying to escape. Nor, to-morrow morning, would she. After lunch she would announce that she had dropped something—an earring, say—among the trees and was going to look for it. She would remember the path she had taken and was sure she would find it. Perhaps it would be safer to say a book —she could settle that detail later. Then—then—with the letter she had written in the secrecy of the woods during the morning she would look for a way out. Forrester had told her that the upper part of the woods was impenetrable. But how could she be sure this was the truth ? It might be possible to break through some gap and come into the lane above the house, and so make her way to the village. The postman was the son of the old lady who kept the village shop—a little soft in the upper story, Forrester had said—but that wasn't important. The important thing was to establish the fact of her existence, to let some third person know that she was staying at The Cottage, to mention her name and her address and perhaps add a detail or two about herself. Villagers, she had always heard, liked to gossip a bit with strangers. They might refuse to talk about themselves, but since she wanted to do the talking that would be eminently satisfactory. Then she would leave her letter and on her return she would recount her doings to one or other of her hosts. Or might it be better to say nothing of the letter, at all events until it had left the district ? She knew that letters once posted are supposed to be irrecoverable, but Forrester had an engaging tongue, and he might tell so disarming a story that the old lady would fish the letter out of the bag and hand it over to him. That would be fatal. No, on second thoughts better say nothing. She would ask Mr. Matthews to ring up The Cottage, and she made a mental note to jot down the number before leaving the house. The Forresters could withhold a letter, they couldn't prevent her hearing the sound of the telephone bell. She would make a point of not leaving the house once the letter had left her hands until the message had come through. If one of the

Forresters answered it, as of course they would, and said there was no such person as Emily Watson staying at that address—well, she would have warned her lawyers to expect just such a reception, and that surely would bring a representative of the firm hotfoot to Swinnerton. She might even suggest that if such an answer was received they might get in touch with the police. Still, it was important to be careful about mentioning *them*. Albert, her touchstone for worldly wisdom, said the country was full of slightly deranged middle-aged and old women, with or without fortunes, going round suffering from persecution mania demanding protection for the money they didn't possess and the lives of which no one wished to deprive them. So, hour after hour, she brooded, planning, discarding, rebuilding, and it was startling to see Forrester enter with her evening cocktail. She thought she saw him throw a rapid glance round the room, but she had nothing to hide. No pen was in sight, the zipped writing-case Desmond had given her (out of her own money, she reflected wryly) lay where it had lain that morning. Surely, she thought, she had thrown dust in the eyes of both.

Dinner was as excellent as usual. She resolved to go to bed in good time, and it wasn't until Berta entered with a cup of hot milk that it went through her mind that, if she had been planning, so perhaps had they. The hot milk wasn't an innovation; she had it every night. But she would run no unnecessary risks. She took the cup with a pleasant, friendly smile, saying she was tired and would drink it in bed, but when Berta's footsteps had died away she cautiously poured the contents of the cup down the bathroom basin. She left a drain of milk in the bottom and stared at it closely. Was it imagination or was there really a tell-tale sediment, showing that her suspicions were justified? She couldn't be sure. Still, since she had not drunk the milk, it didn't matter.

She had expected to lie awake half the night, so tense was her mood, but to her amazement she was scarcely in bed before she was overcome by drowsiness. She could, as they say, hardly keep her eyes open. Resolutely she opened her book and tried to read, but all the lines of print ran into one another and none of the sentences had any meaning. Next the book itself began to waver in her hands and though she drew up her knees and propped it against them it was no help. She couldn't stay awake.

" But I didn't drink the milk," she told herself. And then the thought came, " Of course ! Not the milk—the coffee. They might expect me to be suspicious of the milk, so they wouldn't doctor that. But why ? "

To make sure you didn't write a letter, said her commonsense.

Before she could continue the argument the book crashed to the floor, and she was asleep with the light still burning.

When she woke it was with a start, to find the room in darkness. Hurriedly she pushed the pin of the lamp but nothing happened. So it was after midnight and she had been sleeping more than two hours at the least. To her horror she found she was shivering, not just a gentle tremor because the eiderdown had fallen off the bed, but great shudders that shook her whole frame. In vain she tried to control them. Her instinct was stronger than she, and it was her instinct, she believed, that had wakened her so peremptorily to warn her of approaching danger. With cold hands she felt for the matches, struck one and got the candle alight. Now she was aware of sounds and movements, faint and careful but, to her over-sensitive ear, unmistakable. Someone was standing just outside the door ; perhaps if she had wakened a few minutes later, whoever it was would have been inside the room. For she had never locked her door at night since her arrival at The Cottage, and she had not done so last night. She must give the appearance of absolute normality. Yet now, by the candle's shooting beam, she was half-persuaded that she could see the knob of the door slowly turning. She put one hand to her throat in a gesture that in someone else would have seemed unnecessarily melodramatic, but she was unaware of the movement. The candlestick shook in her hand, a guttering trail of wax ran down into the silver tray, immense ludicrous shadows were suddenly painted on the pale distempered walls.

" If it is Forrester he has come for the letter," she told herself. " That is all. If you call out he will say that you called out in your sleep and he came to see what was wrong." Or would he say he had found her on the stairs or by the front door, and had just guided her back to bed ? In any case, there was no need for this shuddering terror. " He's not going to murder you," she told herself, and then thought, " But how do I know ? *How do I know ?* He must realise that if ever I get away from this house I shall talk, and if it's his idea to go on luring rich, silly women down that would put a spoke in his wheel." Being a doctor, she thought vaguely, he could probably contrive her death to look like suicide or accident.

At this juncture the candle fell out of its stick with a noise that seemed to her as loud as an earthquake ; she had been tilting it unconsciously as she pursued her thoughts down their avenue of terror. As though that sound were a warning she heard another, the unmistakable closing a door a little way down the passage. So someone had been there and—had gone. Gone ! She fumbled for the candle, found it and lighted it. At least, she thought, she was now safe for the remainder of the night. He had expected her to be asleep, but the falling candle had warned him. Then another more alarming idea came to trouble her poor desperate mind. What if that closing door was part of a plot ? Perhaps both Forresters were waiting in the passage five minutes ago and now one had gone back. Or perhaps they were both there still. She must, she must be reassured before she could risk once more falling asleep. Shaking but resolved, she stole out of bed and went barefooted across the floor. Now in the passage absolute silence reigned. She laid her ear against the panel of the door, as though in this way she could hear the noise of breathing from the other side.

But there was nothing—nothing. With the last remnants of self-control, she flung the door wide.

The passage was empty, the house pitch dark and as silent as the proverbial grave.

## 14

The next morning she was hard put to it to believe in the events of the night. She knew if she spoke of them to Forrester he would tell her she had had a nightmare, and to-day in the brilliant sunlight, with the birds shouting with glee beyond the window, she could have believed him. Only when she was dressing did her glance happen to fall on the carpet near the bed and she saw the trail of candle grease where the candle had fallen. And she saw, too, that the candle itself was burned right down. After she got back to bed she had not dared to extinguish it, and for the second time had fallen asleep with the light burning.

Sometimes Berta asked her visitor if she had a good night, but to-day she said nothing, which confirmed Emily in her conviction that a watch had been kept on her room and that, if she had not awakened just when she did, it might have turned into an invasion. It did not, fortunately, occur to her that she might have been aroused by the closing of the door as Forrester left the room.

When Berta came to clear the breakfast table Emily said casually, " It seems such a lovely morning I thought I would take a book into the woods. Your husband says I can't lose myself if I keep the house in sight."

Berta said seriously, " If you do get lost, Mrs. Watson, you may never be found. They tell ugly stories in the village about the woods."

" I shan't go far," Emily promised her. " Albert—my husband—used to say I had no bump of locality and could lose my way even in my own house."

In the passage she met Forrester and asked him pleasantly if he thought it would stay fine.

"You're safe for this morning," he told her; "but there's a storm in the distance."

"Are you sure? It seems such a perfect day, all blue and gold."

"I told you the views here were magnificent. Better than the suburbs." He smiled. But Emily thought, "Suburbs!" as she might have thought "Heaven!" She had visions of Maisie and Dossie and Mrs. Durrant, all the safe women who didn't know how blessed they were, going into their rooms, doing a little dusting, running round after the 'daily woman,' deciding which hat to wear, going forth to keep their unimportant engagements with the dentist, the hairdresser, the dressmaker, standing in the fish queue, the bread queue, the horsemeat queue for darling Fido or Carlo or the Pussies, complaining in tranquil tones of the dullness of the post-war world. She told herself that if ever she got back safely to Southwood she'd never grumble at anything again.

She found her book, her writing-pad, one of the women's magazines she had brought with her that would conceal the pad, put a handkerchief and a powder puff in her pocket and opened her bag to look for her pen. And it wasn't there. Oh, botheration, I've put it down somewhere, she thought. On the dressing-table, the mantelpiece, the bookcase. It wasn't on any of them. She looked round in dismay. Of course, she could write in pencil, but would Mr. Matthews take a pencil letter seriously? She thought vaguely that pencil signatures aren't valid, and, anyway, pencil fades so soon, the address might get rubbed out en route. Besides, the pen must be somewhere. She tried to remember when she had used it last. The fact was that at The Cottage she had hardly needed a pen. She had written no letters since her arrival. Her glance fell on the big chesterfield, and she thought, Perhaps it has fallen out of my bag and slipped down the side. It was amazing how many things did get lost in that way. She had found spectacle-cases, pencils, even library books hidden between the side of the frame and the cushion.

The first thing she fished up was a hairpin, a sturdy silver hairpin. It must have been there years, fallen from the head of one of Thorold's guests, since the Forresters hadn't used these rooms, and in any case, Berta wouldn't use silver pins. What was it she had said about the dead artist ? " He liked all kinds evidently." She had said that after finding the bundle of letters. In spite of the fact that it must have been there six or seven years it wasn't at all tarnished or rusty. It might only have slipped down there a week or two ago. Her exploring hand, diving deeper, found something else, though it wasn't her pen. It was a diary with a blue leather cover, and a little white silk marker. If Thorold was really famous this might be worth quite a lot one day, she thought fantastically. But when she had opened the cover and seen the name written on the front page she decided the diary had probably belonged to the owner of the silver hairpin. Someone—presumably the owner—had written in it : (Mrs.) May Courtenay and an address in Hilton Green.

" Did she miss it ? " wondered Emily, letting the cover fall back into place.

And then, as if a fire bell had suddenly started clanging, she knew why the hairpin wasn't rusted, how it was that the diary had stayed unnoticed. For the date on the cover was 1947 !

" This year," she whispered, and that fearful shivering began again. She couldn't control it. In a moment, she thought, she might find herself screaming aloud, and she folded her lips very tight and even put one hand over them. Forrester had said she was their first visitor, the rooms stood just as Thorold had left them, hadn't been used since his departure from Swinnerton early in the war. And here, on her lap, lay a diary for this year, filled up to—when ? Her hands shook so that she could scarcely turn the pages. They were covered in a rather large, sprawling writing that somehow seemed vaguely familiar. Albert used to say you could tell character from handwriting. His own had been small, pointed, very efficient. He told Emily hers spoke of a markedly female temperament. But I am a female, Emily had protested.

To which Albert replied rather obscurely that you could overdo anything. She wondered what he would make of this Mrs. Courtenay. A neurotic woman, he'd have said, seeing that large nervous hand, probably someone good at making mountains out of molehills. And if he had troubled to read the diary he would have observed complacently that he was right.

Emily, however, found no such consolation in the really terrifying story that the record unfolded. Curiosity changed to apprehension, apprehension to outright fear when she discovered that the last entry had been made on the 16th April, the day on which Forrester had both received and answered her letter. After that—nothing. Yet was it probable that a woman who liked to record her doings, thoughts, suspicions and intentions in such detail would suddenly stop unless for some reason it was impossible to continue?

Turning the thin closely-written sheets, Emily felt the horror mounting until she was like someone threatened by a tidal wave. On and on it came, inescapable, enveloping. For the story she now read was, in its general outline, the counterpart of her own. Even their ages fitted. There was an entry early in the year. "58 to-day. But Helene swears I don't look a day over 45 when I've had a treatment." A little later. "Dr. Purdy came. He says my general condition is much better, and I can look forward to many more happy years with C."

Emily pieced the story together from the fragments at her command. Mrs. Courtenay had fled to Swinnerton because of a husband who, she was convinced, was plotting against her life. She had committed that supreme blunder of the middle-aged, well-to-do woman, she had taken for her second husband a penniless man many years her junior. It was easy to see what had happened. He had supposed that her expectation of life was short, and had thought he was earning a good life-income in the easiest possible way. Then came the bombshell of the doctor's declaration. His wife was no fading invalid, she was a woman approaching sixty with many years of tedious life ahead. Tedious to Cecil Courtenay, that is.

The diary had no secrets. *He saw M. again to-day. M. telephoned this morning. I followed C. this afternoon. He said he had to meet a man about a business matter, but it was another lie.*

Emily thought she'd never realised how lucky she had been in Albert. Sometimes she had envied other women their more personable, more attentive husbands, but now she realised how grateful she should have been. Albert had never thought of poisoning her, not once, not even as a sort of joke. He hadn't even said as husbands sometimes do, " One of these days I shall put arsenic in your coffee." She'd heard husbands say that, thinking, " If it were Albert I'd never know another minute's peace." Because, even if it was only an idle threat, it showed the direction in which their minds were pointing. She read on. The difficulty was you couldn't be sure how much ground Mrs. Courtenay had for her suspicions. A jealous woman must suffer as much as one in physical torment, she reflected, and such people voice the most outrageous accusations that have no foundation whatever in fact.

Then she came across Forrester's name and her thoughts switched back to her own miserable situation. She read on with painful absorption.

Mrs. Courtenay had reacted to a similar advertisement in precisely Emily's manner. There was the record of the secret reply, the stolen meeting, the unspoken decision, even the taking advantage of Cecil's appointment at the golf club. (" Golf club " ? gibed the diary. " He has gone to M. for the week-end.") For once, however, she seemed not to have pleaded with him. It all fitted in too well with her own plans. While he was away she packed a bag, crept out of her house like a thief and came to Swinnerton. She had even brought her pearls sooner than leave them for M. Emily couldn't help wondering why a rich woman didn't divorce a husband with murderous impulses, to say nothing of infidelity, or get a legal separation, but it became obvious that, in spite of everything, his unfaithfulness, his cruelty, his heartless exploitation of her, even his attempts to rid himself of her in order to enjoy her money, the foolish woman couldn't uproot her love for him.

" If I had stayed at Hilton Green I should be dead by now. He used to bring me hot milk at night. I never drank it. Soon he would have found some other way."

Emily thought impatiently, " What did she see in him ? An unimaginative clod. How unenterprising men are, always taking the old, hackneyed path to freedom. Didn't he give her credit for any intelligence ? Think her so easily fooled ? " But then, she, Emily, had been fooled successfully by Desmond for years. Albert was right. There was no sense arguing with or about women ; they lived by their own codes that no man would ever understand.

Mrs. Courtenay had been nearly a fortnight at The Cottage when she proposed an excursion to Oxbridge, a proposal to which Forrester readily agreed. Feeling as though she were following a familiar path, Emily read of the obstacle that had prevented the outing, the new plan, its inevitable frustration and at last the rousing of Mrs. Courtenay's suspicions. Something unrecorded must have happened to wake doubt in her breast. On the 7th April she wrote :

> I was wrong. I am no more safe here than at Hilton Green. Somehow I must get away. Yet he is determined to keep me a prisoner. When I was out yesterday someone went through my jewel-case. I set a simple trap with a piece of thread. It is my pearls he is after. I was a fool to show them to that girl. Still, rather than that M. should wear them I would fling them away in the woods.

She must have been badly scared for the next day, April 8th, she wrote to Cecil asking him to come and fetch her away. When no reply was received to this desperate plea she began to believe that the letter had never reached its destination.

> April 10. If C. had heard he would have come by now. He needs the money. So they have kept my letter back. Now I am lost indeed. I would telephone but they tell me the line is disconnected since the big storm.
> April 12. Wrote to C. again. I am sure someone tried my door last night.
> April 15. Dr. Forrester says he will take me driving to-morrow. Somehow, when we are in Oxbridge, I must contrive to send C. a telegram. I feel this is my last chance. I must not, dare not miss it.
> April 16. Mrs. Forrester has just come in to say that 'he' is ready. I should like to take my pearls, but that might increase my danger. What have they schemed between them? To-night I will finish the record or never write in this diary again.

The last word was written crookedly as though the unfortunate lady had been interrupted, and in a fever of dread had closed the little book and thrust it far, far out of sight among the springs of the chesterfield where, but for the accident of Emily mislaying her pen, it might have remained for years.

That was the end of the story. She had never finished the record on paper. Her prophecy had been true. And the Forresters were denying her existence. You are our first guest, they said to Emily. Had they said the same to Mrs. Courtenay? And had it been equally false in her case? Was she, Emily Watson, one of a trail of nameless, lost women who came blindly seeking refuge at The Cottage, never to emerge alive? The mystery of the hat in the ruined cottage was solved now. It had belonged to Mrs. Courtenay or to Mrs. Courtenay's predecessor. As to why it should be found in a closed cupboard, with a mud-stained spade close at hand—oh, even a poor fool like Emily could see the connection now. Then, with a sense of vertigo, she knew where she had seen that handwriting before. Time rolled back ; she was standing between the Forresters in the room she had just entered ; a piece of scorched letter-paper floated out of the fire to her feet. She stooped to pick it up. " I beseech you . . ." and then Berta had taken it from her. " It is one of many I found in the cupboard," she had said scornfully. " It is easy to see the kind of man that Thorold was."

No, easy to see the kind of people the Forresters were—unscrupulous, brutal, pitiless. . . .

Suddenly she thought she heard steps pause outside the door, and jumping to her feet, she thrust the diary into the pocket of her cardigan. Now she knew only one desire, to escape from the house at once. Not that she intended to let panic jeopardise her careful plan but if she could include the diary in the letter she intended to write, that surely should convince Mr. Matthews she wasn't simply an hysterical woman treading an inevitable path to the lunatic asylum. She flung a final glance round, saw the pen in some obvious place, and went quickly out.

She saw Forrester in the hall, and he said laughingly, " Going into the woods ? Be sure you don't get lost," and she forced herself to make some commonplace reply. She wouldn't look over her shoulder to see if she were being watched, or hurry her pace. Steadily she forged ahead, only turning now and again to be sure that The Cottage was still in sight. At last she thought she had come far enough ; she had reached a very pleasant little copse whose shady trees seemed to promise privacy. Certainly by stepping in it she momentarily lost sight of the house, but it was only a matter of five or six paces, and all she had to do when her letter was completed was retrace those steps and find her simple way home. She walked round the copse looking for the most comfortable place in which to settle herself and soon she had unscrewed her pen and had begun to write her letter. She had supposed it would be quite simple to outline the facts to her correspondent, but set on paper they seemed outrageous, fantastic, quite incapable of proof. And if Matthews did come down, would he not be more reassured by the doctor's cool professional manner than by her own troubled protestations? She wrote and destroyed, wrote and destroyed. Even the little diary did not seem the sheet-anchor it had appeared at first, for a level-headed man like Mr. Matthews would consider its writer in her dotage. Crook might believe in poisoning husbands, because he dealt in violence, but Mr. Matthews wouldn't. All the same, she resolved to enclose the diary, but at the last minute changed her mind. Because if, by some desperate chance, her letter miscarried, then all her proof was gone. Eventually she tore out the front page of the diary and enclosed it in her letter, and slipped the diary itself back into her pocket. Surely, surely, Mr. Matthews would make discreet inquiries and discover if Mrs. Courtenay ever reappeared at Hilton Green?

Then, suddenly, she changed her mind again. Abandoning Mr. Matthews, that frail reed, she resolved to approach the police direct. She had heard Albert say that if a citizen reported his suspicions that a crime had been committed, particularly the crime of murder, the police were bound to make inquiries. She had spent more than two hours trying to write to Mr. Matthews, her letter to the police was scribbled inside of twenty minutes. She told them who she was and said they could verify the facts of her departure from Miss Dossie Brett, she gave them Desmond's name and address, she spoke of Mrs. Courtenay, and as an afterthought she mentioned who her husband had been. Albert might be dead, but his reputation had survived him. And she slipped the front leaf of the diary into the letter and prepared to return to The Cottage.

It was only when she was once more on her feet that she realised the tremendous change that had overtaken the day. This morning's vivid blue sky had turned to an ominous purple, like grape bloom; low clouds hung round the tops of the trees; the wind had risen and the trees moved their branches menacingly or so she thought. She remembered now that at breakfast, when she commented on the brilliance of the day, Berta had said, " My husband thinks there will be a storm later. They come up here with no warning at all."

"I must hurry," she told herself, hastily collecting her belongings. "I can't be caught in that." She had a nervous dread of storms. "But there's no need to be caught. I didn't come far. I shall have plenty of time if I keep my head."

That, unfortunately, was what she failed to do. When she left the copse she forgot that on entering it she had walked round the bases of the trees looking for the one that promised the most comfortable seat, and so she had not left the copse at the precise point at which she had entered it. She had taken several steps before she realised that there was no sign of The Cottage and she took several more before she would agree that she was on the wrong path. But fear of the woods, of the loneliness, of the creaking trees, of the senseless cruelty of storms, sent her hurrying back. But in her haste she must have left the original path, for now the copse was nowhere to be seen. She wouldn't believe this until she was brought up short by a clump of scarlet toadstools that she knew she had not seen before, and from which she instinctively recoiled. Hurrying back, she took what seemed to her a likely path only to find herself a moment later confronted by such a tangle of brambles and low-growing bushes that it was impossible to thrust a way through. Then panic took her, as the thunder began to roll in the sky and the trees to stoop earthward; utterly lost to any sense of direction, she dashed hither and thither, perpetually tripped and entangled by the spiny undergrowth. Low branches touched her shoulder and neck, wringing from her low screams, her feet slipped in the mud, once she came full-length in the slime, another time she saved herself only by a wild snatch at the nearest support, a thorny bramble spray that drew blood and left the vicious little red thorns in her hand. Now she could believe the rumours that circulated in the village, that the trees could tear themselves up from the earth by their roots and leave no trace. The thunder reverberated, the rain came down like a curtain. She fought against it as though it were some living thing; her stockings were slit from knee to ankle, a thorn caught her coat, there was mud on her face, blood on hands, wrists and ankles. Her hair hung lankly round a countenance so devoid of intelligence that no one would have thought her sane.

"I must get out, I must get out. I shall be caught in this wood, battered, drowned, beaten into the earth. No, I shall survive to stamp round and round looking for a way out and never finding it. Let me get out, God, and I'll never try and find my way through the hedge. Let me see The Cottage. That's all. Never mind what plan the Forresters have in mind. Just let me see The Cottage."

Tears poured down her cheeks, the dye from her scarf stained her throat; once she thought she saw lights and ran hysterically towards them, but they receded as she approached. "They were a figment of my imagination, they weren't really there," she sobbed. "So long as I know that, I'm not really mad."

Voices sounded, but not the voices of humans; the wood was coming closer, the trees moved and whispered. Emily Watson's mad, they said. Emily Watson's mad. Poor mad Emily. Suddenly she ceased her wild gyrations. It was no use. She knew it. She was lost. Irremediably. It would suit Forrester's book—unless he thought she had escaped. But, of course, he'd know she hadn't. And Berta would wear the diamonds when other people weren't by, just as now, presumably, when she and her husband were alone, she wore Mrs. Courtenay's pearls. Anyway, it wouldn't matter any more to her, Emily Watson, lying a faceless, fleshless thing among the trodden roots of the wood. She propped herself defiantly against an adjacent trunk and stared up.... The Cottage was just ahead of her, and from her feet ran a path to the very door. The shock was so great that for an instant she was paralysed. Then recognising the nature of her deliverance, she started forward, hesitated in case this were only another illusion, and staggered in its direction.

It wasn't a mirage. The Cottage was where it appeared

to be. The garden gate was open and Berta Forrester came hurrying down to meet her. When she saw the pitiful streaked scarecrow, a bundle of rags, its face distorted with terror, who came hurrying to meet her, any vestige of pity she might have cherished for the unfortunate woman died still-born.

"I lost my way," stammered Emily, and at the sound of her own voice she began to weep. "I lost my way."

Berta saw the futility of argument. "My husband is out looking for you," she said. "He has been out for an hour or more."

But all Emily could do was make those queer animal noises and repeat, "I lost my way. I thought I should die in the wood."

"You had better have a hot bath and I will get you a hot drink," said Berta. "It is half-past two and your lunch is spoiled, but I will bring some sandwiches."

All Emily wanted was to be left alone to conceal the precious letter and the diary. As soon as Berta had gone, she hurried into the sitting-room and thrust the letter into the safest hiding-place she knew. They might creep into her room in the dark, feel under her pillow, examine her clothes, but they wouldn't look in the back of the couch. As for the diary—but here she was brought up short, for when she felt in her pocket it was no longer there.

## 15

At first she could not believe it. She hunted in this pocket and that, shook out her clothes, searched again and again. But always with the same result. What had happened was clear enough. In one of her headlong falls the little book had been jolted out of her pocket and now lay, being pounded to pulp somewhere in the sodden woods. Now despair filled her heart. She had no real proof that her story was justified; never again would she dare venture among the trees searching for her treasure.

Emily, who had been brought up in a perfunctory sort of way on the poets (and who indeed sometimes broke into facile rhymes on her own account, a faculty Albert had heavily discouraged) remembered a tag from her childhood. *And oft apart his arms he tost, And often muttered, " Lost! Lost! Lost! "* But when, reluctantly, she left her room and lay utterly exhausted in her hot bath, a still more alarming thought came to torment her. Suppose, in his search through the woods, Forrester should stumble on the diary and realise the meaning of its presence there. She had worked herself into a fever when it occurred to her that, even if he found it, he could not be sure that she had dropped it there. The unfortunate Mrs. Courtenay might have dropped it when she went into the woods. Nevertheless, she was convinced that its loss increased her own peril.

" I must not only post that letter, creep down early to the gate and hand it myself to the postman, I must make the doctor understand that I have written to someone in the outside world. Then perhaps he won't dare do away with me as I'm convinced he has done away with the unfortunate Mrs. Courtenay."

(Besides she reminded herself once more, if she could be seen by a third person, that would be evidence of her presence at The Cottage. That alone, she hoped, would save her.)

When she came back from her bath she heard voices in the passage below, and knew that the doctor had returned. He was asking about her.

" Oh, yes," said Berta carelessly, " she came in about half an hour ago. She looked demented."

" Being lost in the woods in a storm like this is enough to send any one demented," returned Forrester. " I'll come up presently." Then a door shut, and if they said anything more Emily did not hear it. There was nothing to show that he had found the diary and she was inclined to think that he had not. Resolutely she dismissed the thought of it from her mind and set herself to evolve some plan by which she could escape their joint vigilance and contrive to post her letter in the morning. She had no intention of letting it out of her possession until she actually placed it in the hands of the postman.

When she had recovered somewhat and had taken some hot soup and a dish of eggs prepared by the still ungracious Berta, Forrester came up and asked her very kindly how she did. She found herself apologising for the trouble she had caused the household, " though, really," she added, " I still don't understand how I lost sight of The Cottage. One instant I could see it over my shoulder and a moment later it seemed to have taken wings."

He refused to allow her to blame herself, prescribed aspirin and a quiet afternoon with her feet up. He didn't urge her not to repeat this morning's experiment, because it was obvious she had no heart to do so. In the circumstances, he pointed out, there was no possibility of his trying to get the car back before to-morrow, but if he was fortunate then, he promised, she should have her long-delayed outing. Up till this instant his manner had been so much that of the family doctor, grave, concerned, advisory, that she had almost forgotten her suspicions. It seemed impossible that he could effect such a metamorphosis all in a moment, as it were. Then she remembered Dossie and Desmond, how easily they had fooled her, and her resolve not to accompany him in his car strengthened. Mrs. Courtenay had gone out—and never come back. Again she saw the fantastic hat on the rusty peg, the earth-stained spade leaning against the cottage wall.

" I think," she said with commendable composure, " I shall give myself a day or two to get over this. Storms always upset me, and this one sounds as though it were going on for ever."

She spoke, she thought, with just the right degree of casualness, but in the light of subsequent events she believed she must have aroused his suspicions by her tacit refusal, and so have spurred him to immediate action.

All the afternoon the rain wept and wailed at the windows and the storm increased in fury. Roaming round the room, looking for something to read to distract her own disagreeable thoughts, Emily found a book of short stories and opened it at random. She began to read without at first taking in the sense, but presently the gruesome plot began to force itself on her mind. She turned back to look at the title—*The Pit and the Pendulum* by Edgar Allan Poe. Vaguely she remembered hearing it described as a classic. A classic in horror certainly. It seemed to her that at every turn she was reminded of her own condition. Here also was the helpless prisoner, enclosed in a locked cell, threatened by the razor-edged pendulum. And even when he was unexpectedly rescued from that peril by the action of the rats he was faced with a new, more horrible torment when the walls of the cell began to shrink. She could read no further. Horror blinded her eyes. There was, it appeared, no end to the fiendish ingeniousness of debased mankind.

" I must keep my head," she told herself. " If I behave naturally they will suspect nothing. To-night I will keep a light burning from the instant the electricity goes off, and in the morning, too early for them to suspect me, I will go down to the gate and hide until the postman appears."

Unable to concentrate on anything else, she rehearsed over and over again what she would say in the short time at her disposal.

" I am Mrs. Watson, Mrs. Emily Watson of Kozicot, Southwood, Middlesex. I am being kept here against my will. This is a letter to the police. It is very urgent. If you see them tell them what I have said."

Would the fellow take that in? Or would he merely think she was a maniac? Already Emily was convinced Forrester had spread the word that no inmate of The Cottage except himself was in full possession of his senses—her senses, she corrected herself painfully. She wouldn't have much time. As soon as Berta discovered she was not in her room she would come looking for her, and after to-day's fright they would know she wouldn't be in the woods.

Her reflections were interrupted by Berta herself who came in with her dinner, saying, " I am afraid you did not sleep well last night, Mrs. Watson. I see your candle is burned right down."

She said uncomfortably, " I was reading."

" I have given you a new one," Berta continued. " We have no long ones left, so I will leave you another before I go to bed—just in case."

Emily thought, panic-stricken—In case of what ? But Berta had nothing more to say, and Emily ate her meal in silence. Later she turned on the wireless and found herself involved in a play about a murder on Hampstead Heath—a woman's body crammed into a perambulator. And now night was truly drawing on. She had thought that afternoon interminable, but as the darkness closed round the house she would have given anything for the power to push the hours back. Nothing, nothing was so terrible as the dark. She made and abandoned plan after plan for escape. None was foolproof, none offered any real hope of security. Round and round like a dormouse on a wheel went her desperate thoughts.

She had refused to drink her nightly hot milk when Berta brought it, pouring it away as she had done the night before, but the Forresters must have been aware of her suspicions and put an appropriate dose into the coffee, for, despite every effort, she found her head beginning to nod soon after ten o'clock. She had resolved not to undress, to await any opportunity of escape that might offer. She was even ready to steal out in the dark hours and hide in the ditch beside the gate. The difficulty would be to unfasten the big door without attracting attention. If she was discovered she could plead sleep-walking, though she didn't believe Forrester's story. Still, a woman in her wretched situation clutched at any floating straw.

She slept suddenly while the light still burned ; when she woke her watch stood at half-past one, but the light was still on. She didn't believe he would go to bed and forget to turn off the plant, so he was still up and about

—waiting, perhaps. Waiting for what ? For her to take the first step ? For the narcotic to take full effect ? But if so, why hadn't he come into her room before this ? Or did he guess she was going to try and get away, and would he be waiting for her down in the dark hall ?

The dreadful sequence of her thoughts formed themselves into crazy rhymes.

> Tick tock, tick tock,
> The light is burning at one o'clock.
> What will be done ere to-morrow's sun,
> That the light is burning at half-past one ?
> What does the doctor plan to do
> That the light is burning at nearly two ?

Now she felt she was really going mad. Wheels were revolving furiously in her brain. Mustn't sleep, mustn't sleep, she began to say aloud ; her voice increased till she thought they must hear her at the village a mile and a half away. *Mustn't sleep.* MUSTN'T SLEEP. She clapped her hands over her mouth. Pull yourself together. Listen. Plan. Scheme. Evade. What outlets are there ? Door ? Not locked. Then lock it. But—if he can't get in, you can't get out. Window ? Too far from the ground.

> Tick tock, tick tock,
> Watch the hands go round the clock.

The words themselves made a sort of fiendish music. She half-crossed the room to lock the door, hesitated, looked towards the window, turned back to the door, all this in an agony of indecision.

While she stood there wondering what best to do, with dramatic suddenness the light went out.

No sooner did she find herself in the dark than Emily felt the need for imperative action. First of all, she must make a light for herself. Then she must somehow get away.

" That's right," she affirmed, nodding idiotically.

First light, then flight,
Run away in the dead of night.

Putting out a trembling hand, she felt her way back to the bedside table, fumbled and discovered the matches, pulled one out and struck it against the emery side of the box. Nothing happened. A dead match, she thought. You got them now and again in full boxes. She threw it away, pulled out another, struck that. But in her feverish anxiety she snapped the slender stick in two, and had to take a third. All this while she was certain that Forrester had silently mounted the stairs and was standing outside her door, listening, listening. Should she let him know she was awake by making some exclamation, some movement ? Or should she let him enter and be taken unawares ? The fourth match scraped across the emery board with a defeated sound. For the first time she realised that here also something was wrong, Four matches that wouldn't strike was too much of a coincidence to be accepted. The truth flashed upon her. They had filled an ordinary match-box with safety matches which could only be ignited by their own box.

Now she was lost indeed. Fool, fool, not to have kept the fire burning. She turned desperately to the hearth but there was not even a smouldering gleam among the blackened embers. She remembered now noticing that the coal basket was empty ; she had paid no particular attention to that fact at the time. There had been so much else to think of. She crossed to the window and tore back the curtain. The rain had ceased, as Forrester had prophesied, but the outside world was pitch black and ice-cold. No stars, no moon, even the birds and creatures of darkness had not ventured out on such a night.

Now she was certain she heard a movement in the corridor. At any instant now the door would open.

Tick tock, tick tock,
Now his hand is on the lock.
Tock tick, tock tick,
Hear the latch begin to click.

She remembered that she had a torch in a drawer of the commode and, flinging aside the useless match-box, stumbled across the room to find it. If they had taken this, too, she thought. But they hadn't. Her fingers closed over its smooth sides. But when she pressed the button there was no answering beam of light. The battery's gone, she thought stupidly; the battery's gone. And that was exactly what had happened. The thoughtful Forresters, resolved to leave no stone unturned, had left her the empty container. It was too much. It was the last straw. Throwing back her head, she began to laugh.

Ha-ha-ha! Ho-ho-ho. Maniacal laughter. If any one had been within earshot he must have stirred uneasily in his bed to hear those wild sounds come pealing through the dark. The watcher on the threshold paused in his stealthy advance. Had he betrayed himself? Did she know? Did she guess? He had a torch in his pocket, but he didn't dare put it on. Only a few feet of black space separated them. Desperately Emily pushed the switch of the torch again, as though some miracle might take place. But of course it was no good.

Not a spark, not a spark,
Emily's got to die in the dark.

A phrase from one of the romantic novels that were her normal fare rushed through her mind. Selling your life dearly. Only in the novels it was her honour the woman was preparing to sell. And honour was always saved. Life was another matter.

Hearing that lunatic laughter, knowing now beyond all doubt that she was awake and aware, the enemy resolved to act. Softly he began to cross the room towards the bed, while not three yards away Emily waited motionless. It was all a matter of seconds, she knew. What chance had she against this ruthless pair? But still the cliché rang in her ears.

"At least I needn't be taken like a rabbit in its burrow," she told herself, and as Forrester came to a dead stop beside the bed she made her frantic, desperate bid for freedom.

# PART TWO

## I

When Miss Brett returned to Kozicot after lunch on the 25th April she stood in the hall calling in girlish tones, "Emily, Emily! Come and see what a clever girl Dossie's been." When there was no reply she impatiently flung open the door of the room she and Emily called the lounge and was surprised and annoyed to find it unoccupied. But it was more than unoccupied; it had that mysterious emptiness only known to rooms that have been abandoned. Closing the door Dossie ran upstairs, still calling to Emily.

"Where are you? Having forty winks?" She opened the door of the best bedroom with complete lack of ceremony, and stood looking round her with a dismay she could not immediately explain. After all, why shouldn't Emily have gone out? Probably she had suddenly had a brilliant idea about getting something special for Desmond's tea. If only she would leave things to people who really understood them! All the time these reflections were passing through Dossie's head, her small inquisitive eyes roamed round the big comfortable room. Something was wrong, though she could not at first identify it. Then, suddenly, she knew what it was. The dressing-table had been swept bare. Brushes, comb, mirror, powder, toilet-water, all gone. Dossie swung round. The nightdress-case on the bed was gone, and so was the familiar dressing-gown from its scented hanger on the door.

"Gone!" exclaimed Dossie in stupefaction. "But—I don't understand. Why? And where?"

She tore open the wardrobe door; there were plenty of clothes still hanging on the hooks, for Emily was a careful body. She bought good things and took good care of them, and even if she wore a suit no oftener than three or four times in a year she couldn't bring herself to part with it. Dossie suggested boisterously that she might sell what she didn't really need for the benefit of her friends. Her intention was obvious but Emily only replied with dignity that she hardly thought her friends would care to wear her old clothes and she for one couldn't bear to see them doing so.

"You could sell one of your three fur coats," Dossie had urged. She had never had a fur coat, and since the war their price had risen to figures she couldn't hope to pay. But Emily was stubborn, she wouldn't take a hint, and the mink, the beaver and the musquash remained hanging, cheek by jowl, as Dossie said violently, in her wardrobe. Now Dossie saw that the only one of the three that was missing was the beaver. Not going anywhere very smart or she'd have taken the mink, she reflected. There's nothing wrong with the mink or she'd have sent it away. What does that mean ? What did this sudden flight mean in any case ? Can she have rumbled us ? Dossie asked herself. How did we give ourselves away ? She's not all that bright. . . . She had forgotten Desmond's mis-addressed letter ; anyway, she would not have believed that Emily could have had it without betraying the fact. Still, the salient fact remained. Emily had gone and with her two suitcases and a quantity of clothing as well as all her toilet accessories. It was then that Dossie thought of the diamonds. She can't, she thought, have taken those. Emily always kept them locked in a special case in a locked desk, so that, short of breaking the various locks, there was no way of finding out if the diamonds were there or not, and even if she had no conscience about breaking locks Dossie didn't know how it was done.

She had a fair idea of the clothes Emily possessed so she could make out a reasonably comprehensive list of what was missing. Sly, thought Dossie, indignantly. I thought she was very pleasant about Doris going over to her mother. She ran downstairs and picked up the telephone. But there was no answer at Desmond's end. He, too, must be out. When she emerged into the hall again she noticed what, in her hurry, she had previously overlooked, the two letters Emily had left on the hall-table. She tore hers open. You could hardly say Emily had been confiding.

MY DEAR DOSSIE (she had written),

I am going away for a little holiday. I am sure you will keep things going very nicely in my absence. I enclose a cheque for Doris' wages and any outstanding expenses there may be. Please don't hesitate to help yourself from the store cupboard. My letters can wait till my return. Will you give Desmond his letter when he comes this afternoon.

EMILY WATSON.

That was all. No explanation, no hint of how long she intended to remain away. Not long, reflected Dossie, grimly, if the size of the cheque was anything to go by. She tried the telephone again with the same result. After a third effort she tore open Desmond's letter. Perhaps she had been more detailed writing to him. But his was even briefer than her own.

MY DEAR DESMOND,

I am afraid I cannot stay to see you this afternoon. I am going for a short holiday. No letters are being forwarded.

PENNY.

"Desmond was right, she's completely dotty," said Miss Brett viciously. "I thought she was being very peculiar lately. All that dashing up to London, pretending she was going to her dentist."

She was in a fever of impatience, perpetually dialling Desmond's number and getting no reply. Perhaps he's gone off somewhere, too, she thought. Or is he celebrating in advance the fortune he isn't going to handle?

It was almost four o'clock when Desmond turned up, carrying a small bunch of flowers. As soon as Dossie opened the door he said, " When Penny decides to get a new companion you'll be able to get a job as a human barometer. Outlook stormy ? " He grinned.

" That's right," Dossie advised him. " Laugh. Make the most of it. You won't laugh so heartily when you know."

He threw the flowers on the table. " Know what ? "

" She's gone. Don't ask me where. Eloped, perhaps." She had spoken savagely, but at the sound of her own words her face changed. " I wonder if she has."

" Eloped ? Be your age, Charm Girl. What need would she have to elope ? She'd be married in purple feathers with " The Voice that Breathed," sung over her. Look here, what are we talking about ? "

Dossie told him.

" I must say you've got a nerve opening my letter," he exclaimed.

" I couldn't get you on the telephone. I tried about twenty times. And there might have been some hint in her letter. . . ."

" Pygmalion to you. Whatever Penny has done she's made sure we shan't know. Look here, you must have been pretty dumb these last weeks. A woman can't walk out of a house without any preparation and you living under the same roof noticed nothing."

" I noticed she was a bit peculiar," Dossie defended herself warmly. " But, then, she so often is. How could I imagine . . . ? I wonder if she ever did go near her dentist."

" Is that what she said she was doing ? "

" Yes. Though now I come to think of it she was very careful I should never pick her up there."

" It'll be easy enough to find out if she ever went." Desmond picked up the telephone, flipped over the pages of the little blue book in which Emily carefully noted her special numbers and dialled Mayfair exchange.

" Mrs. Watson ? " said the dentist's secretary. " No,

she's not been in to-day. No, she's not expected. As a matter of fact, she hasn't been to see us for some time."

" Pulling my leg," said Desmond at his most charming, and hung up the receiver. " And yours, Charm Girl," he said.

" She must have been meeting someone in town," hazarded Dossie hazily, and Desmond replied in a nasty sort of voice, " You're so bright, darling."

" Perhaps," suggested Dossie, paying him back in his own coin, " she realises you're likely to ask her for more money next week."

They bickered for a few minutes and then MacKinnon arrived. He cheered them up by refusing to be downcast by the news.

" It'll all help," he told them. " Normal women don't creep out of their homes without a word. Unless, of course, she really has eloped, in which case her husband will doubtless see to it that nobody else touches a bean."

" If she's mentally deficient can she get married, legally ? " inquired Dossie in hopeful tones.

" She's never been certified."

" Only a mentally deficient person would want to marry again at Emily's age. It isn't as though she needed a home."

" Perhaps he does," said MacKinnon cynically. " Any notion who it could be ? "

" She hasn't got married," said Dossie suddenly. " She'd never have left her mink coat. And that's in her wardrobe."

Then she remembered the diamonds. " And I don't know whether she's taken them or not, because she always keeps them locked up, and the desk is still locked. Still, if she's only gone away to escape from us, she'd hardly take her jewel-case."

" She'd be even less likely to leave it here," objected MacKinnon.

" The obvious thing would be to send them to the Bank. When did you last see them, Dossie ? "

" As a matter of fact, she was looking at them only yesterday. You know what she's like, always pinning on something sparkling, like a human magpie. I used to tell her she was crazy to keep them in the house, but she said she had no next generation to think of, and why shouldn't she enjoy them in her own way ? One of these days you'll be found dead in your bed, I told her, and she said that was probably true of most people, whether they had diamonds or not."

" She must have had a busy morning if she packed her belongings, parked her diamonds and got away by lunch-time. Confound it, Dossie, you might have watched her letters better."

" It's just occurred to me," said Dossie," that if she was having letters they weren't coming to this address. That might explain all her visits to town about which she was so secretive. If she really has eloped . . ."

" If she really has," interrupted MacKinnon, " she'll probably end in a nameless grave in a wood, like most Bluebeard victims."

" She's as mad as a hatter, this proves it." Dossie was like Don Quixote in that she charged windmills with complete recklessness. " If we don't find her and stop her, she may do something irretrievable."

" Like changing her will ? " That was MacKinnon again, calm and derisive. He was Desmond's generation with as few scruples and more finesse.

" She might think it romantic. She's just the age. And whatever dear Albert was it wasn't romantic."

They considered all the other possibilities, like loss of memory, but ruled that out because whatever Emily had lost—her wits, for instance—it wasn't her memory. She remembered who she was and who they were and that Desmond was coming to tea and presently, when Desmond calmly picked the lock of the desk with an expertness that argued some experience, they knew she hadn't forgotten about the diamonds either.

" I believe I have it," said Dossie as the three sat round the tea-table. " She thinks if she goes away long enough without letting any one know where she is, I shall disappear and Desmond will get a job. Then and only then she'll think it's safe to come back."

"In that case, she's certainly *non compos mentis,*" contributed Desmond.

MacKinnon wanted to know if she usually kept a hoard of spare cash in the house, and Dossie said No. Albert had told her only fools did that. The result was that it always 'got about' and you were either burgled by a gang or (more politely) by your own circle of friends and relations. People borrowed money and conveniently forgot to repay. Or they told a hard luck story and women were fools anyhow where money was concerned, unless they had to earn it first. And even if none of these factors operated, every man knew that money burns a hole in a woman's pocket and, being creatures of infinite leisure, they were always poking their noses against shop windows and buying things, out of sheer ennui.

"Then she must have gone to the Bank sometime this week. She can't have disappeared for an indefinite period with a couple of half-crowns in her pocket."

"She wouldn't need cash if she had the sparklers," said MacKinnon.

"Perhaps Desmond, who's so clever at picking locks, can find out about her bank account," suggested Dossie, nastily.

There may be honour among thieves, but there is seldom much liking.

Desmond, however, was going through the pigeon-holes of the desk and now he looked up to say, "Here's a rum go. She hasn't taken her cheque-book."

He held it out and Dossie snatched it away from him. "Oh, she's mad all right. She can't get on without this. She pays for everything by cheque."

"Well, wherever she's gone it's where she doesn't need cheques," was Desmond's grim comment. And MacKinnon added, "Perhaps she's counting on some-one else paying for her now."

Dossie said, looking meaningly at Desmond, "Once

bitten, twice shy," but Desmond, flipping through the counterfoils, could afford to disregard that.

" She's not counting on that whatever she's counting on," he announced. " She drew two hundred pounds in cash this morning."

MacKinnon said thoughtfully, " Hush money ? "

But Desmond laughed the idea to scorn. " Not Penny. She wouldn't know how to get into a mess. All the same, there's some method behind her madness. If she's taken two hundred quid she's not just gone for the week-end. I'd be inclined to agree with Dossie that there's a husband, if only in the sight of God, in the case if it weren't for the mink coat. Even Penny wouldn't be mad enough to leave that for someone else to enjoy."

" Could she be going abroad ? " hazarded Dossie, but MacKinnon said she wouldn't get much farther than His Majesty's jail if she tried to sneak two hundred pounds out of the country.

And, anyhow, further search of the desk revealed an out-of-date passport. It was Desmond who said gloomily, " Bet you anything you like she's told old Matthews where she's gone and told him not to pass her address on to us." And MacKinnon said that seemed to show a degree of sanity, anyway.

" Who's going to pay the rent when it falls due ? " Dossie continued. " That cheque she left isn't going far."

MacKinnon said the rent wasn't due for a couple of months anyhow, and as for gas and electricity, she'd probably left things in her lawyer's hands. Then he suggested that he might be shown the two letters, but had to agree they were singularly uninformative. Dossie, indeed, was shaken by such a paroxysm of rage when she re-read hers that she tore it up and threw it in the fire.

" That was a silly thing to do," said MacKinnon. " Suppose later on someone suggests she's been murdered you've no proof she left a letter at all."

Dossie said sulkily he was talking nonsense, and, anyway, Desmond had his letter.

They went on talking round and round about Emily's

extraordinary behaviour without getting a step further. Both men seemed, quite unjustly, to think it was Dossie's fault, but Dossie snapped that she wasn't hired as a watch-dog, she was a paying guest. She was furious with the way things had turned out, just when she and Desmond had been getting so friendly. She had no more illusions about him than Emily had, but he represented a side of life she had never known. She had quarrelled with him furiously when Emily was there and bit his head off when Emily wasn't, but she measured her life by the days he called or rang up or wrote. She couldn't endure the thought of existence without him now. It wasn't love as novelists understand the word, but that wretched, deluded creature, Mrs. Courtenay, of whom at that time none of them had heard, would have understood. A psychologist might look wise and call it infatuation, but the net result was the same. Dossie wouldn't have plunged a knife into Emily's breast or put arsenic into Emily's tea, but short of that she would do anything to strengthen the link between her and this charming, unscrupulous, utterly unreliable, not-so-young young man. Ten years earlier she would have despised him ; ten years later she would probably be indifferent ; now she stood at the parting of the ways and he represented the only touch of romance and youth that had ever come her way.

It was when Dossie broke the news to Doris that she began to realise how very awkward the situation might become. Doris simply stared.

" Gone ? " she repeated. " Bit sudden, wasn't it ? I mean, she never said a word to me."

" Why should she ? " snapped Dossie.

" She's the one that pays my wages," retorted Doris, who saw no reason to kow-tow, as she put it, to someone whom she regarded as a poor relation, and not even a relation at that, simply a sponge. Worse than Desmond really. " All the same, it's funny she's gone off and left her mink coat in the wardrobe. Didn't you know that ? I was just Flit-ting it this morning in case of moth, and I saw it there."

She was never one to boast that she kept herself to herself and pretty soon all Southwood, that is all the members who knew Emily, and it is a compact suburb where news circulates rapidly, agreed with Doris. It was very peculiar indeed. Dear Emily had never said a word—and if you could believe Dossie, it came as just as much of a shock to her.

" What about her letters ? " they inquired eagerly, and Doris said, Well, there they were piling up, and some of them were bills, and Mrs. Watson had always been ever so careful about paying things the minute they became due. And the milk not cancelled, and if you asked her (and at the moment she was receiving more attention than she had ever done in her life) it was ever so queer. And she added that she wasn't going to take orders from that Miss Brett.

Inevitably as the days passed and Emily's silence remained unbroken, the talk increased. Now Emily had been gone a fortnight, and there were bridge dates she surely wouldn't have broken without a word of apology. Some people perhaps, but not kind, scrupulous Emily. Maisie Easingwold remembered how worried she had been about that nephew of hers. A bad hat, Maisie was convinced, and it wasn't natural for a man to be so charming, not if he was honest. Of course, Emily had never actually *said* anything, but the ferocity with which she had always defended him showed you how ill-at-ease she really was.

Then, too, contributed Mrs. Durrant, it seemed rather *odd* that Dossie should know nothing. She didn't mean to suggest that Dossie was untruthful, but surely if the pair had been *on good terms* Emily would naturally have confided in her. So gradually the idea got about that Emily's disappearance was in some mysterious way linked up with Dossie. During that first fortnight no one, except perhaps Doris and then only to her boy-friend who served behind a grocery counter but liked to be known as Sherlock Holmes Taylor, had suggested anything sinister about Emily's silence. They implied that it was owing to bad behaviour on someone's part—Dossie ? Desmond ? —they remained charmingly vague on that question— but presently something else happened that turned their thoughts in a darker direction. One morning the postman knocked twice and handed in a long registered envelope addressed in a flowing old-fashioned hand. Doris, who thought it was up to her to keep her finger on the pulse of any establishment where she obliged, recognised it immediately. Messrs. Matthews and Tring always addressed their envelopes in handwriting, though the letters inside were typewritten correctly enough.

" Fishy," observed Doris to Dossie, putting the envelope on the table. " Looks as though Mr. Matthews doesn't know Mrs. Watson is away either."

Dossie seized on this letter as an excuse to get Desmond round. Desmond said, " Long envelope, eh ? What do you make of that ? "

" I suppose it's some dividend or something she has to sign." Dossie was vague.

" The old girl's always very close about what she's got," remarked Desmond a little unfairly ; " though we know dear Albert must have left her rolling. Pity it's sealed."

" I shouldn't have thought it was too much for you to break a seal and replace it," observed Dossie, sarcastically. When she was alone she would wonder why she was such a fool as to say the very things most likely to antagonise him, but she was so terrified of betraying her burning interest in him that she put up a smoke-screen of active dislike in the belief that everybody would be deceived by it. Desmond, of course, wasn't deceived in the least. " Dossie'll do anything I say," he told MacKinnon in careless tones. " Chaps tell you to leave women out of your affairs but personally I've always found it paid."

Dossie hadn't, as a matter of fact, expected Desmond to take her suggestion seriously, and she drew a sharp breath when he replied, " It's your idea, remember," and calmly broke the seal.

" Emily will be furious," Dossie exclaimed, but Desmond only said, " Emily won't know. How many people notice the particular design of the stamp that's been used? And there's nothing special about this one."

He drew out a long folded paper. Then he whistled softly, and though his voice was as cool as ever his face deepened into an angry red.

"So Mac was right. She was thinking about her will." He looked through the paper. "All for her one living relative. Now—why does she want to change it?"

"Because she'd rather leave it—her money, I mean—to someone else," suggested Dossie, dryly.

"You have a positive gift for the obvious, my sweet," said Desmond smoothly. "But does it imply a secret lover?"

"Or just prove she's not so infatuated as you supposed?"

Desmond finished reading the will, glanced at Mr. Matthews' letter which told him nothing he didn't know already, glanced up at Dossie with his charming smile, and said, "Darling, do you have to lay all your cards on the table? And you in the Binding-on-the-Marsh Bridge Four!"

Doris was no fool. She had noticed the arrival of the letter, and when, two or three days later, she went to lay the morning offering with all the others, she saw that the envelope had disappeared. She spoke to Dossie about it at once. Dossie said, "I locked it up in Mrs. Watson's desk. Registered letters are important."

"Well," said Doris in dissatisfied tones, "if you're sure it's all right—only I don't want to get into trouble."

"Do you have to?" asked Dossie, and Doris turned rather red and immediately repeated the conversation to her boy-friend.

"And if that old maid thinks she's throwing dust in my eyes she's got me taped wrong," she remarked darkly. "I know there's something fishy. And how could she lock the letter up when Mrs. Watson left the desk locked and took the key with her?"

"You don't want to get mixed up in any funny business," her companion urged. "Say what you like,

Doris, you won't get a better job. She's not like some that are always picking on you."

"Shouldn't stay if she did," said democratic Doris. "It's a free country, isn't it?" Lots of people would have said No, but it was free enough for Doris. "All the same, poor Mrs. Watson was being bled white by that Desmond, that I do know, and as for Miss Mighty Brett, I wouldn't trust her as far as I could throw her. No, say what you like, Fred, there's something wrong. That mink coat." She brooded.

"You seem to have got the mink coat on the brain," said Fred. "Why, she might have been going somewhere where mink wouldn't look right."

But Doris told him scornfully mink would look right in the courts of Heaven.

"Maybe," said Fred, "she wasn't going to Heaven. Anyhow," he added quickly, seeing Doris beginning to smoulder, "if you really think there's been foul play you ought to stay on and keep an eye on those two. Don't let 'em see what you're after, but just notice. It's the little things that give chaps away." He spoke knowingly, as one of those amateur sleuths who, remaining in the background, nevertheless outwits the pros.

"I never said anything about foul play," objected Doris. But now that Fred had planted the idea in her mind she couldn't think of anything else. Because suddenly that seemed the obvious solution. She kept going over and over the events of the past two weeks or so in her own mind. It was queer, wasn't it, that Mrs. Watson, a considerate employer if a bit of a fusser, should never have dropped a hint about going away? Never have left a line as to her plans. Of course Dossie said there had been a letter, but when Doris practically asked to see it, saying perhaps there was some reference to herself, in a postscript, say, that Dossie in her haste had overlooked, Dossie had snapped that of course she hadn't overlooked anything, that it was deplorable how nosy some people were, but that she'd show Doris the letter and welcome, if she hadn't thought it so unimportant that she'd destroyed it. Doris went on with her own line of thought. Funny that Dossie, who was so self-centred as a rule, had been positively sympathetic about Doris going to her mother and staying as long as she was needed. Funny, too, that it was the very afternoon that Desmond was coming to tea that Mrs. Watson vanished. And since then no letter, no telegram, nothing at all. And the post pouring in and the telephone ringing, and people getting more and more curious. And, as always, Doris came back to the inexplicable presence of the mink coat hanging in the vanished woman's wardrobe.

It was Mr. Matthews who gave her the final push that drove her into action. Mr. Matthews telephoned anxiously a few days after the arrival of the registered letter to know if it had arrived and if Mrs. Watson was all right. Doris said, " Mrs. Watson's away. She's been away for nearly three weeks."

" Could you give me her address ? " asked Mr. Matthews and Doris thrilled by this conversation, said, No, she hadn't left one.

" What is happening to her correspondence ? "

" It's waiting for her return. Miss Brett says she's locked up your letter, seeing it was registered."

" Does Miss Brett not know where Mrs. Watson is ? "

" Nobody knows. As a matter of fact, Miss Brett said probably Mrs. Watson had written to you. I mean to say, there's the gas bill in and some of the tradesmen's accounts, and I did hear Miss Brett say she wasn't going to pay them."

Mr. Matthews sounded troubled. He asked if Emily had been ill, and Doris said, Oh no, but she'd left a note for Miss Brett saying she was going for a little holiday, and that was all anybody could tell him. She would have been happy to prolong the conversation, but the lawyer rang off abruptly. He rang up again the next day, when Dossie answered the telephone but her story was substantially the same as Doris', except that she said she had thought Emily's manner distinctly queer for some time, and mentioned the mysterious visits to town.

When the conversation ended Dossie got in touch with Desmond, who said, " Interfering old fool! Y'know, Doss, you may be right, after all. Suppose she has gone off with some seducer? " And Dossie would have agreed with him but (like Doris) she couldn't get over Emily's omission to wear the mink coat. Desmond laughed at her but she refused to be shaken. Any woman, she said, would agree with her.

Later, a lot of women did.

There was no doubt about it that Dossie had put herself lamentably in the wrong when she destroyed Emily's note. But that was nothing compared with her folly a week later when she deliberately put a noose round her own neck.

## 2

By the end of the third week Emily's silence was beginning, in his own phraseology, to get Desmond down. The fact was, as Dossie had surmised, he was in an even worse jam than usual. In a sense you might say it was his aunt's fault. She had been too soft with him, with the result that he had got it into his careless head that he could always count on her, quick or dead. Quick, she would help him. Dead, he would be able to help himself. But now she was, as it were, in some No Man's Land between the two. He couldn't make a touch because he didn't know how to get at her, and he couldn't raise a further loan on the strength of having money coming to him when the lawyers had done their stuff, because, so far as he knew, she wasn't dead.

He found himself forced to confess his predicament to Dossie.

" A jam? " repeated Dossie. " You're never in anything else."

" That's right," agreed Desmond sourly. " Rub it in. If Penny were here, she'd be the first to help me."

" And the last. If you were looking to me for a little

assistance, I must tell you frankly that I recently heard from my so-called man of affairs that he's taking all my money out of six per cent industrials and putting them into three-and-a-halfs. When I wanted to know why he said he had inside information. Silly old sausage!"

"Shows how much he trusts the Government," commented Desmond.

"So, in the circumstances, it was a bit of left-handed luck that my landlord did dispossess me, if that's the right word. I certainly couldn't have gone on paying the rent."

"So I'm not the only one to profit from Penny's benevolent tendencies. And you can't even claim that your mother was Penny's sister."

"Safe!" observed Dossie, following up her own line of thought. "That's what he called them. Safe to fall, if you ask me."

"I shall tell this chap I've heard from my aunt and she'll be back by the end of the month. That ought to keep him quiet."

"What's the odds you'll find him standing on your doorstep like Love Locked Out?" gibed Dossie. She couldn't have explained why she always went out of her way to torment Desmond, but he, with a far wider knowledge of life and women than would ever be hers, understood it all perfectly well. If he had been less certain of her he would probably never have made his next suggestion. As it was, it came to her as a considerable shock.

It was two or three days later that he remarked casually, "While the cat's away . . . How about a week-end at the sea just by way of a break?"

At first Dossie thought he was joking. "Lovely," she said. "Tell the chauffeur to bring round the car."

Desmond sighed. "Can't you ever be serious? Well, my dear girl, you're not likely to have much fun when Penny does come back. Surely you've a mind above Bridge Fours and Lectures on the Palestine Problem?"

"But—where do you mean we could go?" Dossie was nervous, uneasy.

"Oh, plenty of places. If you don't like Brighton there's Maidenhead, or there are more select spots along the river that must be looking rather nice just now. Don't you ever let your back hair down, Dossie?"

Dossie was in a state of complete confusion. In Desmond's circle people presumably thought nothing of weekends. It was a tough world and you took any fun that came your way. She wasn't deceived into thinking that Desmond was in love with her or anything absurd like that. He was being friendly, true, but then he'd be friendly with a black mamba if it suited his book. She did wonder what he expected to get out of it and decided cynically that if she did go away with him he would have something to hold over her head in emergencies. She didn't know the nature of the latest jam, but it was quite likely to be something dishonourable and it would be worth his while having a friend at court. It was not this argument, however, which made her agree to his proposal. She didn't want to particularly, she was frightened of all it might involve, but she was still more frightened of his appreciating her attitude, and worst of all, of losing him out of her life. He knew, quite as well as though she had explained it to him, that she had been reared to the knowledge that she wasn't attractive to men, that no one had ever expected her to marry and that she had not the smallest notion how to attract or hold a husband. She'd never been kissed, never even been dated. This was a wry sort of romance to be tossed her way, but it was the only kind she was ever likely to know, and desperately, shutting her eyes to all possible consequences, she said in as cool a tone as she could contrive, "Well, why not? A breath of country air would be quite a treat."

"What a hypocrite you are, Dossie!" remarked Desmond, but he said it quite nicely. He had not been at all sure of his success here and everything in the immediate future depended on his winning her assent to his proposal.

Twenty-four hours later he told her he'd been through to Rennies, a well-known road-house at King's Ditton, a bit more select than Maidenhead or Bray, he told her, and he would pick her up on Saturday morning.

Dossie told Doris that she would be staying with a friend for a day or two, but would be back to lunch on Monday, and Doris said in her impudent way, " Well, don't you go getting lost, too. One in a house is enough."

" If I were married I wouldn't have a girl like that about the house," Dossie told herself, and abandoned herself to a day-dream in which Desmond made even more improbable proposals than the last. " Women of my age are always getting married," she told her reflection defensively. " And I know I have a great capacity for feeling, only so far no one has aroused it."

All the same, she was full of nervousness as Saturday morning drew near. Doris didn't come on Saturdays, on the ground that she wanted the afternoon to go to the pictures, which involved queueing all the morning, and though Dossie had often thought how selfish a girl she was, on this particular Saturday she was relieved to know her departure would be unobserved. When she was ready she looked at herself in the glass. She had fallen some way from grace in accepting Desmond's outrageous proposal, but she was still too honest to pretend that she looked like the sort of partner any one as personable as Desmond would choose for a week-end on the river. " Except," she thought, cynically, " he might feel he would have to settle the bill if it were any one else, whereas he wouldn't have the smallest scruple about asking me to lend him money."

She wondered feverishly if she had got enough. It would be appalling if between them they couldn't pay the account, and there was a row and it got into the papers. She wished passionately she had never involved herself to this extent. Still, it was too late now. She belted her sensible spring-weight coat round her narrow waist. Her figure was her one good point. Lots of girls of five and twenty might have envied it. Still, nothing took away from the fact that most people seeing the pair of them would imagine that Desmond was being kind to his aunty —a comparatively young aunty, certainly, but an aunty for all that. Probably most of Desmond's week-end companions wore nylons and fur coats—and it was then that she remembered Emily's mink.

From the moment she let herself lift it from the wardrobe and slip it on, she was lost. It was long on Emily, but on her it hung perfectly. It was, perhaps, a little loose, but then you didn't button a fur coat like this. The little motoring hat she had bought the day before looked twice as good allied to the mink coat, and even her serviceable tweed suit took on a sort of allure seen through the film of shining silky fur. And what harm was there? Emily wasn't using it. The house would be empty for the week-end, since Doris said she wasn't going to sleep there by herself. Sometimes to oblige Emily she had done this, but she certainly wasn't going to put herself out to oblige Miss Brett. And Emily was really quite generous. If you asked her to lend her coat for a great emergency. . . . But here Dossie's conscience pricked her heavily. In no conceivable circumstances would Emily lend her best fur coat to a member of her Bridge Four planning to spend an illicit week-end with her (Emily's) nephew. Dossie pushed her uncomfortable conscience into a corner. Stay there till Monday, she told it savagely, twisting and pirouetting to get the full effect of the enchanted coat. She was hardly ready when Desmond drove up and sounded his horn. When he saw her come hurrying down the steps, a neat little case in her hand, he got quite a pleasant shock. She looked younger, more prosperous—well, not younger, perhaps, but more trim, more elegant.

"Broken the bank?" he inquired, leaning over to open the door of the car. "Or merely broken into it." Then he recognised the coat. "Penny's? Well, why not? In fact"—he began to laugh—"I call it a darn good idea. I wish I'd thought of it myself."

It was a glorious morning and Desmond was a skilled and enterprising driver. It occurred to Dossie that no one had ever thought of asking him how he came by his little car and why, if he was so hard up, he didn't sell it. You didn't ask people like Desmond that sort of question.

They knew all the answers. He'd only say, " To take you week-ending, of course," or something equally fatuous. She had expected to be tongue-tied, but on the contrary, conversation was easy and friendly. They stopped half-way for a drink, and it was only after they had returned to the car that Desmond announced casually that he had booked the room at Rennies in the name of Mrs. Watson.

Dossie stared at him. " Are you crazy ? What are you calling yourself ? "

" Oh, I'm sticking to my own name," he said. " They know me at the Blue Boar, so it would be no soap me calling myself Smith, but——"

" The Blue Boar ? "

" The local pub. I'm putting up there. Why, Dossie, you didn't really suppose I'd risk your spotless reputation by staying at the same hotel ? Still, I'm not far off, and——"

" But what was the idea of asking me to pass as Mrs. Watson ? " Dossie refused to be side-tracked.

" Well, you're wearing her coat, aren't you ? " Desmond tried to sound light-hearted. This was the trickiest turn of all ; if he didn't negotiate this corner he was lost.

" That's got nothing to do with it. Why am I supposed to be Emily ? Because that's what it amounts to."

Desmond took his fence at a gallop. " Because Penny's expecting an important registered letter on Monday morning, and she must be on the spot to sign for it."

" A registered letter ? " Dossie's voice was stupid with dismay. " But who from ? "

" The Bank."

" And what's in the letter ? "

" What's usually in a registered letter from a bank ? Oh, not my bank, I admit. They don't bother to register it when they write to tell me I'm overdrawn, but I'm sure Penny's never been overdrawn in her life."

" You mean, it's money."

" Fancy your thinking of that," marvelled Desmond. " Now, Dossie, don't make difficulties. Things are quite hard enough as it is."

" You mean, you've asked the Bank . . . ? But they won't . . . I see." She gasped, as the truth struck her. " You mean, you've forged her signature. Desmond, are you quite insane ? You could get about five years for that."

" Seeing I shall probably get about five years anyhow, I may as well take a sporting chance."

" But why involve me ? " She was sick with humiliation, springing from self-deception. She might have known Desmond was playing a double game. But she wouldn't go through with it. She'd make him put her down at the next town they came to, and she'd take a train back.

Desmond was answering her question. " Do you suppose any hotel clerk would mistake me for Mrs. Watson ? Or that the Bank would send the money to any one else ? "

" Suppose the letter doesn't come ? They may query the signature."

" They won't," said Desmond, simply. " Haven't you noticed what an easy signature Penny has ? "

" No doubt to one of your experience. I notice you didn't tell me any of this before we started. You knew I wouldn't come."

" I did have that idea," Desmond admitted.

" And I shan't go on with it now."

" But that's absurd. If you go back to town everyone will know you meant to go away and something went wrong—why, they'd laugh at you for ever. And it wouldn't help Penny. In fact, if she could join in the conversation, she'd probably urge you to do it. She won't be in the least pleased to come back and find me in quod. And not much more pleased to see you wearing her coat, though it'll help to create the illusion that she's a rich woman."

" How much have you asked for ? "

" Another two hundred." He grinned. " Goodness only knows what the bank wallahs will be thinking. Penny going gay in her old age. Well, that's when it generally happens. You watch your step twenty years hence, Dossie, my girl."

" But when she finds out—as she's bound to ? What then ? "

" She'll pay up," said Desmond in the same untroubled tone.

" You can't go on like this for ever."

" Don't intend to. I'm pulling out. That's why I need the cash."

" You mean, leaving the country ? " Her heart suddenly plunged through her body, leaving her dizzy and sick.

" A democracy doesn't offer anything to an enterprising chap who doesn't want to join a Trade Union."

Dossie quivered with indignant misery. " You mean, you're going to get out, and leave me to bear the brunt. How typical ! "

" There won't be any brunt. She won't know you had anything to do with it."

" As you've just reminded me, no hotel is going to hand over a letter addressed to Mrs. Watson to you. She'll know you had some accomplice."

" But she won't think it's you. Why, we've gone out of our way to give her the impression that we can't stand the sight of each other. So, take that scowl off your face. No woman over thirty can afford to scowl. Now, we may as well amuse ourselves for the rest of the week-end."

" When do you expect the money ? " persisted Dossie.

" Should be here Monday—at Rennies, I mean."

" Won't the Bank think it odd that Mrs. Watson's letter should have a London postmark ? "

" Even if you think a man's a fool, Dossie, you shouldn't tell him so quite so plainly. The letter has the King's Ditton postmark. I sent it off when I came down to see about rooms."

Dossie persisted, intrigued, " Didn't they think it odd you engaging a room for Mrs. Watson ? "

" I said my sister. And if you think they're going to recognise either of us once we've left the place you're wrong. They have several thousand people a week coming in and out, and you and I have no special distinguishing marks, like three legs or hooks instead of hands. Now, for Heaven's sake, ease up. This is a holiday."

" You haven't even asked me if I'll co-operate. Women don't like being taken for granted." (Dossie's mother had told her that men don't value women who make themselves cheap.)

" Now, have a heart. Would you like to think of me doing two years hard ? "

It's bad for women to be neglected till they're nearly forty ; it gives the first man who pays them any attention, even when it's only for his own ends and they know it, such an unfair advantage. Dossie could feel her heart thumping as she met Desmond's sidelong glance. She wasn't illusioned any more ; she knew he was simply making use of her, but she *was* like the unfortunate Mrs. Courtenay or any other deluded woman. She couldn't be rational where her feelings were concerned, and she told herself recklessly she might as well get anything that was going out of this shabby little interlude. Besides, the bank might refuse to send the money, or the world might end before Monday—anything might happen. The only thing that was improbable was that she would ever find herself alone with Desmond again in such circumstances.

When they reached Rennies she was glad she was wearing the mink coat. It was a big hotel, mostly catering for week-end traffic. Desmond was right, a stray visitor calling herself Mrs. Watson would never be remembered here. Desmond put up the car and took Dossie to have a drink, and then she went up and looked at her room, and afterwards had lunch with Desmond, who took a lot of trouble making himself agreeable. He had had so much experience of this sort of thing that he did it excellently. All the afternoon and evening he was very attentive, and they dined together and even danced, though after a short time Desmond said they might cut in at bridge. They played together and won heavily, and Desmond said with any luck they'd make their expenses at the table, and then he said, Good night, and asked her what time she generally got up on a Sunday, and went off to the Blue Boar happy in his conviction that he'd won her over. Dossie spent a lot of time brushing her hair and thinking, and smoking cigarettes before she put out her light. The hotel seemed full of couples. It was normal enough to be alone at Southwood, but here she felt cut off. Fun to be really Mrs. Someone-or-Other. Then she shook herself and remembered that it couldn't have been much fun being Mrs. Albert Watson, except for the diamonds, of course, and the mink coat. She had much more feeling for such accretions than Emily.

Sunday was another brilliant day and she waited about in the lounge until Desmond turned up, and they had lunch at Princes Ditton, and had a pleasant afternoon on the river, and played bridge again that evening, and again were successful. The first rift came on Monday morning when the post arrived, and there was nothing for Mrs. Watson.

" Are you sure ? " demanded Desmond incredulously. " Did you ask at the desk ? "

" No. But surely——"

" You'd better."

But the clerk told her there was nothing. Dossie was immediately distraught.

" I told you it was mad to try it. The Bank must be suspicious——"

" If they were, there'd have been a letter asking for a duplicate signature. No, it's just that the posts are a bit uncertain these days——"

" They'll think I can't pay my bill," exclaimed Dossie in anguished tones.

" Not so long as you've got that coat. It's worth a year of week-ends. Ah, well, may come on the next post."

The letter, however, did not arrive until Tuesday. The Bank, apparently, made no difficulty about cashing the cheque, and the money was sent in a variety of bank and treasury notes.

" I told you it would be all right," said Desmond, putting out his hand for the envelope.

She handed it over with a queer feeling. " There's a

receipt to be signed for the Bank. I signed one at the desk," she said.

"I'll attend to this one."

"It had better have the local postmark, hadn't it?"

"One would almost think you make a habit of this sort of thing." Desmond peeled off some notes and held them out to her. "Your cut," he said.

"Oh, no." She shrank away. "I—I don't want anything."

"I take it back. You don't make a habit of it. Well." He smiled at her. "Nothing else to wait for. Packed yet?"

"It won't take me long."

"I'll bring the car round. I left it in the Blue Boar garage. Wasn't sure if we'd want it this morning. And many thanks for your kind co-operation." His smile broadened into a grin. "Might do it again some time, perhaps."

"I thought you were going abroad."

"I'm not quite sure about it. Anyway, I shouldn't be going next week."

He went out whistling and Dossie went up to her room. "Never again," she vowed angrily, staring at herself in the mirror. "I was a fool to get involved this time. If it weren't Desmond, Emily would prosecute. As it is, I don't know what I shall do if it ever comes out."

Now that the adventure was practically at an end she was left with a curiously flat feeling, though what other consequence she had anticipated from it she could not have said. After all, even if people did think it queer her disappearing for a week-end, she was her own mistress, wasn't she? It had been no part of her plan to become Desmond's, nor, she had to admit, had he considered that possibility either. But she supposed she had anticipated some deepening of their relationship, some mental intimacy, the sense of a shared experience. All she felt was that she had dropped to his level, a woman who stole out to a notorious roadhouse, wearing someone else's valuable fur coat. She wished she could leave it behind, never see Desmond again, return to Southwood under her own steam and her own colours.

" I've finished with him," she promised herself.

But she was reckoning without Doris.

## 3

When Doris reached Kozicot on Tuesday morning and found no trace of Dossie and no message from her (since Dossie could not risk those inquisitive eyes discovering her neighbourhood), she knew a tremor of not altogether pleasurable alarm. There had been enough mystery about this house to be getting on with, in Doris's opinion. " If they're all going to start disappearing, it's time I got out," she told herself. " I don't want to be the third."

She waited till twelve o'clock, but there was no sign of Dossie. It was the girl's habit, when Emily was away, to have an early lunch and go off till evening. In Emily's presence, she had said she wasn't going to put herself out for that Miss Brett, and she had warned Dossie that she didn't intend to cook dinner while Emily was away. Dossie had been furious, but since she did not pay Doris's wages there was nothing she could do, except leave all the washing up until morning. On this particular Tuesday she was grateful that Doris wouldn't be coming back. She had no wish to be questioned or (as she put it) spied on. But as it happened her run of luck ceased at midday. Doris, who was curiosity personified, went to Dossie's room to see what she had taken, justifying her inquisitiveness by saying that you never knew, and it was very fishy, anyway. When she opened the wardrobe she was surprised to find Dossie's well-worn topcoat still on its severely masculine wooden hanger.

" She can't be such a fool as to go without that, not seeing the sort of climate we have," she reflected. " Unless she's developed a boy-friend who's bought her a mink."

The thought not only made her laugh, but reminded her of the existence of Mrs. Watson's fur coat. When she looked in Emily's wardrobe, she saw that the coat was missing. She never had any doubt as to where it was. Dossie had taken it. She looked hurriedly through the rest of Emily's possessions, but could discover nothing else missing. She must be coming back, she argued, otherwise she wouldn't have left so many things here. But on the other hand, she (she in this instance was Dossie, of course) wouldn't have taken the coat if she thought there was the smallest chance of Emily coming back during the week-end and finding it had gone. She shivered more with excitement than with apprehension. Her brain, like a little lively insect, went running through the thicket of facts and conjectures at her disposal. If Dossie knew Emily wasn't coming back that week-end, then she knew where Emily was. Or, if she didn't know that, at least she knew she was in some place where she could not return to Southwood. In her ardent, ungrammatical yet oddly logical way, Doris began to fit the pieces of the puzzle together. To-night she would lay them all before Fred, and get his advice. In the meantime, she would remain on the premises in case Dossie returned or there was a telegram.

Dossie came back in a taxi soon after lunch, congratulating herself that Acacia Avenue was empty of sightseers and idlers. Everyone locally knew Emily's fur coat, which was, indeed, the envy of all her friends. The sooner it was off Dossie's back and on its scented padded hanger in Emily's wardrobe, the more freely would Dossie be able to breathe. She paid off the taxi, seized her week-end case and leaped out. But as she hesitated on the step, fumbling for her latch-key, the front door flashed open and there was Doris in her ridiculous kewpie cap edged with fur, her short fur jacket, her dark-red slacks, nodding and smiling in a knowing manner and completely blocking the hall.

"Well, you did give me a shock," said Doris coolly. "I thought we must have had burglars."

"What's missing?" flashed Dossie.

"The coat. My word, when I saw that had gone——"

Dossie made a lightning recovery. " How did you *happen* to see ? Mrs. Watson's wardrobe was shut when I left the house."

" You can't have noticed," returned Doris shamelessly. " It was standing ajar and that made me think, so I took a look and I tell you, my heart nearly stopped beating."

" I suppose nothing ever makes your tongue stop wagging ? " suggested Dossie, without counting the possible effect of her words.

" Here," said Doris sharply, " what are you getting at ? I've got nothing to hide, have I ? "

" I'm sure I don't know," said Dossie. " Do you mind moving aside and letting me get through ? "

" If I've told Mrs. Watson once that that coat's too long for her I've told her a dozen times. It's just right for you. 'It's not smart that length, Mrs. Watson,' I've said, but it's funny how some people don't know anything about style. Silly, really, her having so much money. Now, if I 'ad a coat like that——"

She moved forward as though to handle the shining fur, and Dossie retreated sharply.

" Has any one telephoned ? "

Doris drew a paper packet of cigarettes out of the pocket of her jacket, lighted one, and then shook her head. " Not while I was here. Anything from Mrs. Watson yet ? "

" I haven't seen any letters that may have come over the week-end."

" Nothing for you," said Doris. " I looked. I thought perhaps you'd heard."

" Why should I ? "

" Seeing you've got her coat. Nice of her to lend it, I must say."

Dossie pushed resolutely past. " You needn't stay for me," she said briefly. " I'm going out."

Just then the telephone rang, and Dossie dropped her case and ran to answer it. She thought it might be Desmond, but it wasn't. It was Mr. Matthews. He asked if there were any news of Emily, and then for Desmond's address. He said he was anxious about his client, and was wondering if she could conceivably be suffering from loss of memory. Dossie assured him quite passionately that she wasn't, but Mr. Matthews did not seem convinced.

Dossie tried to get Desmond but Mr. Mathews got there first so Dossie went upstairs to unpack.

Meanwhile Desmond was having a very uncomfortable three minutes.

He was taken completely aback when Matthews asked him point-blank if he had any idea where his aunt might be.

" No. Why on earth should you suppose I—— ? "

" You are her sole remaining relative."

" I can only assure you she hasn't confided in me. Y'know, there may have been some trouble locally, perhaps she thought she'd like a break."

" What sort of trouble ? " inquired Matthews.

" Oh, how on earth should I know ? " inquired Desmond irritably. " But you know what women are. Anyhow, she's a free agent."

" That's precisely what I wish to be assured of. May I ask, Mr. Raikes, how long you propose to wait before you institute inquiries ? "

" She's only been gone three weeks. Aunt Emily won't spend two hundred pounds in that time." He laughed shortly. " Not unless she's gone to Monte Carlo, that is."

" Two hundred pounds ? Is that the sum of money she took with her ? "

Desmond cursed his folly. " She drew it out of the bank on the morning she went away."

" Then you saw her that day ? "

" No, no. But she left a letter with Miss Brett."

" For you ? "

" Yes."

" Saying she'd taken two hundred pounds ? "

" Yes. I took it that she wished us to understand that she would not be back at once."

" Surely that is a very large sum for her to take in cash ? "

"That's what made us wonder—Miss Brett and myself——" He paused.

"Well? Go on, man. What are you driving at?"

"Whether she'd gone alone. Well, she was easy to deceive."

"I am sure you know," said Matthews suavely. "Are you suggesting that your aunt went off with some gentleman?"

"I don't say so. I don't know. How should I? But you said yourself two hundred pounds is a lot of money, and if she didn't want to hide something, why hasn't any one heard?"

"Quite. No doubt, Mr. Raikes, you have the letter."

"Damn," thought Desmond viciously. "Now I can't produce it." Aloud he said, "As a matter of fact, it was only two or three lines, I didn't think of keeping it. I didn't think it was important. Miss Brett had one, too. I dare say it was on much the same lines. Naturally, we thought she would have written to you."

"It would have been the obvious thing to do," agreed Matthews dryly.

"As a matter of fact, she had been behaving very oddly—I dare say Miss Brett told you—inventing appointments in London and having letters sent to accommodation addresses."

With some difficulty he got rid of the old bore. He'd given him something to think about, anyway. And now, before the matter slipped his mind, it would be as well to destroy Emily's note. When he had done that, he sat down to consider how the forged cheque could be fitted into the plan. Really, it was quite clever of Dossie to wear the mink coat. If Matthews started making inquiries that would be remembered, though nobody would have noticed the wearer. That would establish Emily's whereabouts. He thought he'd better telephone Dossie and tell her the exact position. Then you could be fairly certain that, if questions were asked, they'd both be telling the same truth.

Dossie was anything but happy. She saw Doris as a

potential enemy; there had never been any love lost between them, and now Doris had a hold over her, though there was nothing actually criminal about borrowing someone else's fur coat. There was no question of stealing it. Even the malicious Doris couldn't pretend that.

"He rang me, too," she told Desmond, "and asked for your address. I did try and get through, but you were engaged."

Desmond told her about the two hundred pounds. Dossie couldn't believe him.

"You mean you told Matthews you knew for a certainty she'd taken it?"

"I had to stop the old fool snooping somehow."

"You'd better do something about the cheque-book, then. If he finds she left that at home——"

"That's a nuisance. As a matter of fact, it was probably quite a good stroke my drawing that second cheque. Put 'em off the scent."

"More likely to put them right on it. If Matthews starts asking questions at Rennies—well, I may not look like the run of your chorus-girl friends, but neither do I look like Emily."

"They won't remember you, only the coat."

"And Doris will remember I went away for the week-end, wearing it."

"Damn it, you didn't give it away to her."

"She was waiting in the hall when I arrived. She saw it. I couldn't help that."

"I wonder what she suspects. Still, cheer up. It's not criminal to borrow a coat, and we didn't see any one we knew at Rennies. We're all right. Emily'll turn up when she's ready. I only hope she doesn't turn up with Albert the Second."

It had not occurred to either of them that Doris might be listening on the extension. When she replaced the receiver she could not leave the house soon enough. She had intended to go when the telephone rang, but curiosity triumphed and after she had listened in to Mr. Matthews, she waited and heard the familiar tinkle of the bell as Dossie tried to get Desmond. She slipped into the little spare room when Dossie came upstairs, and when Desmond's telephone call came through a little later she was in the dining-room, where the main telephone was installed, and she listened shamelessly to every word. Then she let herself out of the back door and went to take counsel with Fred.

" I guess it's time for me to do something," she said importantly.

Fred looked a bit dubious. " Police, d'you mean ? You don't want to be rash, Do. A lot of people are going to ask what affair it is of yours if Mrs. Watson goes off in a hurry ? "

" So long as she went of her own free will. But did she ? And how about that other cheque. That's fishy, if you like. Anyhow, who said anything about the police ? No, my idea is to go and see that Matthews. He's the one who's asking questions. There's that registered letter, too. Miss Brett said she'd put it in the desk, but that desk was always kept locked, so how could she, unless she'd broken in ? I don't like it, Fred. If anything funny has happened people might wonder why I hadn't said anything. Besides, I don't like that Dossie Brett wearing Mrs. Watson's coat. It's all right, I'll be careful. I'm just going to tell Mr. Matthews what I heard, and then it's his affair. After all, she may be a fussy old thing, but she always treated me right, and I don't like that Dossie or that Desmond, either, come to that."

The next morning Doris didn't turn up at Kozicot. Instead, wearing a suit in place of her perpetual slacks, her hair neatly combed and tied in a Jacqmar scarf, she went by tube to Mr. Matthews' office in Bishopsgate. An elderly gentleman, looking as though he had stepped out of Dickens, asked her severely if she had an appointment.

" I've got something better than appointment," said Doris, confidently. " I've got some information he's been looking for."

" If you have information you should write for an

appointment," said the old clerk, who didn't believe a word she said.

"Now, look here, I've given up a day's work to come here." Doris sounded truculent. "If you tell Mr. Matthews I came and you wouldn't let me in, there's going to be trouble. Specially if it does turn out to be a case for the police."

"The police?" The old clerk looked up sharply. He didn't like the sound of that. His firm didn't care for police business; respectable solicitors seldom do.

"What is it you've come about?" he demanded sharply.

"I'd rather tell that to Mr. Matthews. Just you let him know a lady's here with information about Mrs. Emily Watson. That'll fetch him. He's been telephoning her house quite a bit lately."

The old clerk looked at her with loathing, but he went through an inner door with the message, and about five minutes later Doris was ushered into Mr. Matthews' room. Matthews had none of those tricks by which small men seek to impress. As soon as he realised that Doris had something of importance to give him, he treated her precisely as he would have treated his most influential client. Doris was subdued, in spite of herself. She told the story well, and he had the good sense not to try to cut her short. Like Arthur Crook, whom he resembled in no other way, he recognised the importance of letting witnesses take their own road. "It's not what they think they're telling you, but what they actually do that matters," both men would have said.

"So, you see," Doris wound up, "I did feel I ought to do something. If Miss Brett's been pretending to be Mrs. Watson and staying at a hotel wearing the mink coat—well, makes you think, don't it?"

"You did quite right to come to me, though you will understand I can go no further than prosecute inquiries at the moment. The authorities can take no steps until we can offer them proof——"

"Here," said Doris, looking angry; "d'you think I'm

making all this up? I'd have gone to the police right away, but I didn't want to make trouble for *her*."

"You did quite right. I've already told you that. But naturally we shall have to get the necessary support for your statement. You may be asked to sign an affidavit."

"You mean, Miss Brett will say she never wore the coat? But the hotel will remember."

"That was what I meant when I said we must get substantiation. Now, have I your address, Miss Stokes? Ah, yes. Now, thank you very much for your assistance."

"Well, our mother brought us up to follow our consciences," said Doris airily, a remark that would have given Emily the staggers.

"I don't like the sound of it at all," said Matthews bluntly to his partner, Anthony Tring. "Mrs. Watson had just written to me, clearly in a state of agitation, to say she was considering changing her will and asking for the document. Now, under that will, everything went to the nephew, Raikes, and I don't doubt he knew it. I've met the fellow once or twice and I've made a few inquiries about him, and I'd say his affection for his aunt is about as stable as the Stock Exchange barometer. If Mrs. Watson meant to change her will, that involved cutting him out to a greater or less degree——"

"Unless there's anything in the suggestion that she was considering remarriage. After all, a rich widow——"

"Albert Watson had thought of that, and if she remarries she retains an income of a hundred pounds a year. That's all. And she can't touch the capital. The rest goes to some charity Watson names. And she knew of that provision."

"It 'ud still give Raikes a motive," speculated Anthony Tring. "So long as she remains a widow and he stays in her good books, he's in the straight for the rest of his days. And if she dies—he inherits. But if she either changes her will, as she's a perfect right to do, or remarries, which again she has a perfect right to do, he's down and out, I fancy more literally than most expectant legatees."

" If she'd been going to remarry she'd have let me know."

" Would she ? The others didn't—the victims of George Joseph Smith and all the rest of the Bluebeards."

" But they didn't write to the family solicitor and ask for the present will to be returned, promising to leave the drafting of the new one in his hands. They sneaked off to some obscure attorney in a provincial city. Besides, if she was considering remarriage the matter of a new will wouldn't arise."

" Then perhaps she was considering marriage in the sight of God only. Watson seems to have overlooked that contingency."

" And you seem to have forgotten what our client is like."

" At that age," said Tring firmly, " you can't put anything past them. What do you propose to do now ? I quite agree we must do something."

" I don't like the story of this Brett woman going off for a week-end in Mrs. Watson's fur coat. And that little bit we had in this afternoon certainly knew her onions, as she would unquestionably put it, when she says that a woman going to meet a lover doesn't leave her mink coat hanging in the wardrobe. I fancy our first step is to make a few inquiries. Pritchard's our man, excellent and discreet."

" He'll need to be. Which was the hotel ? "

" There's only one Rennies."

" You needn't look for much help there. Whoever is behind this, our friend Raikes knows his way about. They make a point of not noticing people at Rennies, don't want to find their staff giving evidence in the Divorce Court, and so long as you pay your bill and don't break up the furniture or assault the servants, they don't care who or what you are."

" There's no getting past the registered letter, provided that girl's got her facts right, and though she's hardly a type I admire, I'm inclined to think she knows what she's talking about. Then, too, there's an ugly suggestion of forgery. I was a bit dubious about Mrs. Watson telling her nephew she was taking two hundred pounds with her, it didn't seem in character, but, of course, if he's got hold of her cheque-book he could find that out for himself. And Miss Brett registers as Mrs. Watson, wears Mrs. Watson's fur coat, takes in a letter containing notes addressed to Mrs. Watson—I'm afraid every step we take brings us nearer to the Police Courts."

" Might even be the Central Criminal Court," agreed Tring grimly. " Funny—you never thought of a quiet little thing like Mrs. Watson getting involved in melodrama."

" It can't happen here," quoted Matthews. " The odd thing is how often it does. There's quite a lot for Pritchard to work on, though. This woman must have signed the hotel register and of course the hotel would demand a receipt for the envelope. Raikes may be an accomplished forger, but I doubt if Miss Brett is in his class, even if she thought of trying to copy Mrs. Watson's writing. Being an amateur, the odds are she didn't, but Pritchard will soon let us know."

As Matthews had anticipated, Pritchard came back with some very useful information. In the first place he asked to see the signature of the psuedo-Mrs. Watson, and after uttering a warning or two as to the results of non-co-operation, he was shown the register. He also saw a similar signature in the hotel book, where a lady calling herself Mrs. Watson had signed " E. Watson " in return for a registered packet, and, comparing these signatures with an authentic one, there could be no conceivable doubt that two people were involved. Of course, signing a hotel register in an assumed name is not a criminal offence, but the registered letter episode was in a very different category. Armed with this information, Matthews made a formal approach to the Bank. He had reason to believe, he said, that someone was forging his client's signature and had recently caused a considerable sum in notes to be sent to Rennies' Hotel at King's Ditton. He added that inquiries as to Mrs. Watson's whereabouts had revealed the fact that the lady calling herself by that name was unquestionably an imposter—for, though Rennie's wouldn't commit themselves to a description, the faked signatures spoke for themselves. No information as to the real Mrs. Watson's present address was forthcoming, and he would be glad to see the letter in which she asked for the two hundred pounds to be sent to Rennies. The manager, appreciating that this was probably going to develop into a police case, and knowing Matthews by correspondence over a number of years, gave all the assistance in his power. Inquiries revealed the fact that Emily had called in person for two hundred pounds on the 25th April, taking it all in single notes. So large a sum would not have been paid to any one else without a written authority from Emily and none had been received. Besides, she had been recognised by one of the cashiers on the day in question. The letter asking for a further two hundred pounds was then produced, and Matthews had to admit that the writing was good enough to deceive any man not looking for blemishes. The letter had been written on a piece of headed notepaper, taken from Kozicot, with the address crossed out and that of Rennies substituted.

"The odd thing is that a cheque drawn to the order of Miss D. Brett on the same day, that is, on the 25th April, for I'm back at the first presumably authentic cheque," continued the manager, "was a subject of some inquiry, as the signature seemed to us a little erratic, but since Miss Brett is known to be a friend of Mrs. Watson and at the moment to be staying at her house, the cheque was duly honoured."

In view of this information and the fact that Dossie had been seen wearing the mink coat—and had unquestionably been away during the operative week-end, and, on top of that, had been recognised by a neighbour driving off with "that fascinating nephew of dear Emily's" Matthews thought himself justified in laying the entire matter before the police.

## 4

When a gloating Doris told Dossie that a policeman had called and was asking for her, she knew it was all up. They had found out about the cheque, and she was, if not the actual criminal, at least an accessory after the crime. She was quite convinced that the fact of her knowing nothing of Desmond's plot until they had accomplished two-thirds of the journey to King's Ditton would make no difference at all. She had supposed that a man in policeman's uniform would interview her, but Inspector Strange wore an ordinary dark suit and might have come about domestic insurance for all the neighbours knew, though Dossie had no hope of concealing the fact of his visit. He did not assail her with the ferocity for which she was prepared, and indeed her automatically defensive manner proved, at first at all events, unnecessary. He said that inquiries were being made about Mrs. Watson's whereabouts, and he asked for her co-operation. Dossie said it would be a relief to her if Emily's present address could be established, it certainly wasn't her (Dossie's) fault that she had vanished like a thief in the night. . . .

" One moment, Miss Brett. I understood that Mrs. Watson left the house in daylight."

" Of course." Dossie sounded impatient. " That was just a *façon de parler*. . . . I doubt whether I can help you very much, but you're welcome to everything I know." Which was, as Strange realised from the start, an exaggeration. Dossie, however, proved very fluent about Emily's peculiar behaviour, her visits to town, the letters she had had sent to accommodation addresses. . . . Once again the Inspector interrupted her.

" Which letters were these, Miss Brett ? "

" Why, the letters she received from whoever it is she's staying with at this moment."

"I thought you didn't know where she was."

"I don't. But it's common sense that she must be somewhere, and she couldn't have gone to any one we know without it having leaked out, so obviously . . ." She looked at him as much as to say that even the police must see that. It appeared, however, that the police were not interested in common sense. All they wanted, like Mr. Gradgrind, was facts, nothing but facts, and presently in his cool unhurried way the inspector demanded them. He was like a drill, thought Dossie, a dentist's drill, going resolutely on and on in some tiny cavity long after you were sure it must be completely hollowed out. Presently he asked Dossie if she remembered the arrival of a registered letter and at once Dossie began to get flustered. Yes, she admitted, Doris had spoken of one coming. No, she couldn't say just where it was now. Yes, of course, she had seen it, though she didn't know who it came from. Yes, she probably had told Doris it was in Mrs. Watson's writing-desk. The writing-desk *was* usually kept locked, but Mrs. Watson must have forgotten. No, the letter wasn't there now, and she didn't know where it was. No, she couldn't explain. No, she didn't think so. No. No. No. (A positive crescendo of Noes.) No, she couldn't remember if she had spoken of it to Mr. Raikes. Yes, she might have done. And, yes, he might have been left alone in this room. Yes, she might have said it was in the writing-desk. Yes, she might have shown it to him. Ye-es. Oh, ye-es. Yes, it was possible. (A positive crescendo of Yeses.) No, she didn't remember. No, of course he wouldn't have it. Well, she wasn't answerable for what Mr. Raikes did. . . . No, of course she couldn't *swear* he hadn't. Why not ask him ? Yes, she had been away at the week-end. No, she couldn't agree it was any one else's affair. No, she had not gone to stay with Mrs. Watson, she had no idea where Mrs. Watson was. She had not set eyes on her since the morning of the 25th. Yes, it was true she had borrowed the fur coat, but there was nothing criminal in that. She hadn't stolen it, she had brought it back unharmed, it had been a cold day for driving.

Driving ? Well, yes, she had gone by car. No, she couldn't agree that it was any affair of the inspector's where she had been. Any one would think she was a criminal. Before answering any more questions she would like to consult her lawyer. NO, she had broken NO laws, but she did not choose to have private affairs bruited abroad. Surely the inspector knew how people in Southwood gossiped. Oh, dear, were they back at Mrs. Watson again ? Well, then, she had assumed that Mr. Matthews had her address. No, she had not rung him up or written to him. If Mrs. Watson chose to go off without a word she, Dossie, wasn't going to worry. Oh, the letter ? Which letter ? The registered letter. Hadn't they done with *that* ? It appeared they had not. Yes, she had already admitted she knew of its existence. No, she hadn't realised it came from Matthews and Tring. Doris had recognised the handwriting ? Doris was too curious by half. No, she didn't say she didn't recognise it. Yes, she supposed if she'd stopped to think she would have known it came from Mr. Matthews. No, she wouldn't have thought it odd even if she had. Mrs. Watson often heard from her lawyer. She had already *said* she would have recognised the handwriting if she'd thought about it. She just hadn't thought. Even if she had recognised it she wouldn't have started thinking things. Mrs. Watson had securities or papers to sign or dividends or something, she couldn't say anything definite. No, she didn't remember if they came at stated intervals. Probably Mrs. Watson had gone off in such a hurry she hadn't given a thought to her business affairs. No, she hadn't wondered what would happen if Emily wasn't at hand to sign whatever it was. Emily's concerns were not hers. She was not Emily's guardian. Neither was she Emily's companion. She was a paying guest at Kozicot until she could find suitable alternative accommodation. No. Mr. Raikes was not a particular friend of hers, as Mrs. Watson's nephew, of course, she had seen a certain amount of him. No, she could say nothing of his affairs. No (very indignantly) certainly he and she had not been staying at the same hotel for the week-end. Well, suppose someone had seen them driving off together, he had just given her a lift. No, she did not consider the police had any right to inquire where she had been or with whom. No, she had not thought of hiring a car. Hired cars were expensive, and if she had a friend—people did sometimes have friends who owned cars. No, she didn't mean to imply that Mr. Raikes was a particular friend, but if he offered her a lift. . . . No, she couldn't say where he had gone for the week-end. No, she could answer no more questions without legal advice. . . .

When at last the inspector went, she flew to the telephone to get in touch with Desmond. A strange voice answered her. Mr. Raikes was engaged for the moment. Could she leave a message ? Dossie hesitated and then gave her telephone number ; she said it was urgent private business. Then she set herself to wait. The telephone rang twice, but it wasn't Desmond either time. At the end of two hours, with her nerves in shreds, she was preparing to go out, convinced that Desmond didn't intend to make contact, when the telephone rang for the third time and at last it was Desmond.

" Are you out of your mind ? " he demanded before she could speak.

" It's no thanks to you if I'm not," stormed Dossie. " Why couldn't you ring before ? I left a message."

" Trust you to make a mess of things. Do you know who took your confiding message ? "

Suddenly she did know. Of course, she ought to have thought of it for herself. It wasn't likely the inspector would give her an opportunity to warn her accomplice (because it was obvious along what road his suspicions ran like a marathon competitor) of what was in the wind. While Strange was interviewing Dossie another police official had Desmond on the rack.

"What did you tell him? I wanted to let you know——"

" Nothing," said Desmond in the same savage voice. " How about you ? "

" Nothing. But I don't think he believed me. Desmond, what did you do with the will ? "

" It's safe enough. You don't suppose I'm going to destroy that. So long as Penny doesn't or can't make another, it's worth a fortune to me."

" You had no right to take it."

" You mean leave it with you, for that so-and-so Doris to get hold of ? "

" You made it very difficult for me."

" Why ? You only had to say you didn't know where it was. Just as I did. Let them think Doris took it."

" It wouldn't be worth anything to her. What about the cheque ? Did they ask—— ? "

" I told them I'd never set eyes on her cheque-book, and if they didn't believe me they could examine the flat."

" They didn't, of course—examine the flat, I mean."

" You need a search warrant. All the same, I wouldn't be surprised if that's their next move. Still, they won't find the cheque-book. I can promise you that. And even if they know about the second cheque, they can't prove I drew it."

" They can prove I collected the money at Rennies."

" Only if you tell them so. They can prove that some lady calling herself Mrs. Watson called for it, that's all."

" Perhaps they'll think it's me. I never thought of that."

" Since you didn't draw it, they can't prove it. Keep your head, Dossie, for Heaven's sake."

" I keep thinking—we can't prove a word we say. If one of us had kept Emily's letter——"

" They might suggest they were forgeries, too."

" Or if I hadn't taken the coat ! "

" Well, for crying out loud. Do you suppose that was the only mink coat in Rennies that week-end ? Why, I counted a dozen myself. . . . And even if they could prove it, they can't have you up on a murder charge for taking a coat."

" Murder ! " Dossie's voice came in a shrill scream.

" Don't yell like that. They'll hear you in Piccadilly

Circus. Why, yes, that's what they're working up to. Doesn't it seem that way to you ? "

" But, Desmond, what can we DO ? "

" Nothing. That's not our job. If the police believe a murder's been committed let them produce the body. They can't move a step without a corpse."

She uttered another little cry. " Desmond, I've just thought. Suppose someone's listening in on the line ? "

" I'd thought of that one. I'm in a call-box. All the same, don't go ringing me up at home. We're in quite enough trouble as it is."

He rang off. Dossie laid down the receiver and sat shivering with terror. For the first time she began to wonder what had really happened to Emily.

Because she couldn't endure the empty house and because the telephone had become a thing of horror, with people ringing up all the time—the story had got round Southwood like a fire before a fanning breeze—she jammed on her hat and went out. She got a tube and went up west and bought herself a seat for a French film. The story dealt with the murder of an old woman by a youthful blackguard, and by the time it was over Dossie was shivering worse than ever. It was now almost seven o'clock and she looked round for some place to have a drink. People at Southwood regarded her with awe because she didn't mind going into a public house alone. She said these fancy drinking places gave you more water to your drink and charged you a higher price than any place outside of hell. The bar was fairly full, and she went to sit at a little round table with a bright-yellow china ash-tray on it, advertising somebody's whisky. Sitting at the next table was a stout, common-looking man with a brown bowler pushed to the back of his head, wearing a brown suit as loud as John Peel's View Hulloah ! drinking beer and reading a newspaper. Dossie bought herself a dry martini and looked surreptitiously at her neighbour's paper. There was a photograph of a woman on the extreme right hand of the front page, and there was something faintly familiar about her. Dossie slewed her eyes a little further round and saw the heading:

RICH WOMAN MYSTERY.

Her heart began to pound; the hand in which she lifted her glass trembled. She must drain it quickly, go out and buy herself a paper. But at this hour the papers would all be sold. She looked round desperately, hoping someone would have left one. But if any one had, it had been collected by the barman before this. She made a casual movement which edged her a couple of inches nearer the next table.

The man in the brown suit suddenly folded the paper in half and handed it to her.

"Take it, sugar. That's a woman all over. Buys herself a fancy drink at three times what it's worth and economises on an evening paper. Still"—his smile was intended to be gracious—"you're welcome. There's nothing in it for me—at present."

Dossie was in such a state of perturbation by this time that she paid no attention to the stranger's peculiar manner and address. She was reading the last column which said:

> Police are inquiring into the whereabouts of Mrs. Emily Watson of Kozicot, Acacia Avenue, Southwood, who left her home secretly on Friday, the 25th April.

And there was a picture of Emily which you would have recognised, even without her name underneath.

"Friend of yours?" asked a cheerful voice in her ear, and she looked up, startled, to see the man in brown watching her acutely.

"I—yes, I know her. I should think it was a case of loss of memory."

"Friends gettin' anxious? Funny, you know, how a poor relation can go on disappearin' for months and no one seems to notice they ain't there, but let a well-lined lady vanish and the Home Office is on the path in no time. And if she has lost her memory," he went on chattily, " I dare say she had a good reason. They mostly have."

" If she's alive she ought to come into the open," said Dossie in choked tones. " It's not fair to other people."

" It could be she don't want to be discovered. Still, if there's no response to that "—he nodded towards the article—" you can bet your Sunday pants there's been foul play."

" I don't see why you should be so sure," objected Dossie. " She might not want people to know——"

" Unless she's turned into a troglodyte and is living underground she won't be able to keep it a secret. You'd be surprised at the number of people who're anxious to help the police in a case like this, though if a bobby was to take their number because their car was causin' an obstruction, there wouldn't be anything hard enough to say about him."

" Why shouldn't she be allowed to go away incognito if she wants to ? " demanded Dossie angrily.

" Unsocial. You ask the town and country planners. They don't want these rebels against the planned age. There's your hole and you ruddy well stay in it. If you want to come out, get a permit. If you don't get a permit, you're up to no good. Can't go against the current, not when it's got a big Parliamentary majority. Even if your name's Arthur Crook, you've got your work cut out."

Dossie stared. " Are you Arthur Crook ? "

" That's what my mother always told me."

" But—I've heard of you."

Crook shoved his bowler hat an inch farther back by way of acknowledgment.

" Gratified, I'm sure. And you don't have to tell me who you are, because I know."

Dossie turned a greenish colour. " What do you mean —you know ? "

Crook gently took the paper out of her hands, turned it over and showed her two smaller pictures on page four.

They were caricatures of herself and Desmond—at least, hers was a caricature.

"Oh!" gasped Dossie. "I didn't know—I hadn't seen——"

"You know," said Crook frankly, "you must be fond of sweets to get yourself into a jam like this."

Dossie looked indignant. "I've done nothing. I couldn't help it if Emily was a bit peculiar. She was, you know."

Crook sighed. "The police are so unreasonable," he suggested.

"They tried to trap me into admitting I knew something. I said I wouldn't answer any more questions till I'd seen a lawyer."

"What did he tell you? Not to fall foul of the police, if he knew his onions."

"I haven't got a lawyer," confessed Dossie. "Poor people don't, as a rule. They don't need them." (She didn't count the silly old sausage who administered her affairs.)

"Maybe if they did have them, they wouldn't stay poor," Crook suggested.

"Lawyers aren't interested in people without money," insisted Dossie. But Crook refused to be insulted.

"If you kept a grocer's shop you wouldn't take much stock of customers who couldn't pay for their goods. It's the same thing with lawyers. We all know they're a race of yellow dogs, but even yellow dogs have to live."

Dossie didn't seem to take much notice of what he was saying. "Mr. Crook," she said, "you've had a lot of experience. How does one prove one hasn't committed a crime?"

"Any one accused you yet? No? Then you don't have to worry. It's up to them to prove you did. What's biting you, sugar?" he added, persuasively.

Dossie hesitated no longer. The words came out with a rush. "I know the police think Emily's dead—you said yourself it was very likely foul play—and that we —that I—between us we know something about her.

But it's ridiculous. What do I stand to gain from her death ? "

" You tell me," invited Crook.

" Nothing. Absolutely nothing. And I should lose the best bridge partner I ever had. It's perfectly absurd to suggest I gain anything. I'm not even mentioned in the will."

" Sure of that ? "

" Yes, of course. I——" She stopped.

" So you did see it ? All right, sugar, it don't matter what you tell me, but think twice before you talk back to the police."

Dossie said simply, " I'm afraid of the police. When they make up their minds about a thing you can't change them. They think Emily's dead." She began to shiver. " And they think I'm involved."

" They need a corpse before they can bring a charge," Crook consoled her.

She turned to him passionately. " That's just it. Suppose—suppose something has happened to Emily ? It seems queer to me she didn't write to any one. It isn't like her. And then—her diamonds."

" What about them ? "

" They disappeared when she did. At least, the Bank may have them——"

" I doubt it. We'd have heard. So she took 'em with her, hey ? "

" That's what makes me wonder if she's gone off with someone. The diamonds and two hundred pounds. Only there's the mink coat she left in her wardrobe. It doesn't make sense. The only way to satisfy the police is to find Emily."

" You think that'll do the trick ? "

" If she's alive. . . . Oh, I see what you mean."

" If she's alive—she can read, I take it ? "

" Of course."

" Not that it would matter, because someone else would tell her she was wanted. But unless she's loco—is that likely, by the way ? "

" Out of her mind ? We did wonder——"
" Lady herself get any idea what you were thinking ? "
" I—no, I don't suppose so. I mean, people who're peculiar never do. But, if she was peculiar, wouldn't that account for her not coming forward now ? "
" Wouldn't account for any chaps who know where she is—and someone must in these days of ration books and identity cards and Form This and Regulation That—wouldn't account for them not coming forward ? Mind you, Scotland Yard will be swamped for the next week by people with extra special information. Chance for all the no-goods, see, the overlooked, the under ten. But it'll all boil down to nothing. There's only three possibilities I can suggest. She's bein' held to ransom. She's payin' someone something pretty handsome not to squeal. Or she's where she can't talk. You pays your money and you takes your choice." He looked at her, whistling dubiously. " What do you think yourself ? "
" I don't know. That is—I begin to be afraid of the last. You see, all we have to go on are those letters in the hall. And—if Desmond was so clever at forging the cheque, how can I be sure he didn't forge them too ? "
" You may have something there. Where did you find 'em ? "
" On the table in the hall. About five minutes after I got back."
" And Desmond wasn't there ? "
" He didn't come for the best part of an hour. But he wasn't at his flat, because I rang him repeatedly. Suppose —Mr. Crook, suppose he had come earlier, when the house was empty of everyone but Emily, and he wanted money and there was a scene and he lost his temper—oh, I don't suggest it was premeditated—and if she told him about the will—he'd know the house was empty because I'd told him about Doris being away——"
Crook laid a big pudgy hand on her arm. " You remember what I told you just now. Talk your heart out to your Uncle Arthur, but keep your mouth shut when it comes to the police. You haven't a grain of proof that any

of this happened, have you ? And you wouldn't like the inspector to suggest that perhaps *you* knew a bit more than you wanted him to guess, and saw a nice chance of passing the buck to Desmond."

"It never occurred to me till now," said Dossie, honestly. "Only—it does seem to fit. The diamonds, too. I can't believe Emily would take those. And, naturally, being a man, he wouldn't think of the fur coat. Emily never wore it in Southwood unless there was something very special on, and if she'd been out that morning—well, we know she had because she went to the Bank—she'd wear one of the others, the beaver or the musquash. And if she was going away, why didn't she hire a car from the garage as she always did ? But she didn't, or Parks would have come forward."

"There's other garages," Crook reminded her.

"But garages always take your name if you order a car, and when it's known that she's disappeared, the proprietor would come forward."

"So he might," agreed Crook. "Give him a chance. Look here. Wait forty-eight hours and if nothing's happened, if she hasn't turned up, dead or alive, and you want me to take a hand—well, I'm your man." He didn't point out there was nothing in this for him, because he knew Dossie couldn't keep him in cigars for a week, especially now the enterprising Chancellor of the Exchequer had whacked up the import duty, but he was one of those fortunate mortals who can afford to indulge their fancies now and again, and for some reason the case attracted him. Of course, if the police found a corpse he'd hold his hand till they made an arrest and then see if there was anything he could do. But if they didn't he'd come in and play 'em at their own game. He always enjoyed that better than the police did.

Dossie, however, was appalled at his suggestion. "Forty-eight hours ? But—anything could happen."

He patted her arm reassuringly. "Now, sugar, be your age. If your Mrs. Watson is O.K. now she'll be O.K. then. No one will dare plant her with the police of the whole country on the looksee, to say nothing of all the nosey amateurs who fancy themselves as Sherlock Holmes, 1947 model. And if she ain't—well, a coupla days won't make any difference. See ? "

And with this for the moment the unfortunate Dossie had to be content.

## 5

There was, as it happened, one witness who could have thrown some very useful light on the affair, and that was a taxi driver called Frank Hardy who had picked up a fare at Southwood and driven her to King's Cross on the afternoon of Friday, the 25th April. But unfortunately he had been involved in a fatal road accident on the very day that Doris paid her visit to Mr. Matthews' office, and shortly afterwards was conveyed, via the mortuary, to the cemetery. So the police were handicapped in their search at the outset.

Within the forty-eight hours for which Crook had stipulated something happened that Dossie, at least, had never anticipated. The authorities arrived at Kozicot with a search warrant.

At first she was inclined to be impatient. " Do you suppose we haven't turned the place upside down looking for clues ? " she demanded. " Do you imagine you will find something we've overlooked ? "

The police, unlike the inspector, were inclined to be curt. They indicated that it wasn't so much the clues as what you made of them that mattered.

" There's nothing to find," insisted Dossie. But the police did not seem to agree with her. It wasn't for some time that she realised they were actually looking for traces of Emily. They were very thorough and Doris at least approved of their activities. She said she was only too anxious to help them if she could, and made no secret of her belief that Emily hadn't left the house of her own free will. Still, whatever they anticipated, the police found nothing.

By the time Crook arrived at the end of the forty-eight hours Dossie was half-crazy with worry.

" They think we've murdered her, I know they do," she told him.

" As I said before, till they find the corpse they can't do a thing. And it could be we shall have found Mrs. Watson before then. Now, let's start going places, the same places as she went."

" But we don't know——"

" What do you think I'm here for ? " demanded Crook indignantly. " All we have to do is find out where she went. No, don't tell me any of her usual places, because if she was at any of those we should have heard by now. No sensible person takes chances with the police, not if there's any question of murder."

" She might be staying somewhere incog," suggested Dossie, when she could get a word in edgeways.

" Sure you're not keeping anythin' up your sleeve ? " asked Crook, keenly. " I don't say open your grief to the police, but don't try keepin' me in the dark. Y'see, if Mrs. Watson suddenly made up her mind to change her will, it does look as if she'd just found out something about her nephew that didn't please her. And that does give said nephew a motive for wanting her out of the way. No, don't tell me again she might have got hitched up, because if so the police would know about it. You have to register a weddin' and though the police and me don't always see eye to eye, you have to hand it to them, they do go round like ferrets when a thing like this breaks. And since you say she wouldn't plump for marriage-without-the-ring it looks as though she don't appear because she can't. Y'see, this picture of her has been sent to every police station in the kingdom and appeared in the press everywhere and though they say we're an illiterate lot, even chaps that can't understand their Income Tax demands can read the news. You go trying to ground and see how long you can keep it up. No, if

Emily Watson could tell us where she was, she'd have done it by this time. And I doubt if it is loss of memory, seein' she must have taken her ration book with her, which would remind her. Unless she's living down a rabbit-hole, sooner or later someone must spot her. And though we haven't any evidence that she ever left the house in the sense that no one actually saw her go, no one who's prepared to testify, anyhow, still, we do know she ain't in it now."

"But where on earth could she go?" asked the distracted Dossie.

"Where would you go if you wanted to get away from everyone?"

Dossie considered. "There are advertisements——"

"Right first time. What paper did she take in?"

"The *Record*."

"So she might start lookin' through that. When did all this start?"

"I suppose, when Dr. MacKinnon came to tea."

"He's a new one. What did he come for?"

There was no help for it. Dossie had to confess to the existence of a plot, though she clung to her statement that Emily really had been very peculiar.

Crook looked at her with less enthusiasm than he usually manifested for his clients.

"You wouldn't like the papers to get hold of this, would you? After all, if you really thought she was loco, why didn't you call in her own doctor instead of this Mac-Whatisname? It begins to look, too, as though dear Emily had rumbled her nephew. When did this doctor come to tea?"

Dossie looked in her diary, and said, "Thursday the 10th April."

"No talk of Emily going away at that time?"

"There was never any talk——"

"No mysterious visits to London?"

"The first was the following Tuesday?"

Crook sighed. "Adds up, don't it? Here we have aunty as happy as a cricket on the tenth and startin' a course of deception on the fifteenth. What happened after that ? "

" She went to London again on the Friday and the following Tuesday, and on the Friday after that she—disappeared. Oh, don't you see, she must have been making plans. Of course, she's all right. This mad suggestion that I—or Desmond—or both of us know anything, plotted anything, is absurd. She knows she's wanted, and she's staying hidden to—to pay us out. Of course she's all right. If only we could find out where she is." And in her agitation Dossie almost wrung her hands in despair.

" Went to London Tuesday," said Crook, quite unmoved by this exhibition of feeling. " Wonder if there was anything in Monday's paper. Where does your girl keep them ? "

" In a paper-rack in the hall, and she uses them for the kitchen table when she wants them. She won't light coal fires now Emily isn't here, says she hasn't any right to use Emily's coal, though, of course, it's sheer laziness and insolence. . . . Suppose there is an advertisement, how will you know that Emily answered it ? "

" I'm like the chap in the hymn," said Crook equably. " One step enough for me. What's the odds that Monday's paper's missing ? "

They were still going through the case like terriers after elusive rats when a latch-key clicked and Doris marched in. She was back in slacks and short checked coat of a pattern almost as bright as Mr. Crook's, and the same Christmas card hood was tied under her chin. When she saw Crook she stopped dead and stared.

" Are you the police ? " she demanded.

" What do you think ? " asked Crook.

" They think up some very fancy uniforms these days," riposted Doris.

" As a matter of fact, Mr. Crook is a lawyer, and he is going to help us to find Mrs. Watson," said Dossie loftily.

Crook looked at her in honest admiration. Help was

rich, he thought. Why, it was obvious he was going to do all the work.

"When the police force of the country are baffled?" Doris had read that in her *Morning Sun*. "You do hate yourself, don't you?"

Crook sat back on his heels. "Ah, but the police are so hampered," he explained. "I mean, they have to respect law and order, all that kind of thing. Red tape. You know. Sign on the dotted line. They're in it for fame and glory, while chaps like me are out for what it'll fetch. Now, angel, this is where you can help."

"What do you think I'm going to do?"

To Dossie's obvious disapproval, he proceeded to explain the situation. "Now, it seemed to me Mrs. W. might have marked a special advertisement or something, and you might remember."

"Wait a minute." Doris's eyes began to shine. She completely ignored Dossie, but she seemed to have forgotten her original animosity against Mr. Crook. "That does remind me of something. I went to put a clean paper on the kitchen table a bit after Mrs. Watson went off and I saw someone had cut a paragraph out of the Personal column. I thought, of course, it was nylons, only the advertisement just above the space was nylons, and it wasn't likely there'd be two together the same day."

"Paper still on the table?" Crook looked like an elderly cherub about to fly down the passage.

"Not likely. I was never one of those who like to cover up my sins. Change the papers every day and throw away the old one. That's my rule."

"You virtuous women!" groaned Crook. "You make more trouble than a dozen of the other sort. If only you'd been a slut you might have got us over the first hurdle."

Doris tossed her head. "I hope I've got a conscience," she remarked.

"If you have, you keep it to yourself," Crook advised her. "We don't want it. It'll only make trouble. Female consciences always do."

He looked through the rest of the papers but not as

though he expected to find anything helpful, then said, " I'll have a word with my friend, Cummings. That ought to do the trick. Vanishing females are right up his street."

He invited Dossie to come with him. " One vanishing lady's as it should be," he said. " Two would be past a joke."

" You mean, you think I——? "

" I mean, I think you'd be a bit safer with me. By the way, told the boy-friend anything about this ? "

" You mean Desmond ? " She sounded dizzy. " No, I hadn't."

" I wouldn't then, not just yet. Hunting in threes never pays."

When Dossie saw the Scourge standing in front of the door she said nervously that she'd come up by tube and meet him at the office of the *Record*.

" What are you afraid of ? " demanded Crook. " Losin' your good name ? That's all right. I don't want it. You hang on to it till Judgment Day." And when Dossie said hurriedly that it wasn't *that*, he grinned (he never took offence) and said, " Is it the car ? You should worry. She'll get you any place, even Kingdom Come if she puts her mind to it."

This, though she didn't dare say so, was precisely what Dossie feared. However, she didn't know how to insist, and five minutes later they were off. Doris watched them enviously from the front step.

" If he'd had any sense he'd have taken me," she was reflecting. " That old maid won't be any use."

At the *Record* office a mincing young woman told Crook that Mr. Cummings saw no one without an appointment.

" Ever heard of Sapphira ? " Crook inquired genially, barging through the office like an elephant going through jungle.

In the editor's office Dossie had another shock. Crook had not been her idea of a lawyer, no white slips to his waistcoat like Emily's Mr. Matthews, no white spats, no beautifully polished pointed black shoes. And Cummings was not her idea of an editor, whom she had pictured as a Conservative M.P., pre-second-world-war vintage. He was tall, incredibly thin, untidy, badly dressed, and had about as much vitality as a human atom bomb.

Crook burst in, explaining, " I'm an old soldier from Botany Bay, and what have I got for you ? "

" I'll buy it," said Cummings obligingly, taking his feet off the table.

" Missing dame," pronounced Crook with as much pleasure as if he were presenting his companion with the Order of the British Empire.

Cummings' eyes gleamed. " Women are always news, specially when they go underground. Is she, by the way ? "

" Could be," said Crook.

" Priority ? " insisted Cummings.

" Your paper started it," said Crook.

" How come ? " asked Cummings.

Crook explained. Cummings looked a bit disappointed. " All the papers have got this," he objected.

" But you're the only paper that's got Miss Dossie Brett. Now don't look so down in the mouth. If the lady ain't young and lovely, she's rich and has a fistful of diamonds Bill tells me are worth a king's ransom, supposin' there were any kings outside this country worth so much."

Cummings brightened up. " Diamonds are always news," he agreed. " Sure she took 'em ? " You could see him shaping the story in his mind. Murder ? Perhaps. Romance ? Well, woman's second blossoming always rated the front page.

" Didn't leave 'em. And they ain't appeared on the market yet. Bill says not, and Bill knows."

Dossie here interrupted to say in shocked tones that dear Emily had been—was—a friend of hers, but neither of the men seemed to see any sense in that remark.

" Be your age," Crook invited her reasonably. " Neither of our mothers thought of christenin' us Galahad. Mrs.

Slapcabbage may be your friend and benefactor, but she's only a sensation to Cummings here and a case to me. It'll make things easier all round if you just bear that in mind."

At this juncture Cummings' messenger returned with the issue of the 14th April, and both men fell on it like starving creatures at the sight of bread.

"Here we are," announced Crook, triumphantly. "Between nylon stockings, bargain, 45s. a pair, and Young Lady, not over-fond of work, wants easy job, good pay. Travel preferred. Y'know, Cummings, you'll find yourself in the police court if you ain't careful."

"I should worry," said Cummings elegantly. "What is it?"

"I saw this," said Crook, thoughtfully. "I wondered then if I'd hear of it again."

Cummings looked over his shoulder. "That's the second instalment," he observed. "The first time that appeared was about three months ago."

Crook looked crestfallen. "How come I missed it?"

"It was in Apartments and Board-Residence last time."

Crook looked relieved. "Ah well, chap can't digest the whole paper. I never seem to get around to the news as it is. Got a note of the chap who put it in?"

The messenger was sent to look this up, and told to consult the earlier records, because, suggested Crook, it could be he was callin' himself something different the first time. It appeared that Dr. Forrester had made no secret of his whereabouts, and Cummings said, "Swinnerton? That's the Back o' Beyond. 'Bout nine miles from Oxbridge."

"Y'know, if this dame is found pushing up the daisies or nourishing the fishes, no coroner will bring in suicide," mused Crook. "What was she thinkin' of going off like this with a fellow she didn't know from Adam? Wonder if she thought to meet him first or if it was a correspondence course first to last."

Dossie suddenly had a brain-wave. She looked up to

exclaim, " Isn't there a place in London, a restaurant, called Parkers ? Isn't there ? "

" There's Parkers of Jermyn Street," said Cummings dubiously, thinking this was hardly Dossie's cup of tea.

" Then that's where they met. I'm sure of it. Perhaps I ought to have suspected something when Emily spoke of it, but how was I to guess ? "

" Guess what ? " asked Crook, patiently.

" She said she was going to town to lunch with a friend, one of the Country Gentlewomen, and when she came back I asked her where she had been and she was very vague. But later in the evening, when she was a bit off guard, I suppose, she said something about Parkers. I said, Is that a new milliner ? because she had been talking about hats a minute earlier, and she said No, it was a place where you had lunch, and she added that it was quiet but quite good. I said we must go there together one day, and I thought she looked a little odd. But she was so unlike herself just then I didn't think very much about it. Oh, and I did ask if it was expensive, and she said Yes, she thought so, but she'd been treated."

" Might be a pointer," agreed Cummings, and Crook asked which day this was.

" Well, she went up first on a Friday and then on a Tuesday, but I don't think it was Friday, because . . ." She plunged into a lot of irrelevant detail. (Cummings said later he wondered how Dossie had ever got herself born at the end of nine months like ordinary people, the pace she set.)

Crook was just the opposite. Once he'd got that bit of information, he jumped into the Scourge to check up at Parkers if a man called Forrester had booked a table for lunch on the 22nd April.

" Will they tell you ? " asked Dossie innocently.

" You don't get tables at Parkers without bookin', and yes, they'll tell me all right. There's only one person that hates being questioned by the police worse than a restaurant manager, and that's a murderer. Once it gets around that the police are gettin' nosey, folk start realisin' they never really liked the joint much. Oh, they'll tell me all right."

It was difficult for Dossie to believe that Crook had been inside a restaurant of the class of Parkers through the front entrance, but she was fascinated to see the respect with which he was treated as soon as he made his identity known. Within a quarter of an hour he had learned that a gentleman called Forrester had booked a table for two for April the 22nd, that he was not known as one of their familiar clientele, and that he had not been there since.

" Where do we go from here ? " demanded Dossie, as they returned to the Scourge. She liked to show that she could talk the modern idiom if she wanted to.

" Next stop Oxbridge," returned Crook, jubilantly. " 'Tain't likely we can get put up at Swinnerton even if we want to qualify for the doctor's private mausoleum. Besides, even in a wood you have to eat, and unless he's a cannibal who feeds on his victims, our Mr. Forrester would most likely do his shoppin' in Oxbridge."

" There must be a Mrs. Forrester," objected Dossie. " Emily was the soul of convention. She'd never have gone to share a house in a wood with a man about whom she knew nothing." Then she had a characteristic brainwave. " Suppose it's a sort of nursing home ? "

" The things you think of," said Crook, admiringly. " Ever hear of a nursing home in the middle of a wood, and one where no other guests are taken ? Wonder if this chap's in the Medical Directory ? "

They consulted one at the next Public Library they passed, but though there were a number of Forresters none of them lived in a wood at Swinnerton.

" Of course, he could be off the register," reflected Crook. " Or he don't have to be a doctor of medicine, does he ? " He didn't seem to think it very important anyway, as he hauled a large, tattered map out of a pocket of the Scourge and identified Oxbridge.

" Might make it this afternoon," said he, casually. " Bring a smicket with you, as we'll stay the night."

" You mean, I'm to come ? " Dossie looked horrified.

Crook said reasonably, " How the heck am I supposed to know darling Emily if and when I see her ? This chap can produce any doll he's got on the premises and call her Emily Watson. Oh, I know about the picture in the paper, but I dare say your Mrs. Watson's as much like W. G. Grace as that. No, I'll pick you up after lunch and with any luck we'll be at Oxbridge by the time they open."

## 6

On the journey to Oxbridge Dossie talked a good deal about Emily and a little about herself. She sketched in a not very flattering picture of Desmond, and Crook seemed completely unimpressed by everything. At last she said, " Suppose Emily's there, at The Cottage, I mean ? What do we do next ? "

" If she's living she's a free agent and can be where she likes, and we shall have saved the police a whole heap of trouble by locating her for them. If she's there but not visible, if you get me, well, we must find out if she ever went there."

" But—we know she went there? " Dossie sounded resentful.

" Don't you believe it. We know she answered the advertisement—no, hell, we don't even know that. We know she cut it out of the *Record* and we know she went to London on Tuesday the 22nd April ; we know she drew out £200 on the 25th and she hasn't been seen since. But we ain't found any one who saw her leave the house or get into the train or out of it for that matter."

" Suppose," continued Dossie, who seemed to enjoy speculation, " this Dr. Forrester agrees that she was there, but says she didn't stop."

" If he lives at the Back of Beyond, then she must have had a car out to the place ; she might even have had labels on her luggage, and the porter might have been vulgar enough to have read 'em. But somehow," he added, taking a corner in a manner that made Dossie's hair rise with terror, " I don't think we shall find that's the way it happened."

Dossie congratulated herself that nobody was likely to recognise her or speculate on what she was doing with this very odd companion. She hoped there would be no question of their putting up for the night at the same hotel, for though Crook couldn't, by any stretch of the imagination, be called amorous, he was not, thought conventional Miss Brett, the kind of person to inspire confidence in a reception clerk.

When they reached Oxbridge, and more than once Dossie thought her last hour had come and was shaken to think that, even in death, her name would be associated with so farouche a companion as Arthur Crook, that gentleman deposited her at the King's Head, and said he was going round the bars to see what there was to pick up.

Dossie looked perplexed. " Pick up ? "

" If Forrester lives in a wood he has to eat something," he reminded her. " If he eats he must buy the stuff and the place for buying stuff is the local shops. He must be rationed, even a bachelor knows that much, and the chaps and more particularly the janes in the shops must know something about him, something that could help us, I mean."

" I don't see why they should," objected Dossie. " I'm rationed but the people in Southwood, the shop-people, I mean, don't know anything about me. Nothing that matters, I mean."

" You'd be surprised. Now the first thing a shopkeeper can tell us is how many ration books there are to a household, if there have been any emergency cards—why, even in towns it's surprising how they remember, and in a little one-horse place like this you can bet your bottom dollar they'll know if there's been a visitor."

" Perhaps Mrs. Forrester does the shopping," suggested Dossie.

" Then that'll be the first brick in the house that Arthur Crook built. That there is a Mrs. Forrester, and that she's been seen. Say she has, then find out if she's been seen lately with any one besides her husband—you can't live in a wood and not be talked about. The only place where you can live and not hope to attract attention is London. The old maestro, G. K. C., found that out long ago."

"It's six o'clock," pointed out Dossie. "Even in one-horse towns the shops are shut by that time."

"All the better," returned the irrepressible Crook. "Where's the butcher when the blinds are down? In the bar of the Red Cow. And where he is there will Arthur Crook be also."

He settled Dossie, for whom he felt as sorry as he could feel for any woman, in the genteel bar of the Queen's Hotel, where she had nervously booked a room for the night, and ordered her a glass of sweetened vinegar, called the Queen's Own Cocktail, and moved off. Like many minor market towns, Oxbridge had one church of each denomination, half a dozen cinemas, its own repertory theatre, a British Legion hall, and innumerable public houses. Crook conscientiously made the rounds, explaining in each bar that he was going to stay at a place called The Cottage at Swinnerton, and asking for directions. Sometimes, of course, he drew a blank. The barmaid either knew nothing or she wasn't talking. But gradually he amassed a nice little store of information, all of which increased his curiosity and interest. He even began to feel friendly towards Dossie.

It was at The Running Horse that he met with most success. Mrs. Grant, who served in the saloon bar, said, Oh reelly, that *was* interesting, wasn't it? He'd be Dr. Forrester's first visitor. Crook said, Would he indeed? He hadn't known about that, but the doctor had been in London a short time ago, in consequence of which he, Crook, had been invited to come down to The Cottage. He didn't, naturally, say that it was Dossie who had issued the invitation, indirectly at all events. Mrs. Grant said he surely wasn't going such a way at this hour of the night, not seeing what the road was like, and Crook inquired innocently was it so bad, the doctor hadn't said. Mrs. Grant assured him that, of course, nobody went there from Oxbridge, they lived in a wood or some such outlandishness, and never seemed to want to see any one, though you couldn't be surprised really.

Crook said didn't they come into Oxbridge pretty often, and Mrs. Grant looked at him in some surprise. " Well, now," she said, " didn't the doctor tell you? About Mrs. Forrester, I mean? "

To which Crook replied truthfully that he only knew there was a Mrs. Forrester, adding he gathered they hadn't been married very long. Mrs. Grant said they hadn't been here long, and Mrs. Forrester had never been seen by any one, and they only knew she existed because of the ration books. Two there were, and neither of the couple ever went away, because it was two regularly, week in, week out. Mrs. Grant's brother was the grocer at Oxbridge with whom the Forresters were registered and there'd never been so much as an emergency card all the time they'd been there. But even Crook knew that didn't prove a thing. If Forrester wanted to conceal the fact that he had a visitor he had only to take the emergency card to a shop where he wasn't known, and take the rations back with him. Still, he reminded himself, in a place the size of Oxbridge it would be difficult not to be recognised, especially with the tale of a mad wife tagged on to you. Because that, it turned out, was the position at The Cottage.

" I suppose Mrs. Forrester's an invalid," Crook hazarded still feeling his way carefully. " I did wonder what made them choose a wood to live in. Not everybody's idea of bein' cosy."

Mrs. Grant leaned her comfortable bosom across the bar. " If you arst me," she said impressively, " if you arst me, Mrs. Forrester's not too well furnished up there." She tapped her forehead and nodded.

" Keeping her in a wood must help a lot," agreed Crook cordially.

" The doctor's afraid of what she'll do, that's my guess.

He told Fred, that's me brother, she'd had a nervous breakdown and wanted rest and quiet. I did wonder if p'raps she'd gone for 'im with a bread-knife—the doctor, I mean. Or it might be herself——"

"If so, I can't think of any better way of drivin' her completely loco than putting her in the Back o' Beyond, can you?" invited Crook. "Look here, just where is this house?"

Mrs. Grant asked suspiciously, "You a doctor?" and he hastily reassured her.

"I just wondered," she explained. "Oh, she's a queer one all right. Dr. Forrester, he says she had a terrible time in France during the war—she's a foreigner, you know. But Ted Darling at the garage told me he's had instructions not to pay any heed to calls from The Cottage unless it's the doctor himself. She gets mad spells when she thinks she's still a prisoner and bein' sent to Belsen or something, and she's got to get out, and tries to hire a car or writes letters. Has to keep an eye on her, he says."

"Anonymous letters?" Crook looked alert.

"Come to think of it," said Mrs. Grant, "there were some a while back, and no one knew for sure who'd wrote 'em——"

"If Mrs. F.'s livin' in the heart of a wood she couldn't be leavin' scurrilous letters on the neighbours in Oxbridge, not without she has a tame carrier pigeon," Crook pointed out mildly.

"And now I come to remember, it was before Mrs. Forrester's time," wound up the gigantic Mrs. Grant, placidly. "You plannin' to stay long at The Cottage?"

"Depends if Mrs. F. takes a likin' to me or not."

"Nice to know just how things are there," insinuated Mrs. Grant.

"If there's any funny business, you'll know," Crook promised her a shade grimly.

Mrs. Grant beamed and offered him one on the house. Soon afterwards Crook left and made his unobtrusive way down to Darlings' Garage, where he asked first for petrol for to-morrow's journey and then for Mr. Darling. As soon as he heard Crook's destination, Ted Darling became as communicative as Mrs Grant had been.

"The Cottage?" he said in surprise. "Goin' there, are you?" He looked speculatively at the Scourge and began to laugh.

"Joke?" inquired Crook, politely.

"You'll never make it in her," Darling spluttered.

Crook remained calm. "You'd be surprised," he said.

"So'll you, when you see the road. How the doctor does it, even in a Rolls, beats me. Why, it's more like a cart-track than a road."

"Does he do it often?"

"Comes in once a week. Well, he's unfortunate, you see. Has to do all the housekeeping himself. His missis has fancies."

"Kind of you to warn me," murmured Crook. "Is she likely to take a fancy to me?"

"Not that sort of fancy. She's a bit out of her head, you see, and starts ringin' up for cars and wants London telephone numbers—ringin' up Mr. Attlee, I dare say, as if he hadn't got enough headaches as it is."

"She must have a nurse or someone to look after her," protested Crook.

"Not she. The doctor does it all, pore feller. Well, she can't do much harm in a wood. Reckon that's why he planted her there." Crook thought the choice of verb ominous and possibly prophetic. "Yes, I reckon you'll be their first visitor, and I wouldn't be surprised if you was their last."

"Very reassurin'," murmured Crook.

Darling became expansive. "T'other day he brought the car in here for me to keep her for twenty-four hours," he confided. "Nothing wrong with her, not a mite, but he was afraid Mrs. Forrester 'ud try and get her out, and first thing you know she'd crash a lorry. And the car, of course," he added, as an afterthought.

"I must say you make it sound a cheerful household," Crook told him. "When was this?"

Darling was a little vague. "Two or three weeks back,

I reckon. It was the night before the big storm. Turr'ble amount of damage that did. The doctor came for the car on a Friday, I remember, so he must ha' brought her in on the Wednesday."

Armed with these scraps of information and knitting them busily into a pattern Crook returned to the feverishly impatient Dossie.

"Made your will?" he asked her, cheerfully.

"I've nothing to leave." Her voice was aggresive.

"Feel like puttin' your head into the lion's mouth in the mornin'?" Crook continued.

"You mean, go to The Cottage? Must we wait till morning?"

"Dear Emily ought to leave you a packet, the way you want to look after her," remarked Crook. "But I don't myself fancy drivin' down an unlighted cart-track at nine p.m. Besides, we've still got a few calls to make that 'ud look better in daylight. Added to which I don't fancy gettin' a shot of lead through the cranium, which is quite likely the way savages livin' in woods greet unexpected visitors after dark."

Dossie wanted him to stay and tell her what he'd found out but he wasn't very forthcoming and soon afterwards left her for his own cheaper but infinitely more comfortable pub. Next morning, bright and early, he appeared at the Queen's Hotel and tooted riotously on his screech-owl horn. Dossie came down, looking flustered and washed out. She said she hadn't slept.

"Plenty of time for that," promised Crook, and she was left wondering uncomfortably just what he meant by that.

"Where are we going now?" she asked, getting into the Scourge and deciding not to ask for an explanation.

"We're goin' to call on Dr. Forrester and ask to see Mrs. Watson."

"You said yourself we've no proof she ever went there."

"Then we'll have to manufacture some. Anyway, attack's the best form of defence. Didn't they teach you that one at school ? If we take this chap by surprise, he might give us something." Dossie remembered his reference to a welcome in the shape of cold lead, and wondered why she'd been crazy enough to embark on this adventure, without even telling Desmond where she was. " I must be as mad as Emily," she reflected. " Besides, if dear Emily's floatin' around we might get a glimpse of her," continued the odious little optimist at her side. " You do a bit of snoopin' if you get the chance, while I put him through it. Say you want to powder your nose or somethin'. They can't refuse a heartrendin' appeal like that."

Dossie turned her usual unbecoming pink and tried to think of something to say. But by the time she had decided on something that wouldn't give the disagreeable Mr. Crook another opening he had apparently forgotten her existence. The little car seemed to eat up the road, yet to both her passengers the journey seemed the longest nine miles they had ever covered. It was a grey day, with rain waiting to fall. The houses vanished after a time, and cottages took their place. Then even the cottages disappeared and they might have been travelling to No Man's Land. Dossie shivered.

" Cold, sugar ? " asked the attentive Mr. Crook.

" If Emily really came to this deserted place on the strength of an advertisement and a lunch at Parkers, then Desmond's right, she really is mad."

Crook thought privately that by this time she might be something even less encouraging, but he did not share his reflections with his companion. For a time Dossie was quiet, but since silence is golden and gold had played little part in her life, she could not maintain that stance for long.

" Are you sure," she protested, " you haven't missed the path ? "

" Nothing's sure in this world. If it was, there'd be no living for chaps like Arthur Crook, but, short of diving through a hedge or into that duck-pond we passed a mile back, I don't see what choice we've had."

" I'm certain it's more than nine miles," chattered Dossie.

" Maybe sums aren't their strong suit in this part of the world." A few minutes later he crowed triumphantly, " What did I tell you, sugar, what did I tell you ? " He indicated a signpost marked SWINNERTON, that stood drunkenly at the side of the road.

" If it says Swinnerton, then there's a village. That's what I was hopin' for."

" If The Cottage is in the heart of a wood, presumably Dr. Forrester doesn't live in the village," snapped Dossie.

" More men know Tom Fool than Tom Fool knows," quoted Crook in his exasperating way. " You wouldn't go in for matric. or one of those toney exams without doin' a bit of swottin' first, would you ? "

Dossie, hopelessly at sea, said she supposed not. " Same like us," explained Crook. " Before we see this chap we want to know all we can about him. Blessed is the man that hath his quiverful," he added, as though that rounded off his argument.

They took the hill into the village at a rate that made the terrified Dossie hang on to the side of the car. Crook, observing this, asked proudly, " Goes like a bird, don't she ? " Dossie thought that, like a bird—a hawk, say—she might drop like a stone at any moment. Swinnerton appeared to consist of half a dozen cottages, a church, where clearly no one had officiated for at least a year, and a general shop. Crook brought the Scourge to a standstill in front of this last. When he got out, he told Dossie, " Back in a minute. Just going in to ask for directions."

But Dossie had no intention of being left alone in a car whose appearance made it seem probable that she would start of her own accord the instant her master's back was turned. On the other hand, she didn't want to be seen too much with Arthur Crook, whose appearance was as peculiar as that of his machine, so she said she'd stretch her legs.

" Take it easy," Crook warned her. " If you stretch

'em much more you'll have to take 'em off to fit 'em into the car. She isn't built for storks." He looked down complacently at his own short legs in their atrocious, ginger-coloured unmentionables. Dossie blushed again—modest violets weren't in it with her, thought Crook—and moved off, while Crook marched into the little shop. As he opened the door, a bell like a burglar alarm began to ring, which startled him so much that he remained stationary on the mat on the threshold, thereby causing the bell to continue to sound the Day of Judgment to the neighbourhood. A door at the back of the shop whipped open, and a two-dimensional little old lady, wearing a straw hat trimmed with a Paisley scarf and four pink cotton forget-me-nots, advanced towards him.

" If you want the police," she began, and Crook, moving belatedly off the mat, said politely that he'd never seen a police station so well camouflaged. " I was going to say, if you want the police he's gone into Oxbridge with the toothache," continued the apparition, severely.

Crook, who had memorised the name over the shop, said, more politely than ever, " Mrs. Holland ? " and the apparition replied, " In the churchyard. Fourth stone from the corner."

Crook abandoned strategy, and asked outright, " Is this the road to Dr. Forrester's house ? "

This time he was successful in arousing his companion's interest. " You visiting at The Cottage ? "

" It's beginning to look like I wasn't," confessed Crook. " Y'know, it's a queer thing, living in the middle of a wood."

The old lady nodded. " What is there to do there but what you shouldn't ? " she inquired, simply.

" Know the doctor ? " continued Crook.

" Poor gentleman. Got a loony wife," confided the apparition.

" Know her ? " asked Crook, invoking the gods for patience.

" My Albert's seen her," announced the apparition, proudly.

This, compared with the progress he had made since morning, was like a stride with seven-leagued boots.

"Albert anywhere about?" he asked. "I mean, could I buy him one?"

"My Albert's silly enough without drink to make him more so," said the apparition, sternly. "Well, if he wasn't silly-like he wouldn't be postman in these parts."

"So Albert's the village postman? Takes the letters to The Cottage?"

"When there are any."

"Not great correspondents?" hazarded Crook.

"Albert says the doctor's a Mormon."

Warmer and warmer, thought the gratified Mr. Crook. "Lots of females around?" he suggested. "Abode of Love and all that?"

"Letters mostly, according to Albert. Silly women with nothing better to do than write letters." She came as far as the counter and leaned over. "I never wrote but one letter in my life and that was to my old gentleman. Havering and havering he was and never coming to the point, so at last I took pen and paper and I wrote: 'You gurt fule, If so be you want to wed with me haven't you a tongue in your gurt silly head?' That fetched him."

It would, thought Crook, dazedly. He was glad Mrs. Whatever-her-name-was hadn't come across him when he was a young man. Girls in London, he decided, must be shy. "As for seeing any wimmen," continued his companion, scornfully, "he's never seen any but this one, and he says she's as crazy as a loon."

"Birds of a feather," reflected Crook, and asked aloud, "Who was the one?"

"Who'd she be but Mrs. Forrester herself, for all her wild talk?"

"How long ago was this? And what did she say?"

"Week or so back," said the old lady, airily. "Albert had gone wi' the letters as usual, and there was a mort of them that day, though there's bin none since, not to mention, and most of them leddies that should know better, when up she bobbed from behind the gate, see ? Her hair was all wild and her face all streaked wi' mud, and her clothes dripping, as if she'd bin out in the storm half the night——"

" Was this the night of the storm ? " interrupted Crook, boldly.

" Didn't I say so ? She wouldn't be all draggled like that in the fine. Albert says she looked delirious or drunk or maybe both, and she leaned on the gate and pushed a letter at him, chattering like a jungleful of monkeys."

" What did she say ? " Crook almost choked in the effort to appear nonchaalnt.

" He couldn't understand the most of it, but she was mad all right. Something about bein' a prisoner and death waiting for her, and would he give the letter to the police ? "

" And did he ? "

The old dame drew herself up like a piece of elastic strained to the utmost. " Albert may be silly-like, but he's not that silly. Getting yourself mixed up with the police is no work for a respectable body."

Crook looked at her, marvelling that the most optimistic dictator could hope to wheel the British nation into line.

" You mean, he didn't deliver it."

" Albert's got a good heart. I've always said it of him, he may not be much in the yead, but his heart's all right. He wouldn't want to make trouble for a poor creature out of her right mind. No, Albert just took the letter and told her to go back out of the rain, and as soon as she was out of sight he just tore it up into little bits."

Crook digested that for a moment in absolute silence. Then he said carefully, " He tore it up ? Right up ? He didn't put it in the hedge or anything ? "

" Why should he put it in the hedge where the doctor might find it and maybe think he'd teach the poor thing a lesson ? "

" Oh, you think he knocks her about, then ? "

Again the old lady, who had relaxed a little during her confidences about the golden-hearted Albert, performed her elastic act. " I'm not saying anything, but—well, he is a husband. You know——"

" Not me," said Crook, hastily. " I'm a bachelor."

She looked at him keenly. Then she sighed. " Who's that bit of stuff you brought with you ? "

Old lady must be like the Beasts of the Revelations, with eyes before and behind, reflected Crook, admiringly. " That's a friend of the lady at The Cottage," he procrastinated.

The old lady beamed. " Albert was right. He is a Mormon. But as for you," her voice changed to one of scolding self-righteousness, " you should be ashamed of yourself, fostering his lust."

There weren't many people who could boast they had silenced Arthur Crook, but the old lady's name in that instant was added to the list. Only the thought of Dossie's face, could she have heard the suggestion, enabled Crook to keep his own.

" She's come for company," he heard himself say. " After all, she's not the first."

The old lady's curiosity overcame her disgust. " Mean to say, there have been others ? "

" Well, haven't any letters ever come for them ? "

" No letters have ever come but for Dr. Forrester."

" And no one's ever seen the others ? "

" If they have any decency left, they'd be glad enough to hide their shameful heads ; if there've ever been any," she riposted fiercely.

At that moment there was an interruption. The moon-witted Albert returned. He was a big, shambling creature, less fluent than his mother, who prodded him as fond parents prod an unwilling child or boastful dog-owners their pets, who don't feel inclined to make an exhibition of themselves before strangers.

" Gentleman's down from London to see Forresters," she announced to her son.

Crook thought Albert was completely unresponsive till he realised that on one side he had a glass eye, which couldn't be blamed for not registering emotion.

" Ar ! " said Albert.

" He's brought another lady down for the doctor," continued the scurrilous old woman.

" Ay," rejoined Albert, peaceably. " Happen she's better furnished upstairs than the other one."

" Tell how she came at you over the hedge like a wild bull," invited his doting parent.

" More like a gert owl," chuckled Albert, " rising up out of the dark and the rain, flapping her arms as it might be wings, and screeching at me in a hoarse sort of voice. Fair gave me a start till I knowledged who she was."

" Quite young, wasn't she ? " hazarded Crook, admiring the other man's descriptive gift.

Albert chuckled. " If she's young, I aren't born yet," he said. Crook kept him in conversation a little while longer, but he had nothing of importance to add. At last he returned to the seething Dossie.

" Get in," he said, swinging open the door of the Scourge. On the way up to The Cottage he telescoped the information he had gleaned from that scarecrow pair at the shop. Dossie became so much excited she even forgave him her interminable wait.

" Do you mean Emily managed to smuggle a letter out, and that—that zany destroyed it ? "

" We don't know it was Emily, but—it all fits, don't it ? The doctor takes his car to the garage, explainin' Mrs. F. may start runnin' amok, and next morning a gert owl, to use Albert's expressive phrase, comes sailing up to the gate with a letter for the police. Now we'll see what Forrester has to say about it."

The road to The Cottage was of a nature to send Dossie's turbulent heart into her mouth, but Crook seemed unperturbed.

They jolted and nearly overturned, they skidded in ruts, they avoided overhanging trees and projecting hedges by a series of miracles. Dossie gasped, " This can't be the right road. No one could live at the end of this."

" Well, not for long," agreed Crook, amiably. " That's the idea, I gather."

" We shan't live long enough to reach the house," panted Dossie. But Crook treated that defeatist remark with the scorn it deserved. If the Forresters had lived at the bottom of the Grand Canyon he would somehow have contrived to get the Scourge there. At last, when Dossie was wishing desperately that she had taken Desmond into her confidence, and was resolving to do so at the first possible opportunity, Crook's quick eye caught sight of a home-made letter-box secured to a post, and he slowed the Scourge's pace.

" Looks like we've made it, honey."

Dossie got back her breath with an effort and said, " And you think we're going to learn——? "

" Who lives here ? I hope so. Whether that's what we want to know is another matter. Roll, bowl or pitch, every time a blood orange or a good seegar. Question is, are we dealing in either to-day ? "

While he talked this nonsense he had jumped out of the Scourge, opened the gate that this morning stood unlocked, driven the car through, and closed the gate behind her. The garage stood on the left, and before resuming his seat at the wheel he ran nimbly round the building to peer in through a small window at the back.

" Car's at home," he announced on his return. " Seems as though Dr. F. might be, too."

" Was there—any one in the car ? " quavered Dossie.

" Not so's you could notice, but it might be piled with corpses for all I could see through the window. Well, we'll soon learn."

The Cottage loomed in sight round a slight curve in the path. Crook had none of the attributes of the velvet-footed sleuth of fiction and film. You could have heard the Scourge almost as far away as Oxbridge.

" Good policy, that," he explained to Dossie above the roar of the engine. " If they ain't expecting us, they won't have the scene set. Now, watch the windows. That's where any one will come who wants to get a looksee before the door's open."

He came roaring up to the front entrance, and Dossie looked up with feverish intensity. At a window on the upper floor a curtain had been pulled across the glass. "That's the one to watch," said Crook, one step ahead of her in thought.

Even as he spoke a hand appeared, and began to draw the curtain back. Another moment and they would see the owner of the hand. But the moment never came. A second person must have entered the room, unnoticed, for the next instant the hand jerked violently backward, the curtain was twitched into place.

Then, before Crook had time to get out of the car and ring the bell, the front door opened and a man came on to the step.

## 7

There was nothing remotely striking about him. Dossie Brett could have passed him in the street on six consecutive days and not recognised him on the seventh. He would have seemed tall, if he hadn't stooped a bit, had an untidy black moustache, dark hair and wore glasses. He looked neither a hero nor a villain. His manner was mystified but polite.

"Good morning," he said, looking uncertainly from one surprising visitor to the other, and probably wondering how such an ill-assorted couple contrived to find themselves simultaneously on his doorstep.

Crook hopped out, slamming the door of the Scourge in a way that would have been a warning to the Seven Sleepers. "Dr. Forrester, I presume. I hope we didn't scare you, but Mrs. Watson didn't give us your telephone number, so we couldn't let you know we were coming. This is Miss Brett. She's probably often spoken of her, Mrs. Watson, I mean. We'd have warned you if we were coming if it had been possible, but it wasn't. And we lost the path so often it's amazing we're here at all."

Dossie admired this dashing frontal attack, but if it was intended to discompose the doctor it was singularly unsuccessful. He said in a slow, pleasant voice, "I'm sorry you had such a tiresome journey and all for nothing. It's a pity, really, you didn't telephone——"

Crook hummed a snatch under his breath that Dossie didn't recognise as the tune of "See any green in my eye?"

"That's all right," he said. "It was a nice drive, anyway. When do you expect Mrs. Watson back?"

"I'm afraid there is some misunderstanding," explained the doctor patiently. "There's no Mrs. Watson here, never has been——" His guileless gaze passed from Crook's hearty red face to Dossie's thinner, quivering one.

"Surely the old girl's not calling herself something else? That's going a bit too far. Still, as a doctor, you'll have the situation all dotted and crossed. And come to that, I dare say you're as glad to see us as we are to see you."

Now Forrester seemed hopelessly at sea. "I can only repeat, there's some misunderstanding. This Mrs. Watson—if any person of that name is staying in this neighbourhood, I assure you it's not at this house."

"What is the lady's name, then?" demanded Crook, firing a broadside. "The one staying here, I mean."

"There's no lady here, except my wife." Forrester was patient, but wary.

"And the *bonne à tout-faire*, of course." Crook liked to show he could be elegant, too, on occasions. "But I suppose she wouldn't count as a lady."

Forrester allowed himself to become a shade emphatic. "I repeat, there is nobody in the house at all except my wife and myself. As must be obvious to any one, we are in a very remote situation and no domestic will come here. Nor do we have visitors."

Crook gave a little sigh of contentment. That was what he had been angling for, to catch the fellow out in a false statement. Now he was tolerably sure he was on the right track.

From the stairs above a woman's voice called down, in a strong foreign accent:

" Vyvyan, you have someone—— ? "

Forrester stepped back. " Come in," he invited Crook. " Even if we can't help you, and I'm afraid we can't, it's a long journey and I dare say you'd like something to drink, or at any rate, the lady would." Crook groaned. It sounded like the wind in the trees outside. " Oh, I do like a nice cupper tea," he hummed despondently. Of course, a chap who chose to live in a wood must be bats, anyway, and his idea of something to drink would be on a par with the Congregational Reunion. If you said licence to this chap he'd think of dogs and wireless. Forrester meanwhile called out to his wife, " It's some travellers, my dear, who have come to the wrong house."

Mrs. Forrester shut a door smartly, and the attentive Crook heard the faint whine of a key in the lock.

" But, Vyvyan, this is the only house for more than a mile."

" I told you, there is a misunderstanding."

Crook edged up to Dossie and nudged her with his elbow. " Keep your eyes open," he muttered, " and whatever happens—WHATEVER HAPPENS, mind—don't say a word till we're outside."

Berta Forrester came downstairs, wearing a coloured overall, and paused at her husband's side. The tireless Crook explained once more the reason for his presence. " We did hope we'd be able to see Mrs. Watson. She came down here a month back. We should have come before but we weren't sure of the address till just lately."

Berta smiled. There was something derisive in that smile. " Takes us for a pair of suckers," reflected Crook. " Well, she'll learn." About him, anyhow, he meant. He wasn't going to be answerable for Dossie. Dossie interpreted it in another way. " Laughing at me," she thought, wrathfully. " Why ? Clothes ? Hair-do ? Or because she thinks I can't find anything better than Arthur Crook to go round with ? She'll learn."

Berta meanwhile had opened a door and said gently,

" And now when you have found your friend's address it is the wrong one. That is too bad. Will you not come in ? I will make some coffee. Oh, yes, my husband and I always have coffee at this hour." She smiled at Forrester. " I am sorry we cannot ask you to stay to lunch——"

Crook drove his elbow into Dossie's side again. Next time she came out with him, she'd wear armour plating, she decided. " We wanted to take Emily to lunch with us," he said blandly. " We've got the car. It's very odd."

Berta went out to get the coffee. Forrester, having offered his guests chairs, asked earnestly, " You're sure your friend wrote from this address ? "

" There couldn't be two houses in Swinnerton called The Cottage ? "

" I've never heard of another."

" Anyway, there wouldn't be two Dr. Forresters. That 'ud be too much coincidence even for a chap like me that's in the Black Market for hope. Still, maybe you can help us, after all. What happened when you met Emily ? "

Forrester's admirable patience began to show signs of strain. " I have told you, I don't know your friend——"

Dossie was inspired to take part in the conversation. " But you gave her lunch, at Parkers," she said. " That we do know, and, anyhow, Parkers can corroborate."

" Bull's-eye, my girl," thought Crook, thinking you can't judge by appearances, and there might be more to Dossie than he'd guessed.

Forrester was no fool, either. He saw they'd got him there and his comeback was admirable. " How foolish of me. I had forgotten the name. Actually, there was no particular reason why I should recall it. But a number of ladies answered my advertisement, of which your friend was one. Actually, I interviewed three or four, but in each case, when I explained living conditions here, the solitude, the remoteness, and when the ladies realised there were no neighbours, no amusements, no cards, no cinema even, they decided not to come."

" You mean no one came ? " Crook's incredulity stood

out like the false light of Rosilly. " But if you advertised——"

" I said we didn't have visitors. In the usual sense of the word, that is true. But my wife is used to nursing, and I am a doctor. Before the war I had my own nursing home for neurasthenic cases. Nowadays, neurasthenia is treated a great deal more intelligently than it was, even ten years ago. In reply to my advertisement, I was asked whether I would take charge of a lady who had had a serious nervous breakdown. Her family were anxious that she should receive kind and careful treatment, but not in an institution. You will know that the stigma of insanity is one that is avoided as far as possible by families in every walk of life."

" Don't they ever open their eyes and look round them ? " asked Crook bluntly. " It 'ud give 'em less of a headache to count the sane people than the loonies."

" Insanity is simply a disease of the mind and no more shameful and in many cases no more incurable than diseases of the body. That is what we are trying to make people believe. I agreed to have the poor lady here for observation, but the experiment was, frankly, not a success. After a very brief interlude I had to warn the relatives that, in my opinion, nothing but an acknowledged mental home would meet the case. Naturally, I promised to observe complete secrecy, but I understand that they have taken my advice."

" And since then they've sailed for South Africa, I expect," said Crook cheerfully. " You're quite sure her name wasn't Watson ? I mean, speakin' as a lawyer, my old dame was suspected of bein' a bit rocky in the upper story, and it sounds to me just the sort of thing her relations might have done. Of course, if you didn't live in the Back of Beyond, you'd have read about the case."

Forrester's head came up with a jerk. " That case ? How absurd of me. I never connected it. The lady, who, it is suggested, may have been the victim of foul play."

" That's the one."

" I understood the police——"

" I represent the family, but I dare say you'll be getting the police down here any time now. Still, as you say, families don't like this sort of yarn to get about, and if you could have helped us——"

" I am beginning to remember," said Forrester. " This lady gave me the impression of being somewhat unbalanced."

" Well, what other sort would want to come and live in a wood ? " asked Crook reasonably. " Unbalanced or wanted by the cops. Unless, of course, the family really think she is a bit screwy and want her put where she can't make trouble."

" Trouble ? "

" Well, I see you like things in black and white. Play ducks and drakes with their money is what I had in mind."

" Their money ? " Forrester's brows climbed up his high, bony forehead.

" When you're countin' on coming into the dough, it ain't long before you start thinkin' of it as yours, even if the bank wouldn't give tuppence for your signature. So, if you can come to some agreement by which the lady can be restrained——"

For the first time Forrester seemed to take offence.

" I'm afraid, Mr—er—what ? Cook ?—Mr. Cook, I cannot have made myself clear. As a doctor, I have a professional reputation. I am scarcely likely to scheme with unscrupulous relatives for their financial benefit, even if they were foolish enough to make me an offer. I don't say that is what you suggested, but that is at all events one interpretation that could be put upon your speech."

" Standin' at the next Election ? " asked Crook, with interest. " I guess it's a long time since you lived in the big, bad world, Doctor."

What Forrester's reply to that would have been was not known, for at this instant Mrs. Forrester relieved the tension by appearing with a tray of coffee cups. Crook gave her a hopeful, not to say a wistful glance, and said that somewhere, was it Russia, he couldn't be sure, he believed they drank coffee from a glass. Dossie opened her mouth to say something, but Crook, rising to bring her her cup, contrived in his carefully clumsy fashion to stamp on her foot, choosing by unerring instinct the one with a bunion, so that she smothered a yelp and repressed whatever it was she had been going to say. Berta had removed the coloured overall and wore a black dress that had no decoration but a brooch at the neck, and managed to look completely Bond Street. Crook thrust a cup in Dossie's direction, putting his fierce pug face close to hers, and she saw the warning it conveyed and said meekly, "What delicious coffee!"

Forrester said something about the inability of the average British housewife to make drinkable coffee, as the French, for instance, understood the word, and Dossie became violently nationalistic, and said, well, really, we'd done a good deal to oblige the French in the past six or seven years, they couldn't expect us to alter our way of making coffee to please them. Crook swallowed Berta's concoction, which was remarkably good if you'd been a judge of coffee which Crook wasn't, and with the air of the martyr he believed himself at that moment to be, he said, "I suppose Mrs. Watson didn't give you any hint where she might be going?"

"We have been over all that ground before," said Forrester. "There was no reason why she should confide in me. If I had had any information I thought could be helpful, I should have communicated with the police."

"Pleasure deferred," said Crook, swallowing the last of the coffee and setting the cup back on the tray. "I dare say they'll be communicatin' with you soon."

"I'm afraid I can tell them no more than I have told you," Forrester assured him. "I can only repeat that I am sorry you should have had this journey for nothing. If you had inquired at the Oxbridge exchange, they would have given you my number, and I could have informed you over the phone that I had nothing helpful to tell you. And you would have saved yourself—and Miss Brett—a very uncomfortable trip."

"Wouldn't have missed it for the world," Crook consoled him. "Y'know what they say—eliminate the impossible and what remains is the answer. Well, you've told me Mrs. Watson isn't here. That's more help than you know. Ready, sugar?"

Dossie got to her feet at once, and they all came into the hall. In one corner a gun leaned, and Crook, nodding towards it, asked conversationally, "Much sport round here?"

"An occasional rabbit for the pot. The woods are thick with them."

"If there are as many rabbits as there are trees you'll never starve. How far do the woods go?"

"I've never penetrated very far, but I'm given to understand they go on for ever."

"And the road?" pursued Crook. "The one we came up, I mean. Suppose we'd shot past the gate, where'd we have landed ourselves?"

"In bog. I doubt if you'd ever have got the car out. That's why there's no prospect of building in these parts. I believe the minister has had his scouts out, but the amount of drainage that would be necessary is so vast that only millionaires could afford to live here. In any case, the road's so narrow above the house even a small car couldn't turn."

"You'd be surprised what my car can do," returned Crook, undaunted. "Must have been a circus horse in another incarnation. Still, we'll take your word for it."

"Would you like me to come and open the gate for you?" asked Forrester politely, as they came out on to the step. The Scourge looked like an impertinent red beetle and nobody but her owner could have surveyed her with such enormous and innocent pride. He jumped in and turned her in a wide sweep that made the doctor skip for safety.

"Thanks a million," he said, opening the other door for Dossie to join him. "We can manage. We'll be seeing you, perhaps." He drove off in fine style. "And if thoughts could kill," he confided to his companion when they were out of sight of the house, " we'd crash in the ditch and he'd bury us under the nettles."

" You wouldn't let me speak," said Dossie, half-eager, half-resentful ; " but Emily has been there."

" And someone, though not necessarily Emily, is there still. Oh, yes, sugar. They say every criminal makes one slip. You noticed someone tryin' to draw back the window curtain as we tootled up ? And someone else stopped her ? And at the same minute Forrester opened the front door, so, unless they've got a tame ghost on the premises, and I hardly think they have, there are three people in that house at the present moment." His thick pugnacious brow furrowed. " How many there'll be this time to-morrow I wouldn't like to guess," he continued. " I don't know how badly we've shaken 'em, but they don't like the idea of the police. And in their shoes I wouldn't either. Now, say your piece," he invited. " How do you know she's been there ? "

" That brooch Mrs. Forrester was wearing, the little diamond bird with the ruby eyes. That was Emily's, though she didn't wear it very often. She had so many, you see. I used to tell her how pretty it was. I have very little jewellery myself, and naturally I like it—all women do——"

" Tough luck, sugar," said Crook sympathetically. " There's times when it's no use just playin' a fish, you have to get a stone and whack him on the side of the head. Mrs. F. seems to have done the trick."

" If the police learn she's wearing Emily's brooch," pursued Dossie, but Crook shook his head.

" I don't suppose it's an exclusive design. Probably, if there's a word said about it in the press, the Home Secretary won't be able to get out of Whitehall for the women who want to show him their sparklets. All the same, it's funny the way these killers can't resist puttin' on their victims' gauds. Time and again it runs 'em right into the little covered shed. There was Crippen, givin' Belle Elmore's whatnots to Ethel Le Neve, and Dougal decoratin' his village wenches with poor Camille Holland's bits and pieces——"

He had been driving rapidly down the lane while he talked, far too rapidly for Dossie's peace of mind. She felt like a middle-aged lady learning to ride. A good seat they called it, and she reflected that was just what you needed when you went driving with Arthur Crook. Or at a pinch a really solid pneumatic cushion might do. They went at this flying pace almost to the end of the lane, when Crook suddenly turned the car towards the hedge. Dossie clutched the side and screamed.

" Take care ! "

" I wish you wouldn't do that," returned Crook pleasantly. " You might upset my nerves, if I could afford luxuries on a peacetime budget."

" I thought you were going to kill us both," quavered Dossie.

" What ? When I'm on a job ? " He was manœuvring the car so that, when he finally brought her to a standstill, she stood right across the mouth of the lane. Then he alighted and suggested to Dossie that she should do likewise.

" But—nobody can pass," she observed foolishly.

Crook beamed.

" So you do notice some things."

" There's no need to be rude," said Dossie, in sharp tones. " Suppose someone wants to come this way ? "

" Another visitor to The Cottage ? But the police ain't caught up with us yet, and Forrester swears he never has guests."

" It might be someone else," suggested Dossie uncertainly.

" Well, sugar, you tell me who."

Dossie had to admit defeat. " Ever started a hare ? " Crook went on, dodging behind the car and beginning to walk back up the lane. " Well, what does it do ? "

" It runs away."

" Just so. And that's what our hare may try to do. But, if he's tellin' the truth when he says there's no way out above The Cottage, and I'm inclined to think he is, then we've got him in a snare. See ? "

" You mean," elaborated Dossie laboriously, " he can't get his car past yours. Yes, I see. Do you think he's likely to try and run away ? "

" No sense takin' chances you ain't paid for," said Crook sensibly. " Even if he and Mrs. F. don't propose to make a getaway, it could be they'll start thinkin' their visitor's outstayin' her welcome. But, myself, I think there'll be three in the car if it comes down the lane."

" And if it don't—doesn't, I mean ? " Crook's colloquialisms were proving contagious.

" Then they'll still be up at the house. Or the body will. There's more ways of killing a baby than poisoning it. But they can't get by till we let 'em." He looked over his shoulder at the Scourge standing small but sturdy in the path. " Come on."

" Where are we going ? " inquired Dossie, bewildered.

" Back to do a bit of snooping. If we've stirred 'em up, as I fancy we have, they'll be precious anxious to blot out all trace of their lady visitor. We might learn something."

" It's very dangerous," objected the practical Dossie.

" It's dangerous to be born at all," Crook pointed out. " If you wanted to play safe, you should have been a stillborn child."

" Do we go back up the path ? Suppose he's locked the gate ? "

" I'm darned sure he'll have locked the gate. Well, wouldn't you ? No, we go through the woods. And don't ask if we fly through the hedge because the answer is I'm no angel. But I keep my eyes open, and I'm a Dutchman if someone hasn't been doin' a bit of jerry building round here lately. And once we're in the woods—well, maybe we'll find something there besides trees. Anyhow, we must hope for the best."

# 8

Crook marched forward, apparently quite undaunted by the dubious prospect in front of him. When he had gone a short distance he stopped and observed, " Well, how about it, sugar ? " and looked at her expectantly.

" How about what ? " asked Dossie, in an enfeebled voice.

" Breaking through here. What's that you say ? Impossible ? Nonsense, Madam. I assure you there's no deception. Great strength returns the penny."

While he jabbered away like an amiable mental deficient he was testing a part of the hedge that, to Dossie's unpractised town eye, looked exactly like every other part. But there must have been something different about it, because when Crook shook the branches they were easily dislodged and after a moment he had forced an entry wide enough to admit them both.

" Didn't notice that, eh ? " he suggested, turning to make good the damage. " Saw it myself as we came by. Someone's been filling a gap, I told myself, and someone must have had a reason. Well, well, looks as if there was a path here. If there's a path, must lead somewhere. And someone's just blocked up the path. Now, why ? Because someone don't want the public walking down it. And if he don't want the public on his premises, it's because he's got something to hide."

" Do you," asked Dossie, in desperation, " talk in your sleep ? "

" I wouldn't know," said Crook blandly, " and seeing I haven't got a girl-friend there's no one who can tell you."

He plunged down the path, followed by the furious Miss Brett, and after a moment he saw round a curve the derelict cottage with its door hanging open an inch or so, its windows smashed, roof in ruins, the whole breathing death and decay. It was just as poor Emily Watson had seen it about two weeks previously, except that now there was no spade in evidence, the necessity for a spade having apparently passed.

" What's the Ministry of Health doing neglecting valuable property ? " Crook wondered aloud.

" No one could live there," said the literal Dossie.

" Perhaps no one wants to. But I suppose any one could die there, if someone else had a mind."

He walked round the little house, peering through the broken panes. As he had anticipated, there was no one inside. There was no furniture at all, except the rusty, black, built-in range ; a dilapidated staircase led to the rooms above, and under the stairs was a cupboard with a closed door.

" Coal," suggested Crook intelligently. " Now, sugar, if this was a film the hero, Humphrey Bogart, say, would fling open the door and reveal Laureen Bacall shuddering on the floor. Or failing that, a new star to British filmdom would find a load of bullion. Being just Arthur Crook, my bet 'ud be a couple of spiders, with a few couponsworth of cobwebs thrown in."

To her surprise, Dossie was shuddering. " You don't think—you don't think Emily——"

" Not if it was Emily at the window just now. Even a magician couldn't do it in the time." He marched over to the door and pulled it open. The inside of the cupboard was pitch-black with his body blocking the doorway, but even when he moved and let a ray of thin grey daylight fill the space he'd vacated, there was nothing to be seen —no body, no bullion, not so much as a black straw hat trimmed with ribbon velvet and a steel buckle hanging on a hook at the back.

" Fifteen, love," ejaculated Mr. Crook philosophically, but Dossie, whose mother had sent her to an old-fashioned school that didn't teach philosophy, exclaimed in disappointment, " Why, there's nothing there."

" Well, what did you expect to find ? Anyway, we haven't half-looked yet." He snapped on a little pencil torch, and went carefully over the grimy walls.

"What are you doing?" inquired Dossie, half-sobbing on a giggle she couldn't repress. "Looking for finger-prints?"

"A rag, a bone, a hank of hair," said Crook airily. But the walls revealed none of these. Undaunted, he squatted like a little brown elephant and splashed his light into the remotest corners.

"There's nothing there," Dossie began again, then caught her breath and choked. For the torch beam shone on some small bright object that had rolled into the farthest corner, under the angle of the stairs. A button? An earring? Crook crawled on all fours to retrieve it, and brought up a slender silver pencil of old-fashioned make, a flat pencil in a flat silver sheath with a cover to protect the point. Dossie remembered her mother owning such a pencil. Nowadays, she supposed, they could only be found in curiosity shops.

"That's Emily's," she exclaimed breathlessly. "At least, it isn't likely there'd be two in this part of the world. It was one of Albert's first presents to her, she told me, and he had his initials put on it. She said it had belonged to his first wife, she supposed, and she did wish it had been one of those gold propelling ones——"

Crook brought their find out into the daylight, and both could decipher the monogram E.W. on the flat holder.

"Even the police must accept that as proof," said Dossie, jerkily. And then, as though the point had only just occurred to her, "What on earth was it doing in that cupboard?"

"Come to that," said Crook, "your guess is as good as mine. Now, sugar, there's no time to lose. If you're going to have high strikes let them ride till you get home. At the moment, there's other things to do."

Dossie said again, "But Emily isn't here."

"We know she has been. Look now, here's a job for you. I'm going to wait in this cupboard while you go back to the lane. When you get to the place where I pulled up the shrubs stop and listen. Got that? Stop—and—listen."

"I'm not deaf," snapped Dossie.

"Well, that's lucky," said Crook imperturbably. "You're going to need all the ears you've got."

"What are you going to do?"

"Stay inside the cupboard and holler."

"Why?" She stared.

"So that you can tell me if I could be heard in the lane. Not that it matters much, seeing no one ever came up the lane except Forrester and his doxy, but—leave no stone unturned. And for Pete's sake, don't get yourself kidnapped, or the odds are I'll go join dear Emily under the daisies or the cabbages or whatever it is they cultivate in these parts."

"How long do you want me to listen?" quavered Dossie.

"Wait a couple of minutes, and then come back as fast as you can make it. If you see any one comin' down the lane, don't bother about the two minutes. Just come back. Got it?"

"Yes," said Dossie, but so dubiously, that he asked in patient tones, "Like me to try again?" But Dossie said, No, thank you, she quite understood, and though he had his doubts he let her go. Then he shut himself inside the cupboard and, giving her time to reach the road, began to yell at the top of his voice.

"Born and bred in a briar patch, Brer Fox," he bellowed. "Born and bred in a briar patch." It had occurred to him that Dossie, resenting the implied slur on her hearing, might not play fair, and if he shouted, "Help! Help!" and she made a lucky guess, he wouldn't be any further on. He shouted for the stipulated two minutes, then dried up.

Dossie was so long coming back he began to wonder if at last he'd backed a loser and if archæologists, years hence, finding the skeleton of a one-time plump gentleman in brown rags in this cupboard, would start building up a story of primitive man. This passed the time nicely till Dossie reappeared.

"Well?" he demanded. "Hear anything?"

" No," said Dossie defiantly. " You can't have shouted very loud."

" Top of my lungs," Crook assured her, " and I dare say they're as good as the old lady's. Well, you see where that gets us."

Dossie did and she shivered. " Do we go to the police now ? Have we got enough proof—— ? "

" Well, pencils don't walk into sheds of their own accord, though all that proves is that your Emily was in the shed sometime, at least, there's reason to suppose she was. Nothin' short of her body, livin' or dead, is actual proof that she is or was here. Still, we've got a few chores to do before we make contact with the force. Not much sense bringin' them here to find the nest empty. What we've got to find out is whether Dr. Forrester is plannin' a getaway at this very moment."

Dossie had her instant of illumination. " So that's why you put the car across the road."

" Ever such a bright girl," Crook complimented her. " Only don't be too bright or you might attract the villain's attention. If you ask me, the Forresters wouldn't have the smallest hesitation in shootin' us down from the windows."

" That would be murder," exclaimed Dossie.

" What makes you think they'd draw the line at murder ? Anyhow, they could say they thought I was an outsize rabbit, and juries mostly are so wooden headed they'd probably believe them."

" What would they think I was ? " inquired Dossie, with spirit. But Crook was too polite (or too intimidated) to tell her.

He was making his way through the woods with an assurance that would have staggered poor Emily Watson. It was his boast that he was like a cat, he could see in the dark, and he was like an Indian brave that he could find a path where no path existed. Dossie was astonished to realise how quietly a stout man could walk. She herself made a lot more commotion.

" Suppose," she said at last, unable to keep silence any

longer, " something really has happened to Emily, where do you suppose—— ? "

" There's about five miles of wood," offered Crook mildly, " and I'm no corpse diviner."

" You aren't looking," panted Dossie.

" All I want to do is locate the house and see what's up there." They passed a clump of scarlet toadstools, and he pointed them out to Dossie, remarking, " Pretty, wouldn't you say ? "

" As if they matter ! " exclaimed the distracted Dossie, and, " Of course they matter," insisted Crook. " In a wood like this with every tree lookin' alike, how are we expected to find our way back if we haven't got any landmarks ? In the old days, when women wore hairpins, they shed 'em in a golden stream, or so my mother told me, but women nowadays only think of their own comfort and not of what's expected of them." Dossie had no breath to make any reply, even if she could have thought of one, and a minute later they came to a little copse of trees standing roughly in a circle.

" Hallo ! " said Crook softly. " Talk about private enterprise ! I'd never have chosen these woods myself for a nice game of hare and hounds, but—you can't keep a good man down."

He stooped, and picked out a few half-pulped fragments of writing-paper scrawled with some washed-out blue blurs that had once been handwriting.

" Now," said he softly, " I wonder who that could have been ? Little Em'ly and Dr. Forrester, do you suppose ? "

He held out the fragments to Dossie, who snatched them out of his hand.

" I believe—I believe——" she stammered in her excitement. " Are there any more ? "

Crook obligingly crawled about and found another specimen. This had suffered a little less than the others and two or three words could, with some imagination, be distinguished. Not that Dossie cared about the words.

" It's Emily's handwriting, I swear it is. It's part of a

letter. Probably the first draft of the letter sent to the police. It must have been her that Albert saw."

"It could be," allowed Mr. Crook. "Yes, sugar, it could be. Though why she wants to write in a wood——"

"Don't you see? It's as clear as daylight. She didn't dare write in the house in case someone tried to stop her or took the letter away. She must have known by that time she was in danger for some reason——"

"The diamonds," said Crook laconically. "Matter of fact, I must get in touch with Bill. He's makin' some inquiries about them. If they've been offered on any market, he'll know. But, of course, now all the stink's appeared in the paper, our Dr. Forrester will likely lie a bit low."

"And these were written before the night of the storm or they wouldn't be sodden the way they are."

"You're coming on," Crook approved. "Might as well tag round a bit and see if there's anything else. We've got two clues, the pencil and these——"

"Three," amended Dossie eagerly. "You're forgetting the brooch."

"Proof from the police point of view is somethin' that can't be disputed. Unless the brooch was a special design we can't prove it was hers. In any case, it's probably down the drain by now."

For once Dossie scored. "They won't have drains in the middle of a wood."

"No more they will, sugar. One up to you. Hallo, what did I tell you? Third time lucky."

He had almost slipped on a small dark object half-buried in the soil. He scooped it up, getting a good deal of earth under his fingernails, and, shaking away the surface mud, revealed a little dark book half-filled in a large, nervous hand.

"What's that?" asked Dossie excitedly. "A diary? It certainly isn't Emily's. At least, I never saw her with one like that. In any case"—she looked over Crook's shoulder—"it's not her writing. Perhaps whoever it belonged to has written her name inside."

Crook flipped open the cover. " Well," he said after a moment, " it could be she did, but some silly ass has torn out the front page so here we are, back at scratch."

He didn't stop to examine his find then and there. More important issues awaited him. Stepping carefully he wove his way among the trees and very shortly the house came into view.

" What——" began Dossie, but she got no further, for Crook caught her unceremoniously by the hand and began to drag her, protesting violently, back the way they had come.

" Let go of my hand ! " she panted. " I've only got two and I need them both—in the future, I mean."

" You're goin' to be lucky to have a future if you don't listen to your Uncle Arthur," Crook assured her. " Did you see what was happenin' ? No ? They're puttin' up the shutters. And that's something you don't do if you're just going down to the local."

At what seemed to Dossie an irrational pace he forced her through the woods, and in a shorter time than she would have believed possible the derelict cottage came into view. They passed it, found the bogus hedge, tore it up, replaced it, and then Crook swung open the door of the Scourge and urged her in.

" Where now ? " asked Dossie breathlessly.

" The police you were so anxious to contact a while back." Crook for once sounded almost surly, and with a shock she realised he had really enjoyed the hunt and hated the thought of turning the matter over to the police.

" You take a look at that diary we found while we're going along," he told her. " See if you can find any clues."

" If the front page is missing," Dossie said argumentatively, but he interrupted with the comment that that didn't matter as much as she seemed to think. " A woman wrote that," he pointed out, " and women love detail the same as they love any other sort of furbelows. You see, somewhere or other she'll say she went to tea with Kitty, and then you'll get a hint who Kitty is or where she lives. Or Kitty will tell her some yarn about Mary Jane, and so brick by brick and silently your boundaries increase, as the poet says. Or if she's a married lady there'll be references to her husband. Now there's no need for you to give your famous imitation of a dyin' duck in a thunder-storm. Persevere and you'll find your Uncle Arthur's right. I mean to say, where's the sense me finding the diary at all if it ain't going to tell us what we want to know ? "

Even the voluble Dossie could find no answer to that one. Moreover, she found herself becoming engrossed in the story.

" She's got a husband," she announced triumphantly after a short while. " She speaks of him as Cecil, my husband——"

" That's known as detection made easy," suggested Crook.

" And the husband's got—got——"

" A wife ? "

" Somebody called M. Or at least, she thinks he has. I wonder if he got her down here by pretending she was crazy and ought to be shut up."

" History repeatin' itself, if so," Crook agreed.

Dossie went on chattering about the writer of the diary, uttering a positive squeal of pleasure when she came to the first suggestion that Cecil had been tampering with the food. She looked expectantly at Crook, but to her surprise he didn't appear to have taken it in. Because, even if he was a bit hardened, there's always something exciting about attempted murder.

" You aren't listening," she accused him. " It's most melodramatic."

" That's what I don't like about it," said Crook. " Y'know, sugar, I think we've underrated Dr. Forrester."

# 9

Dossie suddenly realised that the Scourge was behaving in a most peculiar manner, bumping and skidding and altogether belying the reputation her owner claimed for her.

" What's happened ? " she demanded.

" Just what I'm wondering. It occurs to me I'd have done better to have left you with her while I did my Babes in the Wood stunt solo."

" You mean, you think someone's interfered with her ? "

" Keep it clean," advised Crook. " But—well, it could be just that."

" In that case, it's just as well I wasn't in the car," declared Dossie vigorously. " Another corpse wouldn't have helped you much."

" That's just where you're wrong," Crook assured her. " There's times when nothing helps so much as a fresh body. Y'see, it's harder than an amateur like yourself can guess to commit a murder and not leave any clues."

" You're quite inhuman," Dossie accused him, flushing hotly. " Doesn't my life mean a thing to you ? "

" Be your age," Crook advised her. " Nothing means a thing to me but solvin' the case. And if you're makin' advances——" He had brought the wounded Scourge to a full stop, and now he jumped out and began to examine the damage. Dossie was so angry she was momentarily silenced. Crook, having lifted up the bonnet and jammed it down again, did his best to crawl under the car, almost as though he intended to carry her on his back for the rest of the way. But after another brief pause he reappeared as red as the car herself.

" Caught by the short hairs," he announced grimly. " I ought to have foreseen this. Forrester must have guessed we'd do a bit of corpse-chasing in the wood, so down he comes to investigate, and while we're hot on the scent he comes down and lames her." He paused, thoughtfully.

" Only one thing for it, sugar. That A.A. box can't be more than about a mile. I'll forge ahead and get in touch with the authorities. Pity I didn't get the number of the car, but they can find that out from Darling, if Forrester hasn't changed it in the meantime."

" Are you suggesting I should stay here and wait for you to come back ? " asked Dossie, ominously.

" That was the idea."

" Then you'd better have another. Don't forget I'm an important witness in the case. Why, you couldn't even identify Emily without me."

" It could be we shan't be able to do that even with your help," Crook reminded her brutally. " All right, if you've made up your mind to come, I can't stop you. But it's what I've always said. Steer clear of janes. They always think of their own skins first."

They set out on their mile-long tramp, but before they had achieved more than half the distance they heard the unmistakable sound of a car coming up behind them. Crook grunted. Dossie plucked at his sleeve.

" Perhaps we could get a lift," she said.

" Where ? " asked Crook stolidly. " To the churchyard ? And what do you think will happen to my reputation if I'm bumped off in the middle of a case ? "

" You mean, you think it's *his* car ? "

" That hadn't occurred to you ? "

" But why—— ? "

" Well, what would you do in his place ? Sit on your backside till the police came thundering at the door ? " For a moment he thought of standing square in the middle of the road and blocking the passage of the powerful grey car, but it needed no longer than this to assure him that Forrester would have no compunction whatsoever in running him down and swearing it was his, Crook's, fault. And if the body was found in the middle of the road, the police would probably agree.

" Besides," Crook reminded himself, importantly, " it all depends on me. That Brett woman wouldn't be much use as a witness."

So after an instant's consideration he joined Dossie in the ditch, and the great grey car sailed slowly past, with Forrester at the wheel and beside him, with no attempt at concealment, a bunchy figure lolling ominously against his shoulder, an unfashionable feathered hat on top of untidy grey hair. In the back a rug had been carelessly flung over some luggage and packages and a wooden handle could be seen poking out from its folds.

" That's Emily," agreed Dossie, as the car vanished. " Mr. Crook, that was Emily, after all. In spite of everything he said—and she—she wasn't moving, was she ? "

" No," agreed Crook in sober tones, " she wasn't moving." Except of course as she rolled with the motion of the car.

" Then, what—what—— ? "

For the second time that day Crook said, " Your guess is as good as mine. But didn't you see the spade in the back ? "

" It's the insolence of it," whispered Dossie, half-choked with despair. " To swear she'd never been at The Cottage and then to—to flaunt her like that. He must be mad, of course."

" I wonder," said Crook, stopping dead in his tracks.

" Come on." Dossie pulled furiously at his sleeve. " We've got to get to that telephone."

" Oh, I doubt if that would do us much good," Crook replied. " I fancy our Dr. Forrester will get there first, and when we arrive we shall find the connection cut."

" I never felt so helpless in my life," Dossie raged. " And the triumphant look on his face. I suppose Mrs. Forrester was under the rug. And of course he has method in his madness. He'll take care to be seen, and then, if someone asks about Emily, he can say she's left the house."

" The house he swears she never visited ? "

" Of course. I see. How stupid ! Everyone is supposed to think it's his wife beside him. Aren't they ? Aren't they ? " she added, pulling again at Crook's coat. " What's the matter with you ? Have you gone to sleep ? "

" Thinking, sugar," said Crook.

" What are you thinking ? " Dossie was nearly frantic. She was doing some thinking, too, picturing poor doubly-deceived Emily (deceived first by her nephew and her own friend, and next by the Forresters, though in the circumstances theirs seemed the lesser crime of the two) being carried farther and farther away, destined to lie in a nameless grave (otherwise, why the spade ostentatiously thrust into the back of the car ?) while she and this ridiculous little man teetered in the middle of a country road.

Crook answered her question very seriously. " Thinking it don't always do to go by appearances." Meaning, though he wouldn't tell her this, that people—Dossie, for instance—can look like goofs and sometimes behave like them, and yet have some grey matter, when they choose to bring it into circulation. He turned to her with new respect.

" If this Government don't bring in its Social Security Bill double quick," he assured her, " Arthur Crook will find himself on the rates. Fancy Forrester nearly pullin' that one on me."

" What one ? " screamed Dossie.

" You hit the bullseye with your first shot," he assured her. " When you said Mrs. Forrester was under the rug."

" Well ? "

" Oh, just that she wasn't. That's why we're goin' back."

" Back where ? "

" To the house."

" You don't imagine he'll have left anything incriminating there ? "

" That did occur to me." Crook sounded almost apologetic. " Y'see, he'll take it for granted we'll go poundin' along to the telephone, which a chap of his enterprise will already have put out of action. Then we'll find ourselves stumped in the middle of an empty road. Well, more or less empty. We can't use the car, and we're faced with the choice of walkin' the rest of the way—the longest seven miles in England—or trampin' back to Swinnerton and rousin' up the deaths-head at the Post Office, and gettin' a connection there. That's what he thinks."

To her surprise Dossie found that during this speech Crook had caught her by the arm and was marching her back in the direction of The Cottage.

"But if Mrs. Forrester is at the house, she won't let you in," she protested, her head in a whirl.

"I shan't ask her," said Crook simply. "Now, you be a good girl and don't bother me with questions, and everything'll soon be as clear as daylight."

"I don't like it," whispered Dossie. "I feel we're deserting Emily."

"We can't do any good by following the car."

"We could at least find out what he means to do with her. There are Nissen huts where the squatters haven't settled yet, and there are quarries and pits—why, at this minute she may be in any of them."

"Not she," said Crook with confidence. "Not yet."

"She—she looked so dead."

She waited for Crook to say unsympathetically, "Dead people generally do," but he seemed to be saving his breath. In a shorter time than she had thought possible they had reached the place where they had abandoned the Scourge. Crook gave her a wistful affectionate look as he passed.

"Back soon, old girl," he said.

"I still don't understand," panted Dossie, but Crook only said, "That's all right. You'll get there by closing time. Question is, do we make it?"

Dossie gave up attempting to understand what he was talking about. Anyhow, she needed all her breath to keep up with him.

They reached the mouth of the lane and turned up, still making a good pace, too good for Dossie, who thought it unfair that so short and plump a man should be able to move so fast. When they reached the phoney hedge, as Crook now called it, he stopped.

" Do we go through here ? " Dossie was as lost now as poor Emily had been in the woods a couple of weeks earlier.

" See any difference since the last time we passed it ? "

Dossie stared at it helplessly as if she expected it suddenly to burst into bloom.

" Look at that." He indicated a brown tuft on one of the twigs. " I love little pussy, her coat is so warm. But somehow I never knew a cat with fur that texture."

Then, then at last it burst on Dossie. " You mean, it's part of a fur coat, a beaver fur coat. And Emily went away wearing her beaver. At least, she left the mink and the beaver wasn't in the house. So you think——"

" No sense thinkin' when you've got a chance of provin' your facts. Come on. No need to build up the hedge again yet. We've plenty of time for that. Question is—it's all Lombard Street to a china orange against our bein' in time for—someone else."

The little derelict cottage looked the same as it had done an hour earlier. The broken door swung a little loose on rusty hinges, rust still gleamed dully on the out-of-date range, the cupboard door was still shut. Crook ran forward, turned the key, pulled the door open. Propped against the wall was a shapeless bundle wrapped in a brown fur coat, topped with tangled grey hair.

" Emily ! " Dossie exclaimed in shaking tones.

" If you faint now I'll put you in her place and lock the door on you," threatened Crook ferociously. " Here, give me a hand. No need to be so delicate about it. She's passed right out."

Emily was a little woman and though she was nicely rounded she wasn't heavy ; but an unconscious body always seems a dead weight and it was as much as the two of them together could do to drag her out of the impromptu Black Hole and lie her full length on the floor. Crook peeled off his coat, rolled it into a bundle and pushed it under her head. Then he dropped down on his haunches, pulled up her eyelids, felt her pulse.

" Drugged," he pronounced, " but not beyond hope.

Well, she can't have been there long. There hasn't been time."

" Is she poisoned ? " whispered Dossie.

" Why on earth should Forrester poison her when he could do the job just as well by suffocation ? There can't be much air in that hole, and she was stood upright, so that if any did seep through the crack it shouldn't reach her." He thrust his hand into a hip pocket and brought out a little silver flask. " Never travel without first aid kit," he announced. " They taught us that in the war, though actually——" He had unscrewed the flask while he spoke and was now supporting the unconscious woman's head with surprising gentleness while, with a deftness that surprised Dossie, he tilted a few drops of the spirit between her teeth. " No, she'll be all right, I think. I wonder how many women he's sent to Kingdom Come via that infamous little cellar."

" You think there were more than one ? "

" We know Emily didn't make her first excursion here this afternoon, because of the pencil. And I don't think myself that Forrester tossed that diary into the woods for goops like you and me to find. I think she knew too much for the doctor's peace of mind, and when we started pokin' our noses into his affairs he guessed zero hour had come. What bothers me is why he waited so long."

Dossie had another brainwave. " Perhaps she persuaded him that she had posted a letter and people would be making inquiries."

" Mentionin' the diary ? It could be, sugar, it could be. Then we come buzzin' up the path upsettin' the apple cart, and he plans to get us prettily out of the way while he does his stuff."

" And, of course, that was Mrs. Forrester dressed up in Emily's hat ; she'd never even have walked down a lane without a hat. She was very old fashioned. And the spade was put in the car to deceive us a bit further."

" Well, as to that, he'd need the spade, y'know. While the police were out combin' the roads for a gentleman of no particular distinction, and what a help that is in crime, and an elderly dame lookin' pretty average mops-and-brooms, he and Mrs. F. would be busily diggin' a little hole in the garden, and not the first, I dare say, by a long chalk."

"So it was all an elaborate fake to put us off the scent."

"Partly that and partly he wouldn't want any of Emily's belongin's to be found on his premises. And she had a nice collection of diamonds, by all accounts."

"What I can't understand," said Dossie, "is how Forrester knew that Emily would bring her diamonds to Swinnerton. She'd hardly tell him, surely, and it would be much more reasonable to put them in the Bank, if she didn't want to leave them at Southwood."

"Ah, but you forget, she wasn't feelin' so reasonable then. Besides, it might have started questions. Bank might have wanted to know where she was goin' and for how long. As for tellin' Forrester, I don't suppose she did. But I dare say she met him lookin' like the sky on a starry night, and we know she took a good wad of notes with her, most likely at his suggestion, and even chaps like Forrester are sportsmen up to a point. I mean, they have to gamble."

"Where do you suppose they are now—the diamonds, I mean?" continued Dossie.

"You've just reminded me—there's plenty of Nissen huts and disused camps. You wouldn't expect to find diamonds in a Nissen hut, would you? But it's like I said a piece earlier, you can't always go by appearances."

He had been attending to Emily while he was talking, and now he straightened himself to say, "How strong are you? We've got to get her up the stairs before Forrester comes back."

"You mean, you're going to leave her on the premises?"

"Sure I'm going to leave her on the premises. Well, what do you suggest? Leavin' her out in the wild wood?"

"Are—are we going to stay here and wait for the doctor?"

"That's right, sugar. He's going to have the surprise of his life when he finds a real reception committee comin' to greet him."

" If he has a gun, mightn't he shoot ? "

" Now, sugar, you're old enough to know you can't always bet on certainties. Sure, he might shoot, but I don't think he'll have the gun. Now, heave-ho, my hearties. I'll take her shoulders and you take her feet."

" Wouldn't—wouldn't it be better to wait till she comes round and can walk up the stairs herself ? "

" If we knew exactly what time Forrester was coming back, that might be an idea. But we don't, and since you're goin' to hold the fort for a bit, you can hold it a lot easier upstairs than down. For one thing, if you don't start singing or anything of that sort he won't know you're here."

" He might come upstairs."

" Why should he ? "

" When he finds the cupboard's empty, I mean."

" He won't, not right away. I'll attend to that. Come on. Now, don't put that look on your face. You dragged me into this, didn't you ? You wanted me to save Emily."

Dossie read into his tone the words he didn't say. " You're at least partly responsible for Emily being here. If it hadn't been for you she'd be nice and snug at Kozicot still."

" And he's quite right," Doris told herself sternly. " Suppose you do get yourself killed, you've no one but yourself to thank." So she stopped her protestations and between them, with grunts and mutters and more than once in imminent danger of dropping their burden, they lugged the unconscious woman up the stairs—and no one but Crook, thought Dossie generously, could have manipulated the weak places so skilfully, and laid her out full length on the floor of one of the two minute bedrooms the cottage boasted, with Crook's coat still acting as a pillow under her head.

" Now," said he, " we're goin' to put the fear of death into Dr. Forrester."

He ran downstairs, Dossie following, and began to tinker with the lock of the cellar door.

" I ain't a pro. like Bill," he confessed ; " but at a pinch I can do a bit of damage, too."

Dossie watched, fascinated, as he worked on the lock. After a short time he slammed the door and turned the key. When he turned it back it stuck half-way.

" That's goin' to flummox our friend," he announced gleefully, stepping back and surveying his handiwork. " Can't you see him, twisting and turning and finally trying to smash the lock, because with Arthur Crook on his heels he'll know it ain't healthy havin' a body on the premises ? And it's funny what a guilty conscience will do, even to hardened sinners. Of course, he can tell himself a hundred times nobody but him (and his partner) know there's a corpse there, but there's always the thousand-to-one chance, and if somebody should come prying and peeping and thinking maybe it's funny there should be a locked cupboard in an empty smashed house, well, you see, sugar, don't you ? He can tell himself till he's blue in the face nobody ever comes through these woods, but the fact remains that you and me came to-day, and what Arthur Crook does to-day the police might do to-morrow."

" When he finds the lock's been tampered with he'll know someone has been here," said Dossie.

" It's a lot more likely he'll think the lady came round a bit and started banging on the door, and managed to put the lock out of action. Of course, if he'd guessed we should call his bluff he'd have taken the key with him, but these chaps always slip up on something. Now, sugar, this is your turn. I'm goin' down to give the alarm, and you stay here and keep watch. Yes, I know it's a bit dangerous, but it's our only chance. If Forrester does come back before he's expected, you remember Brer Rabbit, who lay low and said nuffin. Be seeing you."

He went off as casually, thought the slightly resentful Dossie, as though he were going to ring up for a couple of theatre tickets. She watched from the empty window frame that stout little brown figure bobbing away among the trees until the bend in the path hid him from her sight. Then she came back to Emily. Emily was breathing more naturally now. Dossie wondered what on earth she should say if the unconscious woman came round before Crook returned. It would hardly be surprising if she tried to stagger away, believing Dossie to be part of the plot to take her life.

" I wonder how much she knows, how much she remembers. Of course, she'll never speak to me again. You couldn't expect it. But if only we get her out of this jam——"

She stole back to the window but there was no one in sight. She looked at the watch on her wrist, calculated how long it would take for Crook to get down to the Post Office, get his connection, explain the situation and get back. Her heart was beating as perhaps poor Emily's had beaten, waiting in the dark on the night of the storm, though Dossie knew nothing about that yet. Come back, she implored the absent Mr. Crook, oh, come back. Because if *he* is first I shan't stand a dog's chance, and all your work and cleverness will be thrown away.

With each instant that passed she felt she aged a year. " If I had a glass I should probably discover my hair was dead white by now," she reflected desperately. The smallest sound sent her heart into her mouth, she tiptoed to and fro, hoping, dreading, returning to her charge to watch feverishly for any sign of returning consciousness. Suddenly she heard the sound of feet. For an instant she had been off her guard and she had not heard their approach.

## 10

There were two sets of feet and she knew that this was the crisis. " I haven't a chance against the pair of them," she thought ; " but at least I can do something." She went resolutely to the head of the stairs. Once they discovered the cellar was empty, and they would make short work of that, she thought, they would, whatever Crook imagined, come bounding up the stairs. She was unarmed, but she remembered hearing Desmond say once that a good kick in the solar plexus could put even a giant temporarily to sleep. She stood just out of sight ready to give the firstcomer everything she had. But as she swung her foot to and fro, preparatory to this unladylike form of attack, a voice she knew shouted from the stairs, " Hold everything, sugar. It's only me and the law." And the next instant Crook's big red head came round the corner of the stairway.

" The Lord looks after his own," he told her. " I found the sergeant here taking a looksee at the Scourge, and no wonder. You don't see a car like that every day of the week." Even at this juncture the most absurd pride sounded in his voice. " Any developments ? "

" N-not yet," said Dossie.

" The sergeant's rung a doctor, he'll be coming along soon. Then we'll pack up the hedge nice and pretty, and give Forrester the biggest surprise he's had in years."

Emily came round from her drugged sleep before Forrester returned. When she had blinked and stared and as, slowly, recollection began to return to her, a look of terror spread over her face.

" No, no," she began, trying to struggle to her feet. Crook's hand held her wrist firmly.

" That's all right. Don't you take on. It's swings and roundabouts, you see, and you've arrived at the roundabouts. Here "—he beckoned impatiently to Dossie who was hesitating in the background—" your girl-friend's here. In fact, I don't know where we'd be without her."

Emily looked up incredulously. She was still under the influence of the drug, and she spoke with a greater candour than is common among adults.

" Why, Dossie, I never thought I should be so pleased to see your face. But this——"

" It's all right," Crook repeated. " Here's the sergeant——"

Emily struggled into a sitting position. " And about time, too," she said. " If you always take as long as this to answer an S O S I wonder there aren't ten times as many murders as there are."

" You mustn't blame him," Crook assured her. " It's our friend Albert, the loony postman. He didn't think a lady like yourself should have dealings with the police."

" I shall write to the Postmaster-General, whoever he may be at the moment," protested Emily.

" That's the girl," approved Crook. " And what's wrong with the Home Secretary while you're about it ? "

Emily, who was a staunch Conservative, thought practically everything was wrong with the entire Cabinet, but Crook got her back to the subject under discussion.

Considering that, as Crook delightedly phrased it, she had just been dragged back from the gates of death, she put up a remarkably good show. She told them about seeing the advertisement and deciding that, all things considered, it might be a good thing for her to go into retirement for a while. She told them how her first suspicions were aroused and how gradually, though on the whole pretty quickly, she realised that she was being kept a prisoner at The Cottage, and from there to the conviction that she was never going to be allowed to leave it alive, was a short step.

Then she came to the all-important night of the storm. When Forrester came over to the bed, still in pitch darkness, she knew that nothing could save her but her own quickness of mind and body. " And," she said earnestly, speaking mainly to Crook in whom, for some reason, she reposed instant and complete confidence, " it was as if someone else took charge of me, a guardian angel or something, warning me what to do. Because, as Dossie and my nephew both know, I'm not very sharp as a rule to understand what's going on."

Crook was so much enthralled by the situation that he couldn't even spare a glance for the unfortunate and completely routed Dossie.

" And so, honey ? " he encouraged Emily.

" I waited till the doctor had got up to the bed, because though he moved so quietly, I could just detect the sound of his feet, and then I ran out of the room and clattered down the stairs and wrenched open the front door, all before either of them knew I wasn't asleep. Of course, as I had known they would, they came after me. In the rain and the general blackness they couldn't hope to see me, even with torches, so what I did was to crouch against the wall of the house till they were some distance away, and then creep back, not into the bedroom, but into the sitting-room, where I'd hidden the letter. I rescued that, and then I got behind the big sofa that was pushed up by the wall. Of course, if they looked behind it I was lost, but then I was so nearly lost, anyway, I had to take chances. It seemed ages before they came back, and I didn't dare move, though I was in agony from cramp, in case they heard a sound or I tripped and gave myself away. You see, I knew they'd stop at nothing, and I couldn't know that any one would be clever enough to trace me here."

" It's like what you said," Crook told her, looking at her as if she were the one woman he'd ever loved. " You had a guardian angel, and you know the one about entertaining them unawares. Still, I dare say angels get into some queer suits in their time.——"

Emily smiled at him trustingly. " I heard them come in at last, and they looked into my bedroom, but of course they saw no sign, and they didn't search the sitting-room at all. I heard their doors shut—it was absolutely dark everywhere because of the electricity being turned off—and I waited and waited, listening to the clock chime in the hall. It doesn't seem possible that I went to sleep behind the couch, perhaps I had a sort of faint. Anyway, suddenly I heard the clock strike half-past six, and I knew it was now or never. Mrs. Forrester always got up at seven. I sort of edged myself out, and then I knew a pang of horror because I wasn't sure I'd be able to stand up—I was so stiff, you see. I went on all-fours across the carpet, but when I got to the passage I stood up. It was funny. I felt I couldn't bear either of them to come out and see me like that. I knew the front door was open. I'd heard him say when they came in, 'We'd better leave this ajar so she can get in, if she isn't utterly lost in the woods.' And Mrs. Forrester said in that funny voice of hers, 'That would not be satisfactory. It is always best to know.' I went down the stairs, at first trying not to make a noise, and then suddenly wondering why I was taking all this trouble, when, after all, they were sure to get me in the end. So I just went on down almost as usual, and when I got to the door I listened a minute, but nobody was moving, so I went out. The rain had stopped, though it was very sodden underfoot, and the sky was grey and seemed to cover the world. I went down the path towards the gate. I knew the postman came early, and Dr. Forrester often went to meet him, so when I got there I crouched in the ditch. I thought, if he found me, I'd scream at the top of my voice. I meant to scream 'Murder!' because I thought that would attract most attention. But as it happened the postman came along before he did, the doctor, I mean, and I gave him my letter and tried to make him understand I was in great danger. But he looked dazed, not just by me, I mean, but as if that was his natural expression."

"And so it was," agreed Crook. "Carry on, Mrs. Watson. You're doing fine."

Emily seemed so much engrossed in her own story she had forgotten her fear. "As I came back to the house the door opened and Dr. Forrester came out. He said quickly,

'What is it, Mrs. Watson ? Walking in your sleep again, I see.' I said, 'I suppose it was in my sleep I heard you come into my room ? ' And he said, 'You suffer from delusions. I have told you that before.' I felt very brave, quite reckless, now that the letter had gone. Because there was something else in the envelope, a page I'd torn from a diary. But I lost the diary."

"That's all right," said Crook. "We found it. Sometime you might tell us who it belonged to, but finish about yourself first."

"It was a Mrs. Courtenay. She lived at Hilton Green. She came down here to get away from her relations, but I'm pretty sure she never got back. There was the diary, you see, and the hat—— Oh, yes, where was I ? I said to the doctor, 'You'll be able to tell the others that, when they come.' And he laughed, and said, 'What others ? ' So I told him I'd just posted a letter, letting people know where I was. He didn't believe me at first, but presently he did, and he tried to find out who I'd written to, but I wouldn't tell him. I was afraid he'd go into Oxbridge and explain to the police that I was mad, and of course they'd have listened to him, because he's a doctor. Though there was the page from the diary. Anyhow, I told him, somebody knows I'm here now. That man who brings the letters for one thing. He said in an insulting sort of way, 'He probably thinks you're crazy,' and I said, 'Even if he does, you can't murder crazy people without paying for it.' He said they'd found my bed empty and gone hunting for me everywhere, and I laughed. I didn't seem to mind any more. Perhaps he was right. I was a little bit mad." She paused, then said in a shaking voice, "If he'd known about the letter not being delivered I suppose he wouldn't have waited. I used to wonder every morning if I'd live till night. And then I'd think perhaps he wouldn't dare, because if the letter did get into the hands of the police, or any responsible person for that matter, how was he going to explain me away ? I don't know how long he would have waited, but this morning I heard the car, and I thought it was the police at last. I rushed over to the window, but Mrs. Forrester was in the room, and she caught my arm and pulled me back. She's small, but very strong. But the door was open a little bit, she opened it when she came rushing in, and I heard someone say my name. I tried to call out I'm here, but she put her hand over my mouth. I fought and fought, but it wasn't any good. She forced me down and tied my hands behind my back, and put a gag in my mouth. I think she'd done that before, I don't believe the stories about her being a victim were a bit true. After I met her I could believe in the women in the concentration camps. I never did till then. Even then I'd have drummed with my heels, because I was so certain it was someone come for me, but she gave me an injection—they'd done it before when I tried to get away—and it can't have been as strong as usual, because I heard the car driving off. I thought my heart would break."

She used the old-fashioned expression so simply that even the hard-boiled Crook was moved. As for Dossie, she was like a stone.

" I think then I did give up hope. It was the first time. Presently Dr. Forrester came up, and said I seemed so miserable with them he had arranged to take me to another house. I was sure he meant an asylum, and I knew he would try to get me certified. The awful thing was I knew Desmond would agree, but it seemed to me that anything was better than staying at The Cottage. So I put on my hat and my fur coat, and I got into the car. But we hadn't got any farther than the house in the woods, this house "—she looked round with surprised eyes as if she had only just recognised her whereabouts—" when he told me to get out. Mrs. Forrester had come with us, and I saw something shining in her hand, so then I knew it was the end. And I knew they'd only given me a minor injection the first time, so that I should be able to walk to the car, and, afterwards, to this cottage. I would have screamed again, but the doctor stopped me. Between them they marched me along the little path, and then I knew what was going to be the end of me, because of the hat."

"The hat!" exclaimed Dossie in muted tones. And, "Whose hat?" asked Crook in a voice that would have wooed a hippopotamus from its pond during a heat wave.

"Her hat—Mrs. Courtenay's. Oh, you will inquire, won't you, and see if she ever got back. But she didn't—I know she didn't—because I found her hat in the cupboard, and there was a spade outside leaning against the wall, and someone had been digging——"

Crook put his hand into his hip pocket again and brought out the flask. "Take a sip of this," he urged. "Yes, go on, it's only a pick-me-up, and we're not out of the wood yet."

She laughed weakly. "No, we aren't, are we? Where—where is Dr. Forrester?"

"We're waiting for him. Now, don't let that bother you. "Hallo," as footsteps sounded on the threshold of the empty room downstairs, "that our bird? I didn't hear the car."

But it wasn't the Forresters, though the newcomers brought information about them. A large car was coming in the direction of the lane, they reported, introducing themselves to Crook as the police surgeon and a constable. Immediately nerves tightened, Dossie went quite white, but said nothing, Emily exclaimed, "I am safe with you, aren't I?" Crook said, "Crook always gets his man, even if he does have to call in the police once in a hundred times. Now, keep your nerve. Remember, you're all right."

"If he has a gun," quavered Emily, but Crook said, No, he wouldn't have, he wouldn't think he'd want it, and it was a lot easier to explain away a body that hadn't got a bullet in it.

"Where's he been all this time?" asked Emily.

"Giving you a chance to snuff out," said Crook in his reasonable way. "Well, even Forrester probably draws the line at buryin' ladies alive."

The sergeant said sharply, "You put the hedge back?"

And the constable said, " Yes, sir." Crook adding that people mostly saw what they expected to see, and Forrester would be expecting the entrance to be hidden and wouldn't notice if the branches had got a bit tangled up.

For another minute they waited, strained, scarcely breathing. Then the unmistakable sound of a car slowing and stopping was audible to them all, and a moment later Forrester, with no attempt at concealment, came swinging down the path.

## II

It was, however, Berta Forrester who entered the cottage. Her husband, carrying the spade, went round the side and began to dig, flinging up quantities of earth, making a hasty grave. Upstairs no one moved, waiting for the enemy to give the sign. They didn't have to wait long. After a minute Berta called, " Vyvyan, Vyvyan, something is wrong." And on that the doctor came hurrying in.

" What is it ? We gave her plenty of time. She can't——"

" The door is stuck. The key does not turn."

He pushed past her, and began twisting it in the lock. Both were so deeply engrossed they did not hear the stealthy movements overhead, as the sergeant and Crook approached the head of the crazy staircase. Forrester was tugging and even banging the door in impatient rage.

" Confound the woman, she must have tried to beat her way out and somehow damaged the lock. We shall have to break it, that's all."

He stood back, prepared for a rush but before he could move the sergeant said, " Anything wrong, sir ? "

Berta Forrester gave a sudden uncontrollable scream, and flung her hands over her mouth. Forrester stared as if he couldn't believe his eyes, but his control was good, and with scarcely a pause he answered, " You startled me.

I'd no idea any one was here. As a matter of fact, I keep tools in this cupboard, and somehow the lock's jammed. However, it's not particularly important. I'll get a locksmith up some time."

"You won't find that very easy, not in a solitary place like this," the sergeant told him, coming down a couple of steps. "Maybe I could help you."

Forrester seemed suddenly struck by the unusual circumstances.

"By the way," he said, "I don't want to appear difficult but this is my property and—were you looking for me, by any chance?"

"Waiting for you, sir."

"What can I do for you? If you wanted to see me, why on earth come here?"

"Information received," said the sergeant. "Fact is, we've been asked to inquire into the case of a missing lady."

Forrester laughed abruptly. "Are you suggesting she's in the cupboard?"

"I have to ask you, sir, if you know anything about a Mrs. Emily Watson."

"That's the woman that red-haired maniac came bleating about this morning. I told him then I didn't know—— Did he drag you into this?"

"Evidence she's been in the neighbourhood," the sergeant explained. "Now, mind you, sir, you don't have to answer any questions, but if you do——"

"Are you warning me? On what grounds? That I—did away with this lady?"

"Well, dammit," thought that arch-artist, Mr. Crook, "you have to hand it to the fellow, he does know his onions. Believin' as he does that little Em'ly's the other side of that door and bluffin' away like a champion poker player."

The sergeant said, "No, sir, but we'd like to see the inside of that cupboard just the same, and if you can't open it——"

"I tell you, you'll find nothing there, not this Mrs.

Watson or any one else. I don't know anything about her, I don't know where she is——"

"And you never spoke a truer word!" Crook's intervention was as dramatic as it was unexpected. Forrester's face went a sickly green at sight of him.

"Are you at the bottom of all this?" he demanded.

Crook, with a sublime disregard for fair play as understood by the police and applauded by the great British public, fired a broadside.

"No, doctor, ease your mind, they don't want you for the murder of Mrs. Watson, and why should they, with her sitting perky as a cock-sparrow on the top step behind me. But—ever heard of Mrs. Courtenay of Hilton Green? Funny thing, she seems to have disappeared, too. Maybe you have some idea where she's planted."

Berta Forrester uttered a long shuddering cry and seemed about to swoon. The sergeant hastened to her side, but was knocked nearly endways by Crook who, exclaiming, "Fancy catchin' an old bird that way," launched himself straight at Forrester, bearing him down to the ground and contriving to twist his arm in a way not (officially) known to wearers of the Old School Tie. But then, he'd never worn one, and in his sort of school chaps made their own rules and couldn't have spelt Queensberry. Forrester, taken by surprise, was powerless in the grip of this little human dynamo and by the time he had begun to recover the constable had him in a firm grip, and before his horrified eyes he saw Emily Watson, whom he believed to be incarcerated in the coal cupboard, come down the stairs, supported by the doctor's arm.

"Hold your horses!" said Crook, who didn't in the least appear to mind kicking a man when he was down. "It's all over bar the tolling of the bell. And there's no need to bother about that cupboard, sergeant, because I can promise you there's nothing in it. I looked there not an hour ago just before I locked the door, and it was quite, quite empty."

"It's the oldest trick in the world," he explained to

Emily later. " Lady lapwing distracts the police while the gentleman bites on the poisoned ring. Ladies are supposed to be under the influence of their husbands, so the odds were against her bein' found guilty of murder, and a good counsel could have painted a heart-rendin' picture of her in the tyrant's power. Besides, suicide was too good for a chap who lamed the Scourge. As it is, he'll take his turn in the queue for the little covered shed, and some other chap 'ull start on the same lay. Only this time it'll be a chateau on an inaccessible mountain, and the ladies will stand in rows for a chance to sign their death warrants. Mind you, I didn't want to save the chap's life, but in a better world than this a jury 'ud have brought in a verdict of suicide on that poor lady they found in the garden. I mean, it's asking for it, and next time I mightn't be handy and then where will you be ? "

" At Warrior's Rest," returned Emily demurely. " You know what they say about every cloud having a silver lining. Well, this has taught me two things, one, that the possession of wealth isn't an unmixed blessing, and I really shan't mind parting with some of it—you know, if I remarry I lose a large part of my income—and the other that, as you've just been telling me, I'm too much of a fool to look after myself. I've been deceived all along the line—in Dossie, in Desmond, in Dr. Forrester——"

" Don't tell me," begged Crook, " let me guess. You're going to give another chap the chance of foolin' you. Right ? "

" I'm going to marry Colonel Hunter, who lives in Leaside, not five minutes' walk from my own house. That is actually mine, and we shall sell it, with vacant possession, quite well, so that will be a little *dot* as it were, and I still have my diamonds that you so cleverly rescued from the doctor's car and, of course, Desmond won't take any interest in me after this. The astonishing thing is that, as a result of all this deplorable publicity, which Colonel Hunter has most kindly promised to overlook—I was even asked, you know, to write up my experiences for a Sunday paper, so vulgar, naturally, I refused—Dossie has actually become engaged to some press person, who has flattered her into believing—almost—that it was she Dr. Forrester meant to kill. Well, it will be a new experience for her, and I am all against women of her age getting into a rut, and she really seems genuinely fond of him——"

Crook nodded dubiously. " It wouldn't surprise me a bit," he said. " Probably sees him as Galahad and the Knight of the Burning Pestle rolled into one. Well, when I write my memoirs I'll send you each a copy for a wedding present."

" That will be quite delightful," said Emily, but it was obvious that, with typical feminine ingratitude, she was thinking far more of her prospective bridegroom than of the man who'd made it possible for her to become Mrs. Hunter at all. " And in the meantime, of course, you must let me have the bill for the damage to your car. Oh, yes, Ian insists. And he's really quite well off. I think we shall be very comfortable together."

" Send me a bit of the wedding cake," said Crook. " If I can help any—a lot of my friends are in the Black Market—now, now, lady, it's a free country and, as a Tory, you ought to uphold private enterprise—anyhow, I'd rather have that than the bill for the car."

" But you will be out of pocket," wailed Emily.

Crook winked. " A sort of friend of mine mends cars for a side-line. There's no charge."

For an instant Emily forgot nice reliable Colonel Hunter. " Dear me, Mr. Crook," she said, " you must live a very exciting life. I was telling Ian about you. He does admire you so. He——"

But Crook took her hand and shook it firmly. " Lady," he said, " the colonel's a lot braver man than me, and you can tell him I said so."

And to indicate that the conversation was now at an end he clapped on his brown bowler and went off whistling mournfully, " Another good man gone West."

**THE END**

www.ingramcontent.com/pod-product-compliance
Ingram Content Group UK Ltd.
Pitfield, Milton Keynes, MK11 3LW, UK
UKHW040434280225
455666UK00003B/68